SUSPECTS

Danielle Steel has been hailed as one of the world's most popular authors, with a billion copies of her novels sold. Her recent international bestsellers include *The Whittiers*, *Without a Trace* and *Worthy Opponents*. She is also the author of *His Bright Light*, the story of her son Nick Traina's life and death; *A Gift of Hope*, a memoir of her work with the homeless; and the children's books *Pretty Minnie in Paris* and *Pretty Minnie in Hollywood*. Danielle divides her time between Paris and her home in northern California.

By Danielle Steel

Worthy Opponents • Without a Trace • The Whittiers • The High Notes • The Challenge
Suspects • Beautiful • High Stakes • Invisible • Flying Angels • The Butler
Complications • Nine Lives • Finding Ashley • The Affair • Neighbours
All That Glitters • Royal • Daddy's Girls • The Wedding Dress • The Numbers Game
Moral Compass • Spy • Child's Play • The Dark Side • Lost And Found
Blessing In Disguise • Silent Night • Turning Point • Beauchamp Hall
In His Father's Footsteps • The Good Fight • The Cast • Accidental Heroes
Fall From Grace • Past Perfect • Fairytale • The Right Time • The Duchess
Against All Odds • Dangerous Games • The Mistress • The Award • Rushing Waters
Magic • The Apartment • Property Of A Noblewoman • Blue • Precious Gifts
Undercover • Country • Prodigal Son • Pegasus • A Perfect Life • Power Play
Winners • First Sight • Until The End Of Time • The Sins Of The Mother
Friends Forever • Betrayal • Hotel Vendôme • Happy Birthday • 44 Charles Street
Legacy • Family Ties • Big Girl • Southern Lights • Matters Of The Heart
One Day At A Time • A Good Woman • Rogue • Honor Thyself • Amazing Grace
Bungalow 2 • Sisters • H.R.H. • Coming Out • The House • Toxic Bachelors
Miracle • Impossible • Echoes • Second Chance • Ransom • Safe Harbour
Johnny Angel • Dating Game • Answered Prayers • Sunset In St. Tropez
The Cottage • The Kiss • Leap Of Faith • Lone Eagle • Journey
The House On Hope Street • The Wedding • Irresistible Forces • Granny Dan
Bittersweet • Mirror Image • The Klone And I • The Long Road Home
The Ghost • Special Delivery • The Ranch • Silent Honor • Malice
Five Days In Paris • Lightning • Wings • The Gift • Accident • Vanished
Mixed Blessings • Jewels • No Greater Love • Heartbeat • Message From Nam
Daddy • Star • Zoya • Kaleidoscope • Fine Things • Wanderlust • Secrets
Family Album • Full Circle • Changes • Thurston House • Crossings
Once In A Lifetime • A Perfect Stranger • Remembrance • Palomino • Love: *Poems*
The Ring • Loving • To Love Again • Summer's End • Season Of Passion
The Promise • Now And Forever • Passion's Promise • Going Home

Nonfiction

Expect a Miracle
Pure Joy: *The Dogs We Love*
A Gift Of Hope: *Helping the Homeless*
His Bright Light: *The Story of Nick Traina*

For Children

Pretty Minnie In Hollywood
Pretty Minnie In Paris

Danielle Steel

SUSPECTS

PAN BOOKS

First published 2022 by Delacorte Press
an imprint of Random House
a division of Penguin Random House LLC, New York

First published in the UK 2022 by Macmillan

This paperback edition first published 2023 by Pan Books
an imprint of Pan Macmillan
The Smithson, 6 Briset Street, London EC1M 5NR
EU representative: Macmillan Publishers Ireland Ltd, 1st Floor,
The Liffey Trust Centre, 117–126 Sheriff Street Upper,
Dublin 1, D01 YC43
Associated companies throughout the world
www.panmacmillan.com

ISBN 978-1-5290-2202-5

1 3 5 7 9 8 6 4 2

A CIP catalogue record for this book is available from the British Library.

Typeset in Charter ITC by Palimpsest Book Production Ltd, Falkirk, Stirlingshire
Printed and bound by CPI Group (UK) Ltd, Croydon, CR0 4YY

Visit **www.panmacmillan.com** to read more about all our books
and to buy them. You will also find features, author interviews and
news of any author events, and you can sign up for e-newsletters
so that you're always first to hear about our new releases.

To my beloved children,
Trevor, Todd, Beatrix, Nick,
Samantha, Victoria, Vanessa,
Maxx, and Zara,
so infinitely precious to me,
wherever we are,

You light up my world.
May you be forever safe,
untouched by danger,
and blessed in every way.

I love you so much,
more than words can say,
and bigger than the sky,

Mom / d.s.

Chapter 1

Pierre de Vaumont looked serious and elegant as he left his Left Bank Parisian apartment on the rue Jacob in the fashionable sixth arrondissement. He hated early morning flights, but took them whenever he had meetings in New York. He would reach New York before noon, which gave him time for a lunch meeting and appointments in the afternoon. He was always booked in the evenings for major social events, important dinner parties, or discreet meetings that sometimes slid into unsavory activities, if dictated by the people he was with. Pierre was versatile, and open to almost anything. Tall, slim, handsome with graying blond hair, he was forty-six years old, and a matchmaker of sorts. He brought people together in order to facilitate unusual deals on a variety of matters. Sometimes even very unlikely endeavors. He knew everyone worth knowing all over Europe and in the Middle East, and his connections now extended into Asia, with Chinese businessmen who had a great deal of money. Almost all his connections were with billionaires. De Vaumont made his living, a very handsome one, on commissions. What he did wasn't illegal, although he brushed along the edge of the respectable at times. The higher the risk, the more money involved, and the greater the profit. He was planning to meet with several different groups of people in New York. He only intended to stay there for a few days, depending on how successful his meetings were.

He was involved in fashion on a massive scale, as well as luxury goods, real estate, technology, and oil. He had worked for years meticulously placing himself in crucial positions so he would be able to introduce the right people to each other. And he took a handsome commission for doing so. People sought him out for his connections. He didn't need to chase them. Not anymore. He had built up his business and his skills over the past twenty years. He was adaptable to all manner of situations and amenable to almost every kind of deal.

He had started working in Europe and expanded to Asia, since he had grown up in Hong Kong when his father was in the diplomatic corps. He returned to France in his early twenties, after his father's death. His mother had died when he was in boarding school in England. He had no family or attachments, and no children. His father had left him some money, but not enough to live the way he wanted to, so he existed by his wits. He had always wanted to live well, envied people with a great deal of money, and had expensive taste.

He spoke fluent Mandarin and Cantonese. Over the past two years he had concluded several very lucrative deals in Russia and spoke Russian as well. His sexual preference was somewhat fluid, and difficult to discern. He was often seen with well-known, very beautiful women, many of them married, and now and then he was in the company of very attractive young men. Whatever the pleasure of his clients was, he was happy to provide it, and had excellent connections for that too. He was a chameleon when he had to be. His reliable sources for difficult-to-obtain information served his clients well. His handsome features and innate elegance contributed to his image, and he didn't look his age. He liked the title of matchmaker, although he was neither sentimental nor interested in romance in the classic sense. In many ways, he was a most unusual man, and a power broker among the ultrarich. He was indiscriminate and open-minded about who his clients were and how they had made their money.

Everyone wanted to know Pierre de Vaumont. Anyone who mattered already did, or they at least knew of him. He had the elegance of the French, the unfussy masculinity of the British, and a hint of Italian sex appeal. He would have made a perfect courtier in the court of Louis XVI—he thrived on intrigue.

He was wearing an impeccably cut dark blue suit made by his tailor in London, as he rode in the back of his Bentley on the way to the airport, driven by the chauffeur he used whenever he needed a driver. When he wished to be more discreet or incognito, he drove himself. He thoroughly enjoyed all the finer things in life.

When he arrived at Charles de Gaulle Airport, two members of the VIP staff were waiting at the curb to spot his Bentley, then two more ground crew rushed out to greet him when his arrival was confirmed. He was well known to the airline of his choice. His luggage was whisked away and checked in immediately. He was then escorted to a private room in the first-class lounge, where a lavish buffet of what he liked to eat was set out just for him. He helped himself to a cup of strong coffee and some fruit, opened his computer, and, after thanking the assembled crew waiting to serve him, disappeared into what he saw on the screen. He would be boarded last, as he preferred, and would settle into his first-class seat, where he would stay for the flight and retreat behind the curtains that gave him privacy. He had flown over a million miles, and his every preference was noted in the airline's VIP file and communicated to the crew aboard any flight he took.

He had several meetings scheduled in New York, and would be returning to Paris in a few days or a week at most. It was a long stay for him. Sometimes he flew in and out the same day for one important meeting. He liked closing most of his deals face-to-face, not by email, text, or phone. He was a compelling person, and took full advantage of it to get the results he wanted.

Pierre de Vaumont had been sitting in his private room in the first-class lounge, drinking his second cup of coffee, when a chauffeur-driven Mercedes had pulled up to the first-class area at the curb. A man got out of the front seat, obviously a bodyguard, and a slim woman in a black hat with a wide brim and dark glasses waited in the back seat. The bodyguard took her passport to the first-class desk and checked her in. The staff at the desk nodded when they saw her name and allowed him to check her in without further questioning. They knew the procedures and had been warned of her arrival ahead of time so there would be no mistakes. She was one of their most valuable clients, even more so than de Vaumont.

It was the first trip Theodora Morgan had taken in over

a year. She was the founder and very successful owner of Theo.com, a well-established internet shopping service that had broken all records of success worldwide. A year before, at thirty-seven, she was one of the most successful businesswomen in the world, and a fashion icon herself, always photographed when she appeared in public, although she kept an intentionally low profile, particularly in the last year. She was also the recent widow of Matthieu Pasquier, who owned more than a dozen of the biggest fashion brands in the world and was the acknowledged multibillionaire mogul of luxury fashion. She and Matthieu had met when she started her fledgling business at twenty-two, fresh out of Harvard. She had started it on a shoestring and rapidly proved the business model's success. Financial journals and the business press began writing about her. Pasquier had made a point of meeting her. He was twenty-five years older than she, and a ruthless businessman. He had fallen in love with her bold, adventuresome, innovative business plan, and her gentle, determined nature behind it, as well as her youth and beauty. After a rapid courtship, they were married a year later, and remained married for fourteen years. She was his third wife and he had no children, and she had enchanted him even further by giving birth to a son, Axel, ten months after their wedding.

Her own family history had prepared her for marriage

to an older man. Her father was almost twenty years older than her mother, and they had had a stable, loving home, where she had thrived as her parents' only child. She had often preferred the company of adults while growing up.

Her parents included her whenever possible. She had a quiet nature and was an outstanding student. Her parents expected academic excellence from her, and encouraged it. Her father greatly admired success in business. He had done all he could to assist her entrepreneurial dreams and help her to make them a reality.

She had spent more time in college working on her business plans for the future than making friends. Her relationship with a much older man who was considered a genius in luxury retail seemed tailor-made for her. Her parents were reserved and only mildly concerned by her relationship with Matthieu initially, but they were supportive over time.

Theo spoke adequate French when she and Matthieu met. She studied diligently to improve it, until she was fully fluent within a year, for both business and social purposes, which made for a smooth transition when she moved to Paris for him. She had missed New York at first, but Paris rapidly became home and now she preferred it.

She was a devoted mother, often working from home, brilliant at her own business, which she never merged with her husband's empire, despite his entreaties. She remained independent professionally, while still being a loving wife to him and mother to their only child. She adored their son Axel, who was the joy of her life. And her business was her passion. Her husband Matthieu had been her mentor and best friend, and the marriage solid. Although strikingly beautiful, she had never looked at another man.

It had all ended brutally a year earlier when Matthieu was kidnapped with their son at their country château, while Theo was in the city working.

Both Matthieu and Theo occasionally worked later than planned on Friday nights, in which case whichever parent was free would drive Axel to their château near Paris, and the other would arrive later. Matthieu preferred having just the three of them on the weekends, without staff underfoot. Theo liked that too. They were both surrounded by employees all week and it was a relief to lead a simple life on Friday nights and Saturdays and Sundays, and to fend for themselves. Sometimes Axel brought a friend, but he hadn't then. They valued their privacy and family time, in contrast to the business pressures they dealt with during the week.

Theo had had a late meeting she couldn't escape on that fateful Friday, and Matthieu had driven to the château with Axel toward the end of the afternoon. By the time Theo arrived shortly after eight that night, they were both gone. She found one of Axel's running shoes on the front steps. The front door had been open. There were signs of a struggle, and with her heart pounding in terror, she called the police. Once they surveyed the scene they in turn called the DGSI, the Direction générale de la sécurité intérieure, the French equivalent of the FBI. After further investigation, when an empty pack of Russian cigarettes was found in the grounds, the case was then turned over to the DGSE, the French CIA, the Direction générale de la sécurité extérieure. The strong suspicion then was that the kidnappers were foreign.

The empty pack of Russian cigarettes had been found in a secluded area where the kidnappers had presumably lain in wait for Axel and Matthieu. Once negotiations began, a translator had to be brought in to facilitate communications with the kidnappers, who proved to be Russian. The DGSE had remained on the case, since the criminals involved came from another country and foreign informants had been used to try to discover who they were. The informants had not been able to provide conclusive information as to who had ordered the abduction, the DGSE had strong suspicions but no solid evidence, and the Russian authorities could supply no factual corroboration of their theories. Not enough to make an arrest. The thugs who had kidnapped Axel and Matthieu had vanished afterwards.

Father and son had been kidnapped by six men who were seen wearing face masks and hoods driving away from the scene in a truck with a chase car, as observed by a neighboring farmer. There was no sign of Matthieu and Axel in either vehicle. Both the truck and car were found abandoned in a nearby village. They were stolen vehicles.

Negotiations for ransom of a hundred million euros began the next day. It was clumsily handled by police who were trying to stall the kidnappers so the various authorities could discover their identities, but they failed to do so. The authorities delayed payment while frantically trying to find where father and son were being held. Theo begged the police to allow her to pay the ransom, which she could have done through her own business and Matthieu's, and they finally allowed her to make a half payment of fifty million, hoping to buy time to find Matthieu, Axel, and the kidnappers in the area. The half payment enraged the kidnappers and caused them to panic. During the negotiations, they proved to be nervous, erratic, and unprofessional, arguing among themselves and with the police. The negotiations went on for seventeen agonizing days, the longest in Theo's life.

The police informed her that most kidnappings were

handled in a businesslike way and were all about obtaining money for some political or personal motive, and the victims were rapidly returned when the ransom was delivered. But given the kidnappers' lack of professionalism, the police convinced Theo that she would jeopardize Matthieu's and Axel's lives if she stepped in with the full ransom. She trusted the authorities and later wished she hadn't. There were too many agencies involved and too many opinions. The police delivered half the ransom money, fifty million euro, to the kidnappers in a remote location, as a further stalling tactic, while gathering more information. The kidnappers panicked, killed the two policemen who delivered it, took the money and ran. Before they left the area, they killed Matthieu and Axel, and buried them in a mound of fresh dirt in a wooded area a few miles from the château, to be sure that they'd be found. The police were able to deduce from the bullet wounds, the threads of Axel's clothing on his father's, and their times of death, that Axel had been shot and killed in his father's arms, Matthieu a short time later. After they were killed, they were found fairly quickly, as were the two dead policemen at the location of the drop. Theo remembered the days afterwards as a blur of grief and despair. She had gone into seclusion for a year, running her business from home, seeing no one except the CEOs of both companies, hers and Matthieu's. She was trying to decide whether or not to sell everything. Nothing had any meaning for her after she lost her husband and son.

The ransom money hadn't turned up anywhere in Europe for the past year. The DGSE had no more evidence than they did the day that Matthieu and Axel died. They had suspicions but no hard facts, and the marked bills of the ransom money had disappeared. Despite appearing to behave like amateurs, the kidnappers had gotten away with committing a seemingly perfect crime. And Theo was left to live with the heartbreaking results.

She hadn't left her Paris home in months, and her CEO, Jacques Ferrier, had finally convinced her to come back to work to solve some problems that no one else could handle as effectively. She had reluctantly agreed, and was surprised that working grounded her. It was something she knew and was good at—problem solving at Theo.com and at Matthieu's company came naturally to her. It distracted her from thinking about her devastating losses, at least for the hours she was in the office. After that she had to go home to her empty apartment and face the ghosts there.

Her CEO's intention in bringing her back to work was his way of getting her back in the human race. He directed her attention to the pop-up stores they were setting up in Dallas, L.A., and New York. Organizing the installations was a lot of work, but they had proved to be a highly efficient tool to attract new customers and increase sales and brand recognition globally. Theo had a magic touch with them. Even not at her best, her creative ideas were infallible, and a year after the tragedy, she was slowly returning to herself and hard at work setting up the opening of the three upcoming concept stores in the States. She was going to travel herself to oversee the openings and execution of her designs for the three temporary stores. They were expensive to create, but it was always worth it.

Although she was American, and had grown up in New York, she had lived in France for almost half her life now, and she combined both a European and an American perspective. She had shifted her thriving operation from New York to Paris when she married Matthieu. This also gave her access to his much bigger organization, and it had worked well. Matthieu had given her office space in a building he owned, and warehouse facilities, but she had never given him a share in her business, which amused him. He had liked to brag about how tough she was in business, and how smart. Her father had been an investment banker who had advised her well about the principles of good business and entrepreneurship. She'd been an economics major at Harvard, and graduated magna cum laude. She had planned to go on to business school, but she had started her business first and it took off at an astounding rate. She had a natural head for business, despite a gentle demeanor and feminine style that fooled people, particularly European men, into thinking they could take advantage of her. Matthieu knew better and had enjoyed watching her operate with an iron hand. He had often asked her advice about his major luxury fashion brands, and the counsel she gave him was always excellent. She had exquisite taste and a definite style, and their marriage had been based on mutual admiration and respect.

Theo had lived in a vacuum, in a lonely, silent world, for the past year. She rarely left their Paris home now and hadn't set foot in their château since the kidnapping. It was empty and closed, and too full of terrible memories for her now. She had met with Jacques, her CEO, to continue to keep track of her business, and Matthieu's CEO too, to keep an eye on his affairs and enormous enterprise. The rest of the time, she wandered her home like a ghost, playing over and over again in her mind everything that had happened, and thinking how it could have been different. The French authorities had made all the wrong assumptions, with disastrous results.

The police had told her at the time that her son's death was an "unfortunate accident of the event" and proved that the kidnappers were amateurs. Professionals would have negotiated more efficiently, and come to some agreement with her rapidly, and neither Matthieu nor Axel would have gotten hurt. French, British, and other European authorities as well as a network of informants had been looking for answers, underground information, and the culprits for the past year, to no avail. No one knew who the kidnappers were or where the fifty million euro she'd paid them had gone. They had wanted a hundred. The only motive that seemed likely to the police and DGSE was one of vengeance for a business venture that had gone wrong. Matthieu had long been leery of opening stores in Russia. Their economy was too unstable, and their business practices too unreliable and often shady. Despite his misgivings, a Russian investor had come along, offering to put up a hundred million euros to help defray the costs of setting up two flagship stores in Russia, an idea Matthieu had begun to like increasingly, and finally agreed to, against his initial better judgment. The investor, Dmitri Aleksandr, was a billionaire himself and knew the Russian market. It was no secret that there was a great deal of money there, and people eager to spend it.

Setting up the two stores had rapidly become a nightmare, with people squandering money on bribes, delayed construction, and the cost being multiplied beyond all reason, with quality building materials being substituted with inferior ones. Matthieu had finally lost patience and abandoned the project before the stores ever opened. It appeared to be the wisest decision, rather than continuing to throw money at the project and losing even more than the two hundred million he had already put in. Matthieu had lost a vast amount of money but was relieved once he decided to get out. Their investor did not accept his losses with equanimity. He lost the hundred million he'd invested, and a little more. Matthieu graciously accepted his own losses, and could afford to. His investor claimed he couldn't, and said the loss would ruin him, which Matthieu did not believe.

The motive the French authorities felt was the correct one for the kidnapping and subsequent murders was that whoever had instigated it wanted to punish Matthieu severely for pulling out, and to recoup the bulk of their losses with the ransom. As far as the police were concerned, they considered it a business deal meant to put the money back in the pockets of the principal investor, Dmitri Aleksandr. He had powerful underworld connections, which protected him and kept him out of reach. According to informants, Matthieu and Axel were supposed to be useful pawns and nothing more. They were leverage to get the money back to Aleksandr for the failure to complete the two stores. But no one had been able to prove the theory. It was all guesswork. And the angry, disgruntled investor was a rich, successful man, who was considered untouchable.

The news of Axel's and Matthieu's deaths had shocked the world and crushed Theo, but the story had slowly faded from the press, with no news since. The money still hadn't shown up, nor had the criminals who had killed her husband and son been caught. There was no justice in the story, nor any consolation for her, having lost a husband and son.

Coming back from it over the past year had been an agony beyond measure, but her CEO had finally been able to convince her to go to New York and oversee the installation of three high-end pop-up stores of her brand in the States. No one understood their business and their customers as she did. She hadn't been seen in public or heard from for a year, and he convinced her it was time to venture into the world again. She wasn't enthusiastic about going, but she realized that she couldn't hide forever. Jacques said that if she wanted to keep her business, she had to take control of it again. Her first days back had been a painful flood of vivid memories.

There was to be a big, splashy party organized by a major New York PR firm to launch the opening of the New York pop-up, which would be open for two weeks. Theo had no intention of going to the event, but she was eager to see that the store was properly set up, and the decor and atmosphere exactly right for their image. Similar events had been planned in L.A. and Dallas in the weeks following, and she intended to oversee them too. No promises had been made that she would attend the events. And there was no one in New York she wanted to see. Her parents were dead now, and she had lost track of old friends there. The brand and the business had been running smoothly without her being seen in public for a long time. Matthieu's business was continuing to function efficiently too, managed by the same people who had worked for him when he was alive. His business was too large and solid to flounder, even once he was gone. She stayed in touch with their top management and sat on the board. She was active behind the scenes, particularly since she was the owner of Matthieu's business now, although it interested her far less than her own brand, where her input made a real difference since it was smaller than Matthieu's empire and rested on her image as well as the products they sold.

The fact that she was going to New York to oversee the opening of the pop-up had not been announced, and she had no intention of being seen by the public before, during, or after the event. She just wanted to make sure that the large store they had rented for a fortune for two weeks on

Madison Avenue would look spectacular. It felt both exciting and terrifying to Theo to be out in the world again. She had lived in the shadows for months now. She wanted to see the action again, but not be in it. She wanted to be invisible.

Because the kidnappers hadn't been caught, she had to travel with a bodyguard, and have one with her whenever she left her house, even for a walk. There was a large rotation of them, which her assistant Martine arranged. Theo liked some of her guards better than others, but she needed protection, in case the kidnappers came back for her too. It was a remote possibility she couldn't ignore, according to the police. For the most part, she detested not having the freedom to go anywhere alone. But thanks to Matthieu, she owned one of the largest, most successful businesses in the world now, and was as big a target as her late husband had been, in some ways even more so, as a woman in that position. The police thought it unlikely that the same group of men would return, but since they hadn't gotten the hundred million they had come for, the authorities felt that it was not entirely impossible that the kidnappers would try to abduct her now for the rest. She had all the correct papers and powers of attorney in place, so the CEO of Matthieu's company could pay the ransom in a relatively short time, if she was abducted. They knew what to expect now.

There were times in the last year when she didn't care

if they took her. Without her son, she had nothing left to live for. She dreaded the long years ahead without him. And neither business was enough to feed her spirit and keep her going. Her passion for her business had waned, so it had been a particularly major victory for the CEO of her own company when he convinced her to go to New York. She had finally agreed at the last minute. She was thinking about what she had to do when she arrived, while she waited in her car for news of the delayed flight. There was supposedly a minor mechanical problem on the plane, which they were promising to repair as soon as possible. She didn't mind the delay. She had no meetings and no set plans. She was just going to supervise the final build-out and look of the pop-up. The temporary New York hires did not even know she was coming. She wanted no focus or attention on her. She hoped to sleep on the flight, since sleep still eluded her on most nights.

Pierre de Vaumont was still in the first-class lounge working on his computer and annoyed by the delay, which might cause him to have to cancel his lunch meeting. He had already had a second cup of coffee, and the ground crew left him alone in solitary splendor, with the VIP team hovering nearby just outside the door of the private salon.

* * *

Pascal Martin sat at his desk as head of security at Charles de Gaulle Airport, in the job he'd had for fifteen years. It had gotten infinitely more complicated in recent times, with mounting concern about terrorism and attacks on other airports. They'd been lucky at CDG so far.

One of the new elements he hated dealing with were the more stringent regulations for all flights with destinations in the United States. United States Homeland Security expected them to hold inbound flights to the U.S. to a higher standard of security, and respect their No Fly List at all times. They required the authorities of the airlines and the airport to submit the manifest for each flight, so the American authorities could run the passenger list through their computers and make sure that no undesirables and potential terrorists would slip in unnoticed. It meant delays on almost every flight while they waited for clearance from Homeland Security, and at times the CIA, in case of some doubt. Meanwhile unsuspecting passengers were told there was a minor mechanical problem on the plane, which was then magically fixed once the manifest was cleared. With fair regularity, passengers who did not meet with U.S. approval were removed from the plane before they boarded. If they let the plane take off without final clearance from the U.S., they ran the risk that the incoming international flight would be refueled on the runway and sent back to its original point of departure without letting a single passenger disembark. It made for hundreds of irate passengers, so Pascal had learned that it was better to let them wait during a delayed departure than to send them home from an aborted round trip, which was much worse.

U.S. regulations about who flew and who didn't were tougher than those in any other country. It was their way of keeping out dangerous elements. And they made it tougher all the time. Occasionally a passenger they singled out was a false alarm, but even Pascal agreed that it was better to be on the safe side, even though it caused him untold aggravation at times. He'd had stomach problems and high blood pressure for the past three years. He couldn't wait to retire in five years.

Meeting the stringent American security procedures took time, and they couldn't explain it to the passengers, since no one officially admitted to the No Fly List.

He'd had a call from the head of the ground crew of a major airline saying a first-class passenger on their early New York flight had been flagged as a potential problem. Worst of all, the circumstances weren't clear. He wasn't on the No Fly List that Homeland Security denied having, but the code that came up next to his name indicated that they needed additional clearance to allow him to enter the U.S. It appeared to be a gray area, which Pascal hated most. If they took him off the flight, he could sue the airline for the embarrassment and business meetings he missed. If they left him on, the plane and its passengers could be turned around and sent back to Paris from New York, without a single passenger able to get off.

"Shit," Pascal said to himself as he read the printout and knew what it meant. "Questionable passenger, clearance required." It was one in the morning in New York, the flight was due to take off from Paris in an hour, and at that time it wouldn't be easy to reach someone at Homeland Security in New York who could give them clearance. He could feel his stomach start to churn and tighten, which was part of the job now. His wife wanted him to take early retirement, but most of the time he still enjoyed his job, when he didn't have a problem like this one.

Pascal knew who to call at Homeland Security at JFK and had the contact's personal cellphone number. He hated to use it if it wasn't a real emergency, but it could easily become one, particularly from a PR standpoint for the airline. He looked for the number on his phone and found it easily. He wondered if his counterpart in New York had high blood pressure too. But Pascal didn't want to make the decision alone. The burden and the fallout were too heavy to have solely on his own shoulders. On mornings like this he didn't enjoy his job and wished he had stayed in the military. Things had been so much simpler there. There were fewer "gray areas" than he dealt with almost daily at Charles de Gaulle.

Rafael Gonzales was awake but still in bed, waiting for the alarm to go off at two A.M., so he could get to his office by four. They'd had a busy few weeks, with fashion week in New York, and the overbooked flights coming in from all over Europe, plus the annual United Nations meetings. These brought people in from countries all over the world, most of them with diplomatic immunity, which was complicated for security. They'd had heads of state and high officials from countries around the globe, as well as the usual traffic of businesspeople coming to New York for a variety of reasons. It was a good time for some of the wrong people to slip in, and it was up to him to see that customs and immigration officers were vigilant about it.

His cellphone rang, and he answered immediately.

"Gonzales," he said, sounding stern and official, as if he was at his desk and not lying in bed in his underwear.

Pascal identified himself immediately and apologized for the late hour.

"No problem," Rafe Gonzales assured him. "I have an early shift today. We've been busy here."

"So have we," Pascal Martin said.

"What do you have?" Gonzales got right to the point.

"I'm not sure if we have a problem or not, but we got an advisory on an outbound flight, about a first-class passenger. He's a French national. I can email you what we've got. There are no details, just that we need additional clearance from you to let him fly. We've delayed the flight until we know."

"Send me what you have and I'll run him through our system. It could be for other circumstances of some kind, or it could be old and should have been cleared." They both knew that would be the best-case scenario. At worst, Pascal was going to have a giant pain in his gut, an irate passenger to deal with, and angry airline officials. It was all part of the territory that went with the job. "Give me five minutes. I'll call you right back, so you don't have to hold the flight."

"Thank you, I appreciate it," Pascal said politely. Rafe hung up and called the operations officer on duty at the airport at that hour and asked him to run Pierre Geoffrey de Vaumont through their database to see what they got. Rafael stayed on the line while he waited, and Charlie, the operations officer, was back in less than three minutes.

"No arrests, no criminal record, nothing from Interpol. The advisory is a little vague. It says he's in investments and has 'dubious connections' with several Russians—at least one involved with the SVR, the Russian Foreign

Intelligence Service—and is possibly under surveillance by them. There's nothing here that we can keep him off a flight for. He may just be one of those slippery characters who knows all the wrong people, or has done some shady deals, but nothing we can nail him for," Charlie explained to his boss, and Rafe nodded as he listened and made rapid notes. "There's nothing here that says to keep him out of the U.S., just to be aware of him."

Rafe was frowning, wondering if he had enough to go on, or needed to dig further. "Thanks, Charlie," he said, sounding distracted. He sat quietly for a minute after the call, and then decided that he wanted to know a little more about de Vaumont before he cleared him for the flight to New York.

He knew the right man to ask, had the number to reach him, and wanted to be sure. He called the number quickly because he knew Pascal Martin was waiting in Paris, and the heat was on him about whether to clear de Vaumont or take him off the flight. Rafe knew what a fuss that would make, particularly if the concern wasn't justified. He didn't sound like a dangerous character, but you never knew.

Mike Andrews was sitting in the room he used as an office when he worked at home, usually late at night, when it was quiet and he had time to catch up. He was a senior supervising operative in the CIA, and head of a local office of the DO, the Directorate of Operations, which functioned primarily abroad with "foreign assets in the field" dealing with clandestine intelligence, terrorism, and weapons. His office worked in conjunction with JFK Airport when needed. He had been in the navy, in military intelligence for eight years after college, then went on to Langley, in Virginia, to be trained for the CIA. At forty-nine, he had been in the Central Intelligence Agency for nineteen years. His office was in an innocuous-looking building in Manhattan that was a rebuilt warehouse on East Seventeenth Street, and he had a fully secure computer set up at home, for when he worked there, so he could easily access any information he needed.

He lived for his work and had no other life. His apartment looked like an office, with bare walls, and a minimum of secondhand furniture. It suited his bachelor existence. Like many top CIA agents, he had the perfect profile: married to his job, no personal attachments, no family other than one sister, no encumbrances. He had done undercover work in Central and South America for his first ten years with the CIA, and then settled down at home, in a spare bachelor pad in the Bowery. He was available 24/7 and didn't mind being called at any hour. Rafe apologized as soon as Mike picked up.

"No worries, I'm still working. What can I do for you?" Mike said easily despite the late hour.

"I think we're okay," Rafe said, sounding uncertain. "We got a call from head of security at CDG in Paris. They got a flag on the computer on a first-class passenger. They're nervous now, since we've started sending flights back. They're being more careful. It sounds like this guy is some kind of businessman, maybe with some dubious connections. Russians. One of them may tie in to the SVR in Russia. They seem to be growing a lot of spies in Russia these days. There's nothing else remarkable in the report about him, nothing with Interpol, no directive that he can't enter the U.S. I just want to be sure I don't make a mistake, and we wind up turning back the flight when they get to JFK, if we don't have to."

Mike listened carefully and was calm when he answered. "That's not enough to hold the flight or take him off." Mike sounded sure of his assessment from what Rafe told him. "It sounds like you're good to go. He may be some kind of creep, but nothing we need to worry about, yet, or stop him for. That can always change, but there's nothing in what you've told me that sets off bells and whistles. Tell them he can fly," Mike said. There was a soothing tone to his voice. Rafael had never met him, but had spoken to him before and liked him. Mike wasn't an alarmist, although he was careful and thorough. They'd denied passengers together before, notably a Venezuelan drug runner, and a Syrian couple who had gotten arrested in England carrying a bomb three months later. They'd dodged a bullet on that one. The woman had been making suicide vests for a terrorist cell outside London. But Pierre de Vaumont was clearly not in those leagues, and a different breed entirely. He seemed to present no serious risk if they let him enter the United States. Being a businessman with Russian connections was not enough to keep him out of the country.

"Happy to help," Mike said.

"I'll give them a call at CDG right away so they can board the flight," Rafe said.

"That'll be good news to them," Mike added, and they ended the call.

Rafe called Pascal Martin back immediately and gave him clearance, telling him he had it straight from the CIA that de Vaumont was clear and there would be no problem with his entering the U.S. Pascal could feel his stomach ease the moment he heard, and advised the airline immediately. The flight was only going to be an hour late, which wouldn't ruffle the passengers' feathers too much.

Mike had asked Rafe to email him the manifest, so he had it, and indicate the passenger in question. It never hurt to take another look, just in case someone else of interest was on the flight. He glanced at it a few minutes later, and only noticed one familiar name. Theodora Morgan Pasquier. He had read the story in the news a year before and remembered how tragic it had sounded. She had lost both her husband and son in a bungled kidnapping situation. He wondered if they had caught the kidnappers, but didn't recall reading that they had. There was no other name that rang a bell on the flight.

He had another thought then, since de Vaumont had some vague link to the Russian Foreign Intelligence Service, either as a suspect or a connection, and decided to put a tail on him when he arrived. At worst, it would be a waste of time and taxpayers' money, and at the other end of the spectrum, they might pick up some interesting information that could be useful to them, MI6 in the UK, or DGSE, the French authorities. Mike thought the Russians seemed to be a noticeable presence these days, more than they had been in a long time. There was a lot of money floating around, being placed in strange places for purposes that were of interest to several governments. He called operations and set up surveillance on Pierre de Vaumont, and gave them de Vaumont's flight number and arrival time. He could always cancel it if the agent said there was nothing of interest going on.

He made another call then, to a friend in MI6 in London,

who had gotten there via Scotland Yard. Mike sat back in his big comfortable chair. He was a tall man with dark hair, brown eyes, and gray at his temples, and had played college football for Notre Dame. He was originally from an Irish family in Boston and had enjoyed his career in national security so far. There was a photograph of a pretty blonde girl on his desk. The photograph was old, and he noticed it often. Becky James. They had gone through Langley together. She had been killed in an undercover operation they both worked on in Ecuador, in his early years in the CIA. She was the only woman he had ever really loved, and he had learned his lesson from that. Personal attachments were high risk when you did national security work, particularly undercover. It was a luxury he couldn't afford, and had avoided after that, but she had been such a sweet girl. Mike was smiling when Robert Richmond picked up his direct line at MI6 in London.

"I haven't heard from you in dog years. Where are you, man?" he said to Mike.

"In New York." Mike always enjoyed talking to him. They had shared information on many cases for several years.

"Working on anything interesting at the moment?" He assumed the call was for business, and he wasn't wrong.

"Nothing much. It's been quiet," Mike said.

"I wish I could say the same. We've got a lot of problems

in Europe. Terrorists, Russian spies, and double agents. It feels like the Cold War again these days."

"We're a little more removed from that than you are. Most of the Russian spies seem to be settling in England," Mike commented, and Robert agreed. "I had a call today about a passenger at CDG. French national. Pierre de Vaumont. The computer flagged him but there's nothing much on him. Supposedly questionable connections, but that could mean anything."

"Do you want me to take a look at what we've got on him?" Richmond offered.

"It might not be a bad idea. Maybe you have more on him than we do. You're closer to home for him."

Robert typed the name into his computer and read what it had. "He sounds more like a lightweight and a nuisance, a bullshitter, one of those connection guys, a networker, who tries to work his way into every kind of deal, and lives off the commissions. He seems to know everyone with big money in Europe. He's a party boy and some of the people he hangs out with in the Middle East and Russia are probably up to some nasty stuff, but there's no hard evidence that he is. I'll send you what we have, if you want. He doesn't sound like a big problem to me, or even a small one. He lived in Russia several years ago and must have met some of his connections then. Anyone else of interest on the manifest?"

"Nothing I recognized, and the computer didn't flag anyone else. The only name I noticed was Theodora Morgan. I don't know if you remember her. She was married to a big deal luxury-brand guy, he and their son were kidnapped last year and both were killed over some mess with the delivery of the ransom. It sounds like everyone blew that one, and she lost a husband and a son."

"I read about it," Richmond remembered. "It sounded like everyone screwed up. Sad that they killed the boy especially. I don't think they ever caught them. Russians, as I recall, but they sounded like amateurs from everything I read. I felt sorry for her too. So what's new with you? Ready to retire yet?"

"I've got another sixteen years to go," Mike said with a smile. "I'm not complaining. I like my job."

"Yeah, me too. Except when everything goes wrong. It happens."

"It does to us too, but it feels great when everyone gets it right and we get our guy."

"It's an absurd job for an adult, isn't it?" Robert said, laughing. "It's like playing cops and robbers for the rest of your life." But the people were real, and some of them died, like Becky. Mike had never been afraid for his life. The risk just went with the job and was a hazard he had expected when he signed up. He didn't mind his solitary life. He was busy, and facing armed gunmen seemed a lot less dangerous to him than falling in love.

He and Robert Richmond hung up a few minutes later, and Mike went to bed for a couple of hours, satisfied about Pierre de Vaumont. If he was up to any mischief while he was in New York, the tail would spot it and report it to Mike. They had all the bases covered. He was sound asleep five minutes later, as the flight took off in Paris, headed for New York.

Chapter 2

Once the flight took off from Paris/Charles de Gaulle, it was uneventful. There were four seats in first class, and only two were occupied, one by Pierre de Vaumont, the other by Theo Morgan. Each had chosen window seats, so they were far apart, and the two seats together between them were vacant. Theo paid no attention to Pierre and sat in her seat lost in thought. She hadn't bothered to draw the curtains and didn't really care if she had privacy. She had taken off her hat, but kept her dark glasses on for a long time. She didn't look forbidding or unpleasant, but there was something about her demeanor that made it clear that she wasn't open to conversation and didn't want to be approached. The cabin crew offered her magazines, champagne, damp cloths to wash her hands, pajamas, a toiletry kit, and slippers, and she refused it all.

Pierre glanced over at her a few times and saw that she hadn't noticed him. He had recognized her immediately when he saw her board the plane with her bodyguard. Pierre had met Matthieu Pasquier several times at major fashion events, but he had only spoken to Theo briefly once, and she seemed not to remember him when she glanced at him when she boarded the plane, and then looked away.

The bodyguard, who was a fixture in her life now, put her tote in the overhead rack, helped her settle in her seat with her jacket and a blanket, and asked if she needed anything, before he took his own seat a few rows back.

Pierre noticed that she had a dazed expression as she sat quietly in her seat before takeoff, as though her mind was full of unhappy memories. She had a tragic look to her that was painful to see. After takeoff, she took a book out of her handbag, and was absorbed in what she was reading. Everything about her seemed to say "I'm wounded, stay away." She was a beautiful woman, with thick dark hair to her shoulders. She would have been sexy if she hadn't looked so sad. She had huge sapphire-blue eyes, very pale white skin, and a creamy flawless complexion. It struck him that she had graceful hands. He noticed that she was wearing her plain gold wedding band, although she'd been widowed for a year.

They crossed paths finally outside the restroom, after the meal, and Pierre seized the opportunity to speak to her. He was determined to connect with her on the flight, and not miss the chance, which was how he operated. He was an opportunist by profession.

"Ms. Morgan," he said with a warm smile, as she left the restroom free for him, and he seemed to accidentally block her path back to her seat. "I'm Pierre de Vaumont. I met you with your husband a few years ago." She had no recollection of it, which was unusual for her. She had a fail-safe memory, which Matthieu had always commented on. It was a little duller now after the trauma she'd been through, but it was starting to improve again. His face didn't look familiar, and he seemed a little too friendly to her. "It's lovely to see you. I'm addicted to your shopping site," he said, smiling even more broadly.

She was about to cut the conversation short when she had a thought. Pierre de Vaumont was seen everywhere, at all important social and fashion events. She didn't recognize his face, but she knew his name. He was in the press all the time, and his attendance was an instant statement that the event was a success. It wouldn't do her any harm to have him attend the opening party of the pop-up store in New York. She thought of it instantly while he spoke.

"I'm actually on the way to New York to open a pop-up store. We're having a party the night it opens." She reached into her bag and pulled out a spare invitation she had with her and handed it to him. "It's a special event, and we have some very exclusive pieces we're bringing in. I hope you'll come and enjoy it," she said with a shy smile.

He noticed how vulnerable she looked, and even he was touched as he took the envelope from her.

"I'd love to come, if you'll be there," he said, appearing to flirt with her, which surprised her. When she first saw him, she had assumed he was gay, but he wasn't acting like it with her.

"I'll be there, of course," she lied to him. She had no intention of attending a big party, or a promotional event, even for her own store. Her plan was to be there, but out of sight, so she had a good sense of what merchandise was working best. But she had no desire to be seen, in fact quite the reverse. She didn't want to play games with the likes of Pierre de Vaumont, who was an entirely social animal, and everything she wasn't, even more so now. She wanted to avoid the press. She didn't want it reported that she was back in the world, and then have to endure a feeding frenzy over her. "I'm going to set up the space for the next few days. It's a lot of work, but I enjoy the manual labor." She was a creature beyond his ken, and the kind of woman he didn't understand. The women he knew loved being in the spotlight, and would have killed to be in her shoes, with a successful business of her own and a conglomerate of luxury brands she had inherited that was worth billions. He wasn't surprised she had a bodyguard, given what she was worth, and what had happened to Matthieu and her son. She was wearing plain black slacks and a black cashmere sweater, with a black cashmere jacket, a heavy gold necklace, a wide gold cuff on her arm, and she carried a large black leather Hermès Kelly bag. She looked impeccably chic, which didn't surprise him. She had when he'd glimpsed her before at an event, but they had never talked. He was pleased with the invitation to her opening party, and slipped it into his pocket. It never occurred to him that she might not show up.

She went back to her seat and drew the curtains after that, lay her seat down flat and settled in under her own cashmere blanket with a pillow, and slept for several hours.

She woke up in time to have a cup of tea and half a sandwich before they landed. She looked fresh from the long nap. With a little rest, she looked younger than her thirty-eight years, but she felt as though a year of sleepless nights and everything that had happened had taken a heavy toll.

She was in her seat with her hat and dark glasses on, looking sleek, as they prepared to land.

Mike Andrews went to his office earlier than usual that day. He wanted to get a head start on a stack of work on his desk. The building was unusually plain. It had a dreary look to it, intentionally, not to attract any notice. The blinds were drawn at all times, and a small plaque on the wall near the door said it was a law firm, which would explain the comings and goings of agents. Once inside the outer door, there were a number of code panels, and others for finger-print and facial recognition as well as a retinal scanner. There were several other buildings like it, discreetly placed around the city, housing CIA offices.

Mike was the highest-ranking agent in the building, and the door released as soon as the codes identified him. He took the stairs up four flights to his office, for the exercise. He tried to stay in shape, with a room of gym equipment at home too, since he essentially had a desk job now, and rarely did fieldwork.

He had already assigned an agent to tail Pierre de Vaumont during his stay in New York, and as soon as he sat down in his big, comfortable leather chair, he saw that

Robert Richmond had sent him an email. It was the follow-up on the Pasquier kidnapping. He opened it and saw that the most recent clipping was six months old. They were all from the British press, and there was a tabloid-style photo of Theo, which didn't do her justice. She looked ravaged.

He read the accounts thoroughly and then called Robert in his office.

"Thanks for sending me the clippings. It sounds like they've done nothing recently about catching the guys who kidnapped and killed her husband and son."

"I'm not sure that's true. But I don't know where in Russia they were from, and if they were amateurs maybe no one on the regular circuit knew them. From what I recall about the information we got, the trail was cold almost immediately." Robert was quick to defend his colleagues in France, who were usually good guys and pretty thorough. But it had been an ugly story, a botched job, and a tragic ending. Every operative's nightmare, especially with a child involved, and with full spotlights shining on them since the victims were so well known.

"But how hard have they tried in the past year?" Mike insisted.

"I don't know. I haven't asked," Robert said. "I was never on that case, other than standard requests to let them know if we heard anything. But I don't think we ever did. None of our informants seemed to know about it at the time."

"That sounds odd to me. Fifty million is a hell of a lot of money. Someone out there must have talked or known something," Mike insisted.

"Apparently not," he said.

"I've put a tail on de Vaumont when they land. I probably won't get much, but I'd like to know what he's up to while he's here."

"Probably a lot of social stuff, some coke and some hookers. That's what those guys do. And somewhere in the midst of all that, they introduce someone to someone else, and they walk away with a fat commission."

"As long as the deals he makes on my watch are legal," Mike said firmly, and Robert laughed.

"You still sound like a military guy. I like old school too. It's a lot more complicated these days. Sometimes it's hard to tell the good guys from the bad guys. And most of the Russians who become spies end up as double agents, playing on both teams. The women too."

"It doesn't sound like fun to me," Mike said.

"It isn't, and a lot of those double agents end up dead in back alleys. They kill each other regularly. Poisoning is their weapon of choice these days. You have to be damn careful. Some of that stuff they use can kill you if you're in the same room with it, or it can leave traces all around a town."

They talked for a few more minutes and then hung up. Mike checked on the flight again. They had made up for lost time, and were only forty minutes late. It had just landed. The passengers were due in customs. He was curious to find out what de Vaumont was doing in New York, and who he was seeing. He didn't know why but something about de Vaumont intrigued him. De Vaumont seemed like a strange creature to him, a bottom feeder, a leech, an opportunist in a very fancy world where he seemed to have easy entrée. Life was a buffet of opportunities for him.

Pierre de Vaumont noticed that two federal agents from Homeland Security met Theo Morgan and her bodyguard on the plane, and escorted them off before everyone else. Two agents from the airline were also with them, and the Homeland Security officers accompanied them through immigration and customs. As a high-profile person with a life-and-death risk from the kidnappers who might come back for her, Homeland Security took on the responsibility of protecting her when she entered the country. She was quiet as she stood with them waiting for her bags to emerge. As soon as they did, the whole group headed toward the street. She never noticed Pierre de Vaumont watching her, standing off to the side, and he made no attempt to approach her again. He would see her at the party in two days anyway, and he didn't want to crowd her. She still had that "don't come near me" look in her eyes.

Pierre didn't notice Rafael Gonzales observing Theo and her entourage move through the airport. Rafe had just wanted to be sure that all went smoothly and, from all appearances, it had. He was pleased that they had done everything by the book and decided to let de Vaumont take the flight.

Pierre emerged from baggage claim onto the sidewalk at the exact moment Theo was stepping into a rented SUV with a driver. A moment later, after she shook hands with the small group, the car pulled away from the curb and headed toward the city.

Pierre had rented a car and driver too. He had half a dozen appointments every day and a lot to do.

He was staying at the Plaza, not far from where her pop-up store was located, and Theo was staying at the Carlyle, just up Madison Avenue from the store. She and Matthieu had always stayed at the Carlyle when they came to New York. She knew it would be nostalgic for her being there without him, but she didn't want to stay at a different hotel. They knew her, and she had memories of Axel running up and down the halls as a little child.

The chauffeur already knew where she was staying, drove

her to the city, and headed uptown. As they sped up Madison Avenue nearly an hour later, the location of the pop-up store caught her eye and she was pleased to see it. The location was perfect, and she could glimpse through the windows that there were about ten people rushing around inside carrying bolts of fabric, ladders, and paintbrushes. It looked like they still had an enormous amount to do. Her work was cut out for her. When they got to the hotel, she told the driver she'd be down in a few minutes and was as good as her word. She was back twenty minutes later wearing jeans and sneakers, a gray sweatshirt, and her long hair in a braid, with her Kelly bag in tow. Her bodyguard was with her. She had a tote bag with a large notebook, a legal pad, a handful of pens, an industrial measuring tape, and a hammer. She was ready to get to work and smiling when she got there.

She looked for Bella, the young woman they had hired as the number two person for the job, or Valentina, the manager. She spotted the younger of the two and introduced herself.

"I'm Theo," she said simply. There was no pretense about her. "The space is fabulous," Theo said with a light in her eyes that hadn't been there when she arrived. "I love it. We can do wonders with it."

"I hope so," Bella said, looking anxious. She had never

met Theo before. She was a legend and Bella was terrified that she would say or do the wrong thing, but Theo was concentrating on the structure, and envisioning what she had planned. They had sent bolts of fabric to attach to the walls with a staple gun, and the space had a handsome natural wood floor, with a pretty garden behind it. It seemed very French, which pleased Theo. She expected to see the Eiffel Tower sparkling at her when she glanced out the windows and was surprised when she didn't.

Theo spoke to the lighting men then, to angle the lights to show the clothes to their best advantage, and to the sound men about the soundtrack for the party. The wall coverings were bright, multicolored silks. And there would be a small group of violinists at the party playing folk music. Bright colors were the core of the new season's collection, and the direction she was taking seemed perfect. The young woman in charge, Valentina, was surprised how fast it started to take shape as soon as Theo arrived. She couldn't have become successful if she'd had a lack of skill or indolence. She flew around like a whirling dervish, wielded the staple gun herself so she could get the colors of the silks positioned just right. She was capable and energetic and for the first time in a year, she was having fun. She wished there was someone she knew to share it with, but there wasn't.

She was surprised when the workmen started to go home.

"It's only eight o'clock," she said, looking disappointed. It was two A.M. for her, on Paris time, which didn't seem to stop her. She was fully energized by what she was doing and seemed tireless. She had been exhausted for a year. But working with her hands in the empty store, she felt alive again. It wasn't serious, in the grander scheme of life, but it was something she could do, a magic she could still create, and that was at least something. It reminded her that she was good at her job, and all its component parts. She hadn't been able to save her son or her husband, no matter how hard she'd tried, but she could take an empty space and make something beautiful of it.

She set up the desk and told them where to put the cash register, just around the corner in a less visible part of the store. By the time she left at nine o'clock, the bare bones were there, and the color palette, which dominated the room, looked like a sky at dawn, with mauves and purples, soft peaches, brighter oranges, and a splash of shocking pink. She was happy when she turned the alarm on, locked the door, and walked up Madison Avenue, with her bodyguard beside her. She didn't speak on the brief walk uptown, but he could see that she was happy, more than she had been in a year.

The agent assigned to Pierre de Vaumont checked in with Mike every few hours, as Mike had asked him to do. He wanted to keep a close eye on who Pierre met with and his activities. He had arrived late at Harry Cipriani at the Sherry Netherland Hotel for lunch, but had called the man he was meeting as soon as he cleared customs, and they had delayed their lunch by an hour. The man had a modeling agency in New York and wanted to open an office in Paris, and he was looking for investors. A friend had told him that Pierre de Vaumont would know who had money and would be interested in the project. Pierre suggested a Russian businessman who loved spending time in Paris and had money to burn. Pierre knew the Russian businessman would view the venture as a never-ending source of women for him to date, who were a cut above the girls he went out with now. Pierre told the man that he would arrange an introduction the next time the Russian came to New York, or they could make a plan to meet in Paris.

At four o'clock, he stopped at an art gallery where he knew the owner, another Russian, who greeted him with open arms. Pierre had found a backer for him.

At six, he went back to his hotel, and changed into a black suit, which fit him to perfection. Then he met with a new Chinese client downstairs at his hotel.

He had dinner at La Grenouille with a group of Saudis he had met in Dubai, members of the royal family, all in their twenties. Pierre went back to their hotel and danced with them afterwards, and then he joined them in a suite at a small discreet hotel, where their assistants had hired the lustful young women they were going to spend the night with. Pierre left quietly when their choices had been made. It was after four by then and had been a very full day.

The agent who had followed him since his arrival that afternoon marveled at his stamina, and had gotten photographs of everyone he met with. He sent the photos to Mike, who had run them through their computers. All involved appeared to be legitimate and had no criminal records, but just looking at them, he understood what Pierre was doing. He didn't know what the projects were, but he was meeting their needs, and they obviously paid for his own lavish lifestyle. He was exactly what he said he was, a matchmaker, for whatever kind of project came along.

The agent went home when Pierre went back to the Plaza. It seemed unlikely he would go out again. The agent would be replaced the next day, so that his face didn't become familiar to Pierre and alert him.

When Pierre got back to his room, and the agent left, Mike was asleep in his comfortable bachelor pad. It had all the technology and comforts he needed for the life he led. And Theo was just waking up at the Carlyle. She was still on Paris time, and it was five A.M. in New York, eleven in the morning in Paris. She had fallen asleep at midnight, in her clothes, with all the lights on, and five hours was enough sleep for her.

She stood looking out the window of her suite, at Central Park still shrouded in darkness, and she remembered all the times she had been there with her husband and Axel. If she closed her eyes, she could imagine that they were still there, asleep in the bedrooms of the suite. Then reality hit her, as it always did. They were gone, and all she could do now was keep going. She could hardly wait for the city to wake up, so she could go back to their store location and get to work again.

They had today to work on it before the party the next day. As it had in the past, work had always saved her. She couldn't afford to let the memories flood in. Their marriage hadn't been perfect. Matthieu was difficult at times, and there had been power struggles between them, but they had been happy enough. The only thing she couldn't forgive him for was that he had had their son with him when they took him, and no protection. She had begged him for years to get private security, particularly at the château, which was fairly isolated, but he insisted he didn't need it. He liked having no help in the house on the weekends, and he thought no one would ever dare attack him, but they had, and none of the happy memories changed that. Their dream life had turned into a nightmare, and she was left to live it alone.

Chapter 3

Theo was back at the store with her bodyguard at eight-thirty that morning. They had given her a key and the alarm code the night before, and she was already hard at work draping fabric on the walls and using the staple gun with her security guard's help. He wasn't adept at it, and she was relieved when Valentina and Bella walked in together and were stunned by the progress Theo was making. The rest of the furniture was delivered that morning, and by the afternoon, it was beginning to look like a real store. Two Damien Hirst paintings had been dropped off that morning, on loan from a well-known gallery. They had the proper insurance that Theo had paid for. When she saw them, she was tempted to buy one of them. She could afford them, but she hadn't bought anything in the past year, not even a pair of shoes. She just didn't care. But she loved the paintings, it was a small sign of her coming back to life. Working on the store had been good for her.

"The place looks incredible," Valentina complimented her. "Wait till people see it at the party. I got confirmation this morning that the press is coming. *Women's Wear Daily*, *Vogue*, and *Vanity Fair*. And I'm sure we'll be on Page Six in the *Post*."

That evening, they set up all the clothes on the racks they'd had built, even though they were only keeping the space for two weeks. But with the kind of prices they charged, everything had to be perfect. It couldn't look like a temporary store, it had to be chic and have substance. It was Theo's unfailing eye and perfectionism that had made her successful, as well as her business sense.

She'd had sandwiches with the crew at lunchtime, and by the time they set up the racks of clothes at the end of the day, she was too tired to eat dinner. The others were going out together, but she said she'd get room service at the hotel.

They had even set up a makeshift back room, curtained off with heavy dark red velvet drapes, which they could use as an office and a stockroom. It was where she intended to stay out of sight during the party. She could manage the stock for them because she knew it well. She said something about it to Valentina before she left for the day, and the young woman looked shocked when she realized that Theo didn't intend to be at the party.

"But you have to," she insisted. "The press will expect to see you, and so will the clients. It won't have the same impact if you're not there. Everyone wants to meet you."

Theo smiled and quietly shook her head. "I don't need to be there. We did pop-ups in Dubai and Hong Kong last year, and we've done several in London. I wasn't at any of them. I was in Paris. This time, I wanted to see how it would work, and how the stock is moving, which affects our buy generally. If the press sees me there, it will distract them. It's much more important that they see what guests are there and how great the clothes are." They had invited three hundred people, and if even half of them came, it would be a mob scene in the store.

Valentina hoped she would change her mind by the next day, but Theo was quiet and firm, and had no intention of being at the party. She had no desire to ever go to a party again, although she and Matthieu had gone to many when they were newly married, and then had been at the heart of the Parisian social scene for their entire marriage. But now it seemed like a travesty to even consider it, with Matthieu and Axel gone. She had brought a simple black dress and high heels to wear, and she intended to stay in the back room, take a peek occasionally, and hear about it from the others. The noise alone would tell her how it was going, and the volume of sales. They had hired a pretty young girl to be at the door with the guest list, and a security guard to stand with her. The food and flowers had been ordered. Everything was set. Theo hadn't forgotten a single detail. They'd invited half a dozen young movie stars, and hoped they'd come too. They'd offered each of them a free dress to wear and keep if they came to the opening party. Five of them had already agreed to do it and were picking up their dresses the next day before the party.

Mike Andrews had called Robert Richmond again that morning.

"I was thinking about Theo Morgan again," he admitted to him.

"I think you're obsessed with her," Robert said coolly.

"What are the French police doing to protect her? She's as big a target now as her husband was, more so because she's a woman," Mike said firmly.

"That's true. But I have no idea. It happened a year ago. They won't have provided her bodyguards for that long. She must have private security."

"Do you suppose de Vaumont followed her to New York for a reason?" Mike asked him, worried and suspicious.

"Were they traveling together?" Robert sounded surprised. Mike hadn't said so.

"Not that I know of," he said sheepishly.

"Then it's just coincidence. If he's following her, which I doubt, it's purely for his own benefit. He has absolutely nothing to offer her. She has all the connections she needs. She's a very rich, important woman. She doesn't need a guy like him for introductions."

"But maybe he needs her." Mike was like a dog with a bone.

"I'm sure he does, but I can't see her being interested or taken in by him. He's a user and she has no need of him," Robert said.

"You're probably right. I just hate what happened to her." It made Mike feel sick whenever he thought of it, especially losing her son.

"It works that way sometimes," Robert said quietly. "We've all seen it at some point or other. Life isn't fair at times. That's not news to us."

"She lost her kid, her only child," he said.

"Your obsessing about her won't change that. You need to go out and get drunk with mates from the office, or have dinner with friends. You're working too hard," Robert warned him. "What's de Vaumont been up to?"

"Meeting with every Russian and Saudi in New York, and

a few Chinese. He's killing my agents with his schedule. He's a human tornado, he's tireless." Robert laughed at the description. "He's out from morning till four and five A.M. every night."

"Hence the term 'hustler,' I think. He's ambitious and on the move."

"He certainly is." They both laughed about it, and Mike relaxed a little.

That night, Theo and her crew worked at the store until midnight. When they left, every last detail was perfect, and they would be open for business the next day with the party that night.

On the eve of the party, Mike was home reading and doing some work on his computer. He was trying not to think of Theo. There was no point worrying about her. Robert was right. It wasn't his case, and he didn't even know her. His obsessing about her wouldn't undo what had happened.

The night of the party, at the store, five of the six actresses came to collect their dresses a few hours before. They picked some expensive ones, but it would be great PR for the store to have them there, looking fabulous in dresses from Theo.com. Two of them said they already shopped Theo.com online.

The staff made sure that their credit card terminal was working so purchases would be easy, and at five o'clock

Theo went back to the hotel to bathe and change, even though no one was going to see her. Just in case, she had to represent the store well, if an emergency happened or if she had to come out of the back room to greet an important guest. She hoped not, but she had to at least be respectably dressed. The dress she had brought to wear was sober and respectable, although her distinctive sense of style shone through whatever she wore.

She was back at the store at seven, in her simple black dress and high-heeled Manolo Blahniks. She wore her hair loose and a pair of diamond earrings Matthieu had given her on her last birthday with him, and she was wearing her wedding band. All her other jewelry had been in her safe for over a year.

She had a chair set up in the back room behind the dark red curtains, where she was going to work the stock for the staff, and hand them the different sizes they needed. She knew precisely where everything was. By seven-thirty, the store was full to the gills with women in cocktail clothes and haute couture outfits. She had peeked through the curtains several times and recognized several well-known socialites and two major actresses. The men were as handsome and well dressed as the women. It was a glittering crowd of fashionable, important New Yorkers, and at a quarter to eight, she saw Pierre de Vaumont among them, in a dark blue suit and Hermès tie. He seemed to know everyone as he walked through the crowd with a glass of champagne in his hand, stopping to greet people.

Valentina burst through the curtains a minute later. "Pierre de Vaumont is here, and he's asking for you. A lot of people are. I told him you hadn't arrived yet, but it seems weird with the party in full swing without you."

It was no weirder than she felt every day now. She couldn't imagine going to a party ever again.

She smiled at Valentina. "It's fine. They don't need me out there."

"You set up this beautiful store, you should be there to see how much they're all loving it." They had been selling expensive items at a brisk pace. The five young actresses had showed up, and the press was outside on the sidewalk. They had gotten photographs of everyone going in and out.

Pierre's CIA tail of the day had called Mike after they got there.

"He's at a party," the young agent reported to Mike. "It's by invitation only so I can't go in. It looks like a big deal, there are a few hundred people here. But there's only one entrance, I think, so I won't lose him." Mike couldn't imagine de Vaumont sneaking out a back door anywhere. He was too bold and arrogant to sneak, and he loved the press.

"Where is it?" Mike asked, wondering where Pierre got

the energy to go from meetings to parties to dinners to nightclubs to hookers all day and night.

"It's at a store called Theo's. It's some kind of opening or something. There are several famous actresses here. Is it okay that I can't get in? They're being strict about the invitations at the door."

Mike thought about it for a minute. "What are you wearing? You could tell them you left the invitation at home."

"I'm wearing a jacket and jeans and running shoes."

"That won't get you far," Mike commented. He was surprised to hear that Pierre de Vaumont was at Theo's store, and he was not too pleased about it. This was obviously why she had come to New York. But why had he? For this or something else? "Stay where you are, unless he leaves," Mike directed him. Mike had stayed late at the office, and he had several changes of clothes there for occasions like this, where he suddenly had to wear a suit or casual clothes, for a meeting or a visit to a field operation. He shaved before he dressed, changed into a suit, white shirt, and tie, brushed his hair, and took off ten minutes later. He had worn dress shoes too. He looked ultra respectable and like the successful lawyer he pretended to be as a cover, so no one would know he was a senior CIA agent, which he never disclosed. Only his sister knew.

An Uber got him uptown in twenty minutes and the party was still in full swing when he got there. He saw the agent out of the corner of his eye, gave no sign of acknowledgment, and walked up to the pretty girl in the attractive black cocktail dress at the door, with the list.

"Hello, I'm so sorry, I forgot my invitation at the office. Theo is going to be so upset if I don't get in," he said with his most alluring, irresistible expression, and she melted at the sight of him. He looked so appropriate she didn't bother to ask his name or check the list.

She smiled. "Of course, go right in. It's pretty crowded," she warned him. He pressed into the crowd and saw de Vaumont in the distance, recognizing him from his pictures. But he didn't recognize Theo from hers. He didn't see her anywhere and wondered if she hadn't arrived yet. He had come to see her himself, and meet her if possible, since he was so intrigued by her case, and why the French authorities hadn't solved it and brought the killers to justice. This might be his only chance to meet her.

He combed the front rooms, looking for her intently and didn't see her, and then he saw the double red velvet curtains at the very back and wondered. He approached cautiously, and with a gentle gesture, pulled one panel aside, and found himself inches from Theo, who had been peeking through them. She looked embarrassed and took a step back as he smiled down at her. He had never seen eyes as blue or skin so white, and her hair looked sexy and voluptuous cascading to her shoulders in waves. He felt as though an electric current had gone through him and struck him dumb. He hadn't expected the impact of seeing her to be so powerful, nor to be so close to her. He didn't know what to say to her, which was rare for him. He usually had the gift of gab of his Irish ancestors. But this time all he could do was stare at her, mesmerized, as he struggled to find the words he needed to put her at ease. She looked startled as he filled the doorway, and a little frightened to be discovered.

"Ms. Morgan, I'm so sorry. I didn't mean to intrude. I was looking for you, and I thought this might be another room for the public."

"It is," she said softly. "We're using it as a stockroom. I'm handling the stock tonight, the others are too busy to do it."

He was sure that wasn't the reason, but he could see in her eyes that she was hiding, from the party and from life.

"I need a birthday gift for my sister, her fortieth, and she said I *had* to talk to you, you'd know just the right thing. She thinks you walk on water, as far as fashion goes," he said, recovering himself, and hiding how moved he felt. She seemed so gentle and so vulnerable, and everything she'd been through was in her eyes.

"Far from it," she said, smiling, feeling as awkward as

he did, and trying to regain her composure. "What does she like?" she asked him as they continued to stand in the doorway of the makeshift stockroom, inches apart, neither of them moving forward or back. She could almost feel the warmth of his body. But she hadn't rebuffed him and sent him back to the party to work with Valentina and the others. She knew how busy they were and it might be a long wait. Her eyes met Mike's bravely as she tried to adapt to the unexpected situation.

"Mike Andrews," he said, smiling broadly, fascinated by her, as he held a hand out and she shook it. She was so much more beautiful than her photographs. She seemed so fragile and human. There was something so kind and mysterious about her. He felt as though he was going to fall into the deep blue pool of her eyes.

"Hello, Mike." She smiled up at him. "What do you think your sister would like?"

It was all a lie. His sister was an artist and hadn't worn decent clothes since high school. She lived in a loft in the village, and everything she owned was splattered with paint. But he could see that Theo wanted to help him. He had hit the right chord with her.

"She likes red," he said off the top of his head, not even sure if that were true. She wore mostly khaki and army surplus, and paint.

"A red mink jacket? A red dress? A red purse," she suggested, and he lit up at that.

"That sounds perfect." She led him deeper into the stockroom and pulled out a box with a Saint Laurent purse in it. It was bright red and very chic, and he smiled when he saw it. He couldn't even remotely imagine his sister with anything like it. "She'll love it."

"Perfect. I can gift wrap it for you."

"I can't believe you're waiting on me. I apologize."

"Don't be silly. I have the time since I'm back here."

"You shouldn't be hiding back here," he said gently, and meant it.

"I don't go to parties anymore."

He didn't ask her why, he knew, and his heart ached for her. His whole body ached for her, and he could barely focus on the purse for his sister. She wasn't even turning forty, she was forty-two.

They completed the transaction with his credit card, with a machine they had in the back room, and when she handed it back to him along with the gift-wrapped box in a Theo.com bag, he handed her his business card, which gave his name, the address of his office, and said he was an attorney. It had his cellphone number and email address on it too.

"You don't live in New York, do you?" he asked her.

"No, I grew up here but I live in Paris now. I'm just here

for this pop-up store. We're doing one in Dallas and another in L.A., and then I'm going back."

"Well, if you need anything while you're here, don't hesitate to call me." He felt foolish for saying it, but he wished he could see her again, and he had no idea how to do it. She was leaving town shortly, traveling and then going back to Paris. She had a life somewhere else, and had survived unspeakable trauma and tragedy. He couldn't imagine how he could be so taken with her. It seemed wrong and like a terrible intrusion, even to him. But Robert Richmond was right, he was obsessed with her. He had no idea why, but she was under his skin. He felt as though he had been meant to meet her, but he had no idea why. It made no sense. And he wanted to protect her, but he was a year too late. There was an otherworldly quality to her, as though she was too gentle to protect herself.

When he thanked her and they said goodbye, he stepped beyond the curtains and Theo retreated behind the curtains again, like a deer into the forest. He wanted to pull the curtains back and see her again just one more time. She was the most beautiful, bewitching creature he'd ever seen. He'd never met another woman like her, or as beautiful.

He made his way back through the crowd to the door, until he reached the sidewalk, and spoke to the young agent briefly and casually on the way past him.

"Is he still here?" Mike asked in a low voice about de Vaumont, and the agent nodded.

"Good. Stay with him. I'm leaving." He walked away then and hailed a cab to take him downtown. He felt as though he was in a daze. He couldn't remember any other woman who had affected him that way before. He had no idea if he'd ever see her again. It seemed unlikely. He felt like a moonstruck boy as he rode downtown in the cab, holding the bag with the red purse he could never give to his sister, or anyone else, except one of his secretaries at Christmas. Theo looked like a lost soul and he wanted to protect her from the evils in her world. He still wasn't sure if Pierre de Vaumont was one of them. All he wanted now was to see her again. She was addictive, and he was hooked.

Chapter 4

Mike took off his jacket and tie, rolled up his sleeves, and went back to his computer when he got home. He checked the clippings Robert Richmond had sent him and read them again—everything about the kidnapping and murder, with all the grim details. In hindsight, it was easier to see the mistakes that the French police had made, withholding the ransom for too long and only doling it out partially, which infuriated the kidnappers and then caused them to panic, afraid of their bosses perhaps. He dug back further then, into articles about Theo's successful internet business. It had been hugely innovative. He saw pictures of her with Matthieu, and read about him too. His name was globally known, with his luxury empire that had earned him a fortune. Mike found one article that fascinated him about Matthieu Pasquier's history. He was an attractive man, but he had a stern, somewhat forbidding look about him. He seemed like an unlikely partner for Theo, being so much older than she was. But as Mike read more about him, he was intrigued by his background.

Matthieu's family had been among the most important industrialists in France at the beginning of the twentieth century. They owned most of the steel business in France, and were the leading members of the haute bourgeoisie. They had been immeasurably wealthy and led a very grand life, and they had profited heavily by supplying the country's need for steel during the First World War in 1914. The Second World War had been equally profitable for them and they had become the most visible collaborators with the Nazis when they occupied France in 1940. They had even advised the Germans on how to make their factories in Germany more efficient. Their alliance with the Germans had filled the Pasquier coffers.

Matthieu's grandfather had been an outspoken supporter of the Nazis, and the family had continued to live extremely well during the war, in great luxury, while others suffered. His wife had been a famous couturière, a rival of Coco Chanel, with the same political views and sympathy for the Nazis. For German sympathizers, it had been a glittering time in Paris.

At the end of the war, the family had been severely punished for collaborating with the Germans and opening their doors and factories to them. Their entire fortune was taken by the French government as restitution. Their factories became government-owned. All of their holdings and possessions were confiscated. Matthieu's grandfather had committed suicide when they lost everything. The only thing left to them was their château outside Paris, and a small apartment in the city. Everything else was gone. Matthieu's grandmother died of tuberculosis not long after her husband's suicide. His father had been a wastrel, a playboy, and a gambler, and had sold the family château to pay for his gambling debts. He had died, shot by the husband of one of his mistresses.

Matthieu had been born in the family's days of poverty and disgrace, fourteen years after the end of the war. His father had disappeared, and his mother had died shortly after he was born. The article said that Matthieu had grown up in Jesuit boarding schools as an orphan, and his mission had become to restore the family name and rebuild their fortune. He worked hard and saved his money, bought back the family château when he was able to, and systematically purchased failing, long-established luxury brands. He restored them to glory, and turned an immense profit, until he owned the largest conglomerate of luxury brands in the

world. It took him most of his life to do it, but his story was
one of extraordinary success, rebuilding what his family
had destroyed and lost, and then donating vast amounts to
French charities. He had a very unusual biography. Both of
his early marriages were unsuccessful, but his marriage to
the American, Theodora Morgan, was supposedly a happy
one. The article said he had one son, who was the heir to
the vast Pasquier fortune his father had built from the ashes
of what his family had once been. Their money was clean
now. Matthieu had atoned for his ancestors' sins, but sadly,
Mike realized, the boy was gone. He had died after the
article was written. It all belonged to Theo now, as well as
the château and all of her late husband's holdings. He was
still alive when the article had appeared in *Le Figaro,* and
there was a photo of the three of them with the château
behind them. Matthieu looked stern in the photograph—he
was brilliant and seemed somewhat tormented, from what
Mike read about him—and Theo had Axel in her arms. He
looked to be about two or three years old. Happier times
for her. Now she was one of the richest women in France,
but had lost what was dearest to her in the world.

Mike thought about having seen her that night in the
back room of the pop-up store, as she wrapped his package
for him—the pretend gift for his sister, who would never
even see it. His sister would have laughed at him if he gave

it to her. He had no idea why, but he had felt compelled to meet Theo. She was such an obvious target for dangerous criminals now, her circumstances were well known, too much so, and there was a fragility to her that brought out all of Mike's protective instincts.

She herself came from a moneyed, respectable, upper class New York family. They were comfortable but didn't have a vast fortune. She was an only child, an outstanding student, and she had caught the wave of internet commerce in the early 2000s after she graduated from Harvard magna cum laude. She was a smart businesswoman, and had built impressive success of her own, though not on the same scale as Matthieu, but she was much younger, and had embraced what she knew best. She wasn't driven by the same demons he was, with an entire family history of treason and betrayal to live down. Her family had been peaceful and her relationship with them had been good. But she had her own burdens to bear now, and her own losses.

It was all so different from Mike's own history. He was from a boisterous poor family in Boston. He had two older brothers and the sister who was now an artist. His father had been a police sergeant and died young of alcoholism. His mother had managed her four kids on her own, with two jobs and doing whatever extra work she could get. She had worked hard and set that example for them, and she had insisted that they get good educations. The best way for her sons to achieve that was to join the military, which she encouraged them to do. He had a football scholarship to Notre Dame, but he lost his two brothers in the Persian Gulf in the Iran–Iraq war, one in an accident and the other in combat. Mike had joined the navy in order to go to graduate school and get a master's in criminology. He wound up in military intelligence, which he loved. He had been decorated for several very dangerous missions in the Middle East. He didn't mind the risks since he had no attachments, no wife or kids, and his mother had died by then. The CIA had been the right job for him for nearly twenty years. It challenged him, and he liked knowing that he was making a difference, even if in unsung ways. The idea of protecting people from the unseen evils in the world motivated him. He had strong protective instincts.

His mother had died young after a life of hard work, and the only family he had now was his sister, Fiona. He helped her with a check every month. She had never married either, but she had a steady boyfriend. She and Mike didn't see a lot of each other, but they did have lunch or dinner together from time to time. She had bad memories of their impoverished childhood. He didn't. Never having enough money hadn't been an easy life. She was an artist and still struggling at forty-two. He was satisfied with his life in the military and passionate about his undercover work for the CIA. He still missed it at times. He had a lot of administrative duties now, which he enjoyed less. But he had no regrets about his life, and he thought he had been lucky with the choices he'd made. He couldn't have made the same ones if he'd been married or had kids. It wouldn't have been fair. He couldn't have consistently risked his life if anyone depended on him, so it was just as well that he had stayed unencumbered. The only time he had ever considered marriage was to Becky, but he was so young then, and it probably wouldn't have worked out in the long run with both of them federal agents working undercover. She had loved the dangerous assignments as much as he did and wouldn't have wanted to give it up either. She had died for her patriotism, protecting her country the best way she knew how. They had been on the same mission when she was killed, and he had blamed himself for years for not dying instead of her. Years later, the agency discovered that she had been exposed by an informant and they hadn't known it, so her killers had been gunning for her. Her death was not an accident Mike could have prevented. There was no way he could have saved her. He knew that now, but he hadn't for years, until one of his superiors shared the classified file with him.

He recognized that he led a strange life. It was very different from that of the people he'd grown up with, had known in college, and even those in the navy. Once he went down the CIA path, it isolated him to a special world of people with similar lives who had made the same hard choices. The way he lived was comfortable for him now.

When he thought of Theo, he thought of a beautiful, graceful bird about to take flight, and he wanted to protect her before someone shot her down. It seemed inevitable that someone would go after her sooner or later, no matter how much security she had. He had noticed that there was no security for her in the back of the store that night. Private bodyguards were never as effective as professional ones, and he suspected that that was all she had to protect her. Robert Richmond had guessed it too. Mike wished he knew her, so he could talk to her about it, but he doubted there would be a circumstance where he would see her again. She thought he was just an ordinary lawyer who had lost his way at the party and wound up in the back room. A kidnapper would have found her even faster and been out the door with her before anyone could stop them. The thought of it made him shiver, as he left his computer and helped himself to a beer from the fridge. The article in *Le Figaro* about Matthieu had given him a lot to think about. He had obviously been an intriguing man with a heavy history to live down. It must have fascinated Theo too. That made the difference in their ages easier to understand. Matthieu Pasquier had exuded power in every possible way, and he was an honorable man. He had deserved better than to be killed by an amateur gang of greedy thugs, so stupid and inept and evil that they left him and his son in a pile of dirt close to a back road near the château. It could have all ended so differently if handled right. It was such a senseless waste that it hadn't been.

Mike got a surprise in his office the next morning when Rafael Gonzales from Homeland Security at the airport called him on his cell. He had forgotten about his earlier call with him after they cleared de Vaumont to fly.

Rafe identified himself and sounded hesitant, but Mike had been helpful before, and always pleasant when he'd called him, including the time he called in the middle of the night about Pierre de Vaumont.

"Hi, Rafe, how's it going at JFK? Keeping the bad guys out of the country?" Mike spoke in the warm, friendly tone that was his style.

"Trying to, Mike. We're identifying more of them these days. They're getting easier to filter out. Other countries are starting to share our concerns, although they still think we're too extreme about it."

"Keep it that way. Less work for me if you don't let them in." Mike smiled as he listened. "What can I do for you?"

"I was actually calling to give you an update on the guy we had questions about a few days ago, Pierre de Vaumont."

"Really? How so?" Mike was surprised that Rafe had intel about him. Pierre had been busy in the city since he'd arrived.

"He met with two men at the airport yesterday. They're Chinese, a couple of big deal types we know about and keep an eye on when they come through. These two are involved with gambling in Macao. I'm pretty sure they're involved in drugs too, but they're careful when they come here. They came in yesterday and flew to Venezuela. They had a long layover, and de Vaumont met with them at one of the airport restaurants. I have no idea what the meeting was about, and we had no reason to question them. We had them under full surveillance. I had two of my men out of uniform sitting nearby. They spoke Chinese the whole time, and de Vaumont did too. He spent about an hour with them, and then he left. We filmed them, nothing was exchanged, no one passed anything. No money changed hands. It appeared to be strictly social, although they didn't look like de Vaumont's type. He's pretty fancy, and these are both rough guys. I'm glad they flew through and didn't stick around. I'm sure they're up to no good."

"There's no way of telling why de Vaumont met with them," Mike told him. "He seems to be all over the map with the people he meets and connections he makes. It could have been anything, as long as there's a commission in it for him."

"I tried to get one of my Chinese-speaking agents in to sit near them. But by the time he got there, they were leaving, and he speaks Cantonese, while they were speaking Mandarin. I just thought you'd like to know that he had a meeting out here, and who he was with."

"He's a hell of a busy guy," Mike commented, wondering what the meeting was about.

"I think it's safe to say it was either about gambling or drugs. What they wanted from de Vaumont, and how they connected with him, I don't know," Rafe said.

"Send me their names, and I'll check them out. I want to see if we have them in our system. Or maybe Interpol does."

"They keep their noses pretty clean in the States. We've never had anything on them we could prosecute them for. They don't want to get arrested here. But we know who they are, so we keep an eye on them when they come to New York."

"Thanks for the heads-up," Mike said, then told him to call anytime and hung up. Their names showed up on his email a few minutes later, and Mike checked them out. The

CIA seemed to have no particular interest in them. They were in the main database, listed as gambling moguls in Macao, living in Beijing. They weren't wanted for any offenses in the U.S., but it was nice of Rafe to call. What de Vaumont was doing with them, Mike couldn't imagine. They sounded a little too down and dirty for him.

Mike checked with the tail who had been with Pierre the day before, and he confirmed the meeting at the airport.

"It's on my list about him that I turned into operations this morning. I don't know who the two Chinese guys were, but it seemed to be a friendly meeting. They had lunch at the Chinese restaurant at the airport. They ate some dumplings, talked for about half an hour, and left. I think they were on a layover between flights, and de Vaumont acted as though he knew them. They spoke Chinese the whole time." The agent didn't, Mike realized.

Pierre de Vaumont was turning out to be a bigger mystery every day. The range of the people he consorted with appeared to be limitless, although Mike was sure there was a motive for his meetings with all of them, and something in it for him. He was like a human cash register, collecting money wherever he went. No one was too low or too high for his attention, and he seemed able to adapt to each one, whether Saudi royals or Chinese gamblers.

Mike would have been fascinated by him if he weren't so worried about Theo Morgan.

The agent who'd tailed him the day before added that he had gone to a dinner party at the home of prominent New Yorkers after Theo's party, and had met with the young Saudi royals again and gone to a nightclub after that. Then he had joined up with two well-known Russian billionaires at their hotel, and a group of hookers had gone up to their suite shortly after that. Pierre had gone back to his hotel, alone, at five A.M.

The question that remained for Mike was who *was* Pierre de Vaumont, really, and what the hell was he doing in New York?

Chapter 5

A week after their arrival in New York, Pierre had gone back to Paris after countless meetings and parties, and Theo had left for Dallas to set up the pop-up store there. They had nearly sold out their merchandise in New York, and the party and resulting press had given them a great send-off. All the fashionistas and social wannabes had arrived in droves when they saw the mention of it on Page Six, and in *Women's Wear Daily*.

Theo had picked an entirely different group of items for the Dallas store, better suited to their taste, lifestyle, and climate, and she had done the same for L.A., where she was going next. Her research had shown that women dressed up more in Dallas and were more casual in L.A., and she had chosen accordingly. She had sent the really high-style items to New York. She was only planning to spend four days in Dallas, and they had arranged for a party there too. They had acquired the guest list from a prominent PR firm, and it included all the best-known big spenders and socialites in town. She didn't attend the Dallas party either. She wandered around Neiman Marcus to check out their stock and merchandising, and the Dallas store in the Highland Park Village area looked beautiful once she set it up.

She felt like a traveling handyman when she boarded the flight to L.A., to do the same thing there. She was going to spend five days in L.A., and then return to New York for one day and night. She was due to land in New York two weeks after the first opening party, and Mike had made careful note of the date that night when he met her. He didn't know how to reach her, although she had his card, but he knew she'd never call him. She had no need for a New York "lawyer," which she thought he was, and he suspected that she was too shy to call him anyway, and there was no reason for her to call him.

He called the store while they were breaking it down. She had given him that number when he made the purchase, and he spoke to Valentina. She was packing all the clothes in cartons to ship back to Paris. There wasn't much left. The pop-up had been a huge success. They usually were, with the merchandise Theo picked. They had sold out of almost everything.

"I'm so sorry to ask you this. I'm trying to reach Theo Morgan, and I'm afraid I lost her number. She gave it to me the night of the party in New York," he said, and Valentina sounded incredulous. "I'm the guy who wandered in the wrong direction and wound up buying the red bag from her in the back room."

Valentina laughed at his description.

"Now I believe you. You're the only person who saw her that night. She doesn't attend social events. She was our stock girl during the party. She'd rather work than make chitchat. I'll get the number for you. She doesn't usually give it out, but since she did, I'll find it. If her phone's not turned on, she's staying at the Beverly Hills Hotel, you can reach her there, or at the store. She's due back here in a few days before she leaves for Paris." She was unusually chatty with Mike, but he sounded solid and sensible, and had a reassuring tone, and Theo had obviously connected with him and given him her number. He seemed like a nice person.

"I know. I told her I'd call her for lunch." It was all a lie. But he told himself that it was his only chance to see her, her one night in town. Otherwise, he'd have to fly to Paris to see her, which sounded too aggressive. She hadn't encouraged him to call her, but he decided it was worth a shot. The worst she could do was say no. He wrote the number down and stared at it for a while on his desk.

He had just hung up with Valentina when Robert Richmond called him. They chatted for a few minutes and then he got to the point.

"I have an odd piece of information for you. I don't know if it matters or not. But I thought you might be interested since you've gotten hooked on the Pasquier case.

"We just got some new info from an informant. He's usually a reliable source. It seems that Matthieu Pasquier had a girlfriend in Moscow, Svetlana. She seemed to be an informant, working for both sides and anyone who would pay her. She was apparently a minor player in the games they play over there. She probably needed the money. She was a young actress. Someone poisoned her and she died two weeks before Matthieu Pasquier was kidnapped. I have no idea if they were seriously involved or if she was just a toy for Pasquier when he came to town. The French DGSE services might know more than I do. She worked for us too, which I assume is why the Russians killed her. They don't take too kindly to that. Apparently she had another boyfriend in the FSB, the Internal Secret Police, formerly the KGB, as you know. They poisoned him too. He's still alive, but probably won't be for much longer. She died immediately."

Mike was startled by what Robert told him. "They don't screw around. Was Matthieu an agent too, for either side?" Mike asked, curious about him.

"I can't imagine it. He didn't need the money. The others all do, which is how they get them. It's not about national loyalty, it's about eating regularly. The actress was a very pretty girl. She was only twenty-two." And dead now. Mike wasn't an innocent, but it all sounded so sordid. He'd been surrounded by the bad elements of the human race for his entire career, but somehow the agents and double agents that Robert told him about sounded particularly sleazy and sinister. And he was probably right. Young women got into it just to have money to buy food, or they got into prostitution. He wondered if the girl had meant anything to Matthieu, or if she had just been a plaything in Russia. A plaything who had risked her life selling secrets to two countries. Maybe Matthieu gave her money too.

"Do you suppose she was involved in his kidnapping in some way?" Mike asked him.

"Probably not. More likely they killed her as a warning to him, or for some other reason. They seem to dish out poison there like caviar. It's their favorite lethal weapon and they've got some damn nasty ones. Some you don't recover from. We've seen it a lot. We have the medications to stop the effects of the poisons if the dose isn't too extreme, and the antidote, Oximes. We use it for our agents. If you ever get in trouble on that front, let me know."

"I'm not likely to run into poisons. Here they just use guns," Mike said.

"I'd rather take a bullet than a dose of what they use," Robert said and sounded serious. "The Russians are nothing to mess with these days. You can kill a whole village with some of the substances they use. There are some great Russians, but some damn dangerous ones too."

"Do you think her death is in any way related to his? Do you think the girl sold him out to the kidnappers?" Mike hated the thought of that.

"Why would she, if he was giving her money, and I would guess he was. He was known to be a generous guy."

Mike couldn't imagine why he would cheat on Theo with a Russian informant. It seemed foolhardy in the extreme, and he felt sorry for Theo, if she knew about it.

"Do you suppose his wife knew about her?"

"That I don't know," Robert answered. "The French agents might. Our informant says the DGSE knew about the Russian girl. It was their investigation, not ours."

Mike nodded, thinking about it. It was all so convoluted, and so tortured and pointless now since both kidnapping victims were dead. And yet he wanted to know what had happened, that Theo was being protected adequately, and that there might be a chance to catch the kidnappers one day—just on principle as a law enforcement agent. Although a year later, it seemed unlikely.

He wanted to protect Theo, but the cast of characters was becoming more and more confusing. And protect her from what, he wondered, and from whom? It wasn't his investigation. The CIA wasn't involved.

He thanked Robert for the information.

"I'll let you know if I hear anything else. You never know what will turn up."

They hung up a few minutes later.

After he spoke to Robert, Mike called Theo on her cellphone in L.A. She sounded distracted when she answered, and he worried that she wouldn't remember him. Their meeting had been so brief, and probably meant a great deal more to him than it did to her. She must meet a lot of clients, when she wasn't hiding in the stockroom.

"Ms. Morgan," he said politely, they hadn't made it to first names when he met her. The fact that he wanted to invite her to dinner at all seemed ridiculous now. He was sure she wouldn't accept. "I'm Mike Andrews," he continued, "the red-bag man the night of your party at the store in New York." She laughed at his description.

"How did your sister like it?" He was relieved that she remembered him. It had been a startling encounter for her too. Unexpected, but not unpleasant, with an odd undercurrent of something she couldn't explain, and wouldn't have known how to put words to.

"I still have it. Her birthday is in two weeks, but I know she is going to love it." He felt like Pinocchio lying to her and was grateful she'd never meet his sister. It was a totally incongruous gift for her. But it had won him a few minutes of conversation and a minor introduction. "I was wondering if we could get together when you come back through New York on your way to Paris. I was going to tell you that I need some fashion advice for my sister, which is true actually. But to be honest with you, I'd just like to have dinner with you, or lunch if you prefer." She sounded hesitant, and he could feel her retreat. She was extremely skittish. She hadn't had lunch or dinner alone with a man for anything other than business in years, and certainly not in the last year since she'd been widowed. She was too traumatized to want to date.

"I'll be back the day after tomorrow. I have meetings with some new designers I want to include in our spring line next year. One of them is at lunchtime, so that won't work." She was dead silent for a minute while he waited, not wanting to push too hard or abort the mission either. "I suppose I could do dinner," she said cautiously, as he slowly exhaled. The gods had smiled on him after all.

"That would be wonderful. What time works best for you?"

"Anything. I'll be finished with my meetings around six. Eight o'clock? If you don't mind, I like simple restaurants best. I don't want to go to some fancy restaurant where everyone stares at me."

"I agree. That doesn't sound like fun to me either. I hate eating when people stare at me," he said as though it happened every day, and she laughed. "How do you feel about burgers? Or Chinese? Thai? Indian? What's your preference?" He didn't want to take her to a restaurant she hated, and he was happy she liked simple restaurants, not elaborate ones where a headwaiter and half a dozen servers would be hovering over them listening to every word.

"I love burgers, and you can't get decent ones in Paris, not real ones." She sounded young as she said it.

"Perfect. I know just the place. Wear whatever you want. Best burgers in the city and I guarantee no one will stare."

"Should I meet you there?" She sounded unsure, and he didn't know what her security arrangements were.

"What's easiest for you?"

"I have a driver who can bring me." He gave her the address so she didn't feel crowded if he picked her up at the hotel. It might be too much for her for a first meeting. As he hung up, he couldn't believe how lucky he had been. He nearly did a jig when he left his office. He couldn't even call it a date, and what right did he have to date Theo Morgan? But she had agreed to see him again. He felt incredibly lucky that she had accepted his invitation.

The following morning he called a number Robert Richmond had given him at the DGSE in Paris, which was part of the defense ministry. It was the branch that had been in charge of the investigation of the Pasquier kidnapping. They co-ordinated foreign intelligence, since the criminals were Russian, and internal protection within the country. They had handled other situations like it, sometimes with better results and a less tragic outcome. The man in charge of the investigation was Agent Guy Thomas. Mike was surprised when he picked up his own extension and identified himself immediately. He spoke reasonably good English, and Mike said that Robert Richmond at MI6 had given him his number. Mike introduced himself as CIA. He didn't share his concerns for Theo immediately, and started with the subject of Pierre de Vaumont, which Mike suspected would be less threatening to Agent Thomas.

"We've had some recent inquiries about a Pierre de Vaumont, who has some unusual Russian connections, as well as Chinese, Saudi, and several others. He seems to be a small-time player from what we've been able to find out. But he had some minor contact with Theodora Morgan Pasquier, which concerned me. He mostly seems like a clever opportunist, but it's hard to say how deep his connections go and what he uses them for, and what his motives are with her."

"We know about him," Agent Thomas said, sounding tired. "His motive is always the same: money. He takes it wherever he gets it. He 'connects' people, for good or bad purposes, and works for whoever pays him."

"That can prove to be dangerous," Mike said in response.

"True. But I think most of the deals he makes are fairly low-level. He's not a big player on the Russian side. He knows them, but he's more involved in their entertainment."

"Did you ever have evidence of a link between him and the Pasquier kidnapping?"

"None," Guy Thomas answered bluntly. "The basic motivation for that was revenge and money. Pasquier opened, or intended to open, two very large, lavish multi-brand luxury stores in Russia. He put in two hundred million and took a Russian partner for another hundred. The project went sour from the beginning. There was so much graft and corruption just in the building process alone. The permits cost them a fortune. Everyone wanted a piece of it—not to put in, but to take out. Pasquier worked on it for nearly three years and decided the project was unmanageable. He had the governing control with majority ownership. He shut it down unilaterally. His investor has powerful connections in the Russian underworld and the government. We think he's had a lot of bad dealings, but he's so well connected, he's considered untouchable. He's got a pretty nasty reputation, which I don't think Pasquier knew at the outset. He was probably ill advised. Aleksandr was looking for a respectable business to put money in, to use as a showcase for how honest he was, which he wasn't. Pasquier lost a lot of money when he shut it down, but he could afford to. So could Aleksandr, but he was vengeful. From what we could piece together, he wanted Matthieu Pasquier to refund him the whole hundred million he'd lost, which of course Pasquier wouldn't. He had lost a lot of money on it himself because it went so far over budget. The bribes alone were outrageous. We haven't been able to prove it, but I will tell you confidentially and unofficially that we believe that Dmitri Aleksandr hired the team that kidnapped Pasquier. There's no solid evidence, but the ransom was exactly the amount that he wanted Pasquier to pay him, the original hundred million of his investment.

"I think Pasquier's wife would have paid it, but the agencies involved, and mainly the police, wouldn't let her. They wanted to bargain with them to string them along, and gain time to try and identify them. They were supposedly in the Russian mafia and a very rough bunch.

"She finally overrode us and paid them fifty million as a start, with a promise of more to come. But they were panicking by then, and probably thought they wouldn't get the rest, and could get caught if it dragged on. We took too long before we moved. They reacted badly to the half payment, and killed Pasquier and the boy to show their displeasure, then ran. We didn't expect them to pull out as fast as they did. We found the boy and his father two days later, they'd been dead since the day the kidnappers got half the ransom and disappeared. None of our informants or others we deal with, like the British, have heard a word about them since they left. Everyone claims they don't know anything. We can't prove that Aleksandr did it, and people are afraid of his connections. He's a dangerous man to mess with. We're still hoping for evidence or a solid informant to tell us what we need to know, so we can go after him. I'm not sure we could ever get near him. And for now, it's been radio silence for a year, nothing. It all went quiet. They took the money and ran. And we can't trace it back to Dmitri Aleksandr. We're just guessing that he was involved because he was so angry about the money he lost because of Pasquier. He had the motive and we think he used men who weren't known in Russian criminal circles so it couldn't be traced back to him. He's smart and careful, and very thorough."

"Aren't you concerned that they'll kidnap his wife now to get the other fifty?"

"Yes and no. It's difficult to believe they would try again. They made a clean escape. Next time we might be luckier and catch them. Maybe they don't want to risk it."

"What are you doing to protect her?" Mike asked him pointedly, wishing he could see Guy's face and his eyes when he did.

"She has good private security now, and I think she's careful. We provided armed police for six months, but we can't forever. This is France, not the U.S. We don't have the money or the manpower. If she had nothing, it would be different. She has the money to pay for good security, and we've advised her to do so. Personally, I don't think they'll go after her again. They got half the money they wanted. They should be satisfied with that."

"Maybe. But are they? Has anyone heard anything at all from them?"

"No, nothing, no threats of any kind. Dmitri Aleksandr warned Matthieu at the time that there would be a price to pay for not refunding his money. A lot of people made money on the two stores he never opened, all the wrong people. I'm sure some of it ended up in government hands too. The only one who really lost money was the Russian investor, and Pasquier of course. Though the Russian investor may have skimmed some off in the early stages. It's a difficult country. There is an undercurrent of violence, and a strong criminal element that is very powerful within the country. Pasquier didn't understand that at first. The whole project was a terrible mistake and ended in tragedy."

Mike took a breath then. "I'm sorry to bring this up, but Richmond with MI6 told me that Pasquier had a mistress in Russia. They have it from a reliable informant. She was poisoned and killed two weeks before he was kidnapped. Do you think that's related?"

"Possibly, but it's unlikely. She was a double agent, selling information to both sides, and the girlfriend of an FSB official. She was playing with fire and with Pasquier. He probably didn't know she was a double agent, or an agent at all."

"Did you know about her during the kidnapping?" Mike was just curious now, but he sounded official.

"We found out during our investigation, shortly after Pasquier and the boy were killed."

"Did you tell his wife about the girl?"

"No, I didn't. There was no point. The girl was already dead, and so was Pasquier. His wife was heartbroken enough over the boy and her husband. She didn't need to know about the other woman. It would have been unnecessarily cruel." Mike was surprised at the delicate touch and decision not to tell her. In the States, they would have, but mistresses were more common in Europe, so they dealt with situations like this more frequently. "She found out later anyway," he added. "One of our younger detectives let it slip, which was unfortunate. In the end, I'm not sure it made things any worse. She was already so distraught about their deaths. She's been in seclusion since it happened. I can't blame her. I'm sorry she was told about the woman though. She didn't need to know."

"No, she didn't." Mike didn't tell him he was having dinner with her. He could only imagine how she felt about the Russian actress on top of everything else. "And you don't think the two deaths are related? Pasquier and the girl in Moscow?" Mike asked him again.

"It's hard to say. And less important. A double agent being poisoned is not an unusual occurrence. And I don't think de Vaumont is involved in any of it. He's an annoyance, but I don't think he deals in murder and kidnapping, just with lining his pockets." Agent Thomas sounded disgusted when he mentioned him, and Mike shared his opinion.

Mike thanked him for the very interesting exchange, and

he asked to be kept informed if anything surfaced regarding Theo or Pierre de Vaumont.

"Do you have a personal interest in the case?" Thomas asked him, and Mike was embarrassed that he should think so. It was very unprofessional of him to inquire about a case he had no involvement in, merely because he was fascinated by her.

"No, I don't, but it troubles me when the perpetrators can't be found. They committed a terrible crime and should be brought to justice."

"We all agree. But we also know that some crimes are never solved. This may be one of them. It may be why they used an unknown team from Russia, so they'd be harder to trace."

Mike thought he was all too willing to accept that outcome, and it was the same impression he'd had when reading about the case. He was sorry for Theo. It wouldn't bring her husband or son back, but she deserved to have closure and for the men who murdered them to be punished for their deaths.

The day after his call to Paris, Mike showered and changed at his office at the end of the day. He put on a suit and new light blue shirt that he kept there and had been saving. He decided to wear a tie, and was freshly shaved. He looked clean and conservative when he left his office in time to meet Theo at the address he had given her. He questioned the choice now. Maybe it was too ridiculous and she wouldn't like it. It was an old diner on the West Side that looked straight out of the fifties. It had been restored by new owners recently, and the burgers were terrific. They had typical diner food, but at a higher standard than previously. They served delicious meatloaf, southern-fried chicken, mashed potatoes that melted in your mouth, classic hot dogs, homemade ice cream sundaes. He loved the food and had been there a few times, and he hoped she'd think it was fun. It definitely wasn't La Grenouille or Le Bernardin, the best restaurants in New York. But it had comfortable booths, and little juke-boxes in each one, with songs from the fifties, sixties, and seventies. It had become popular since it reopened.

She wasn't there yet when he arrived, and he decided to wait for her outside. He had reserved a booth. At five after eight, a chauffeur-driven SUV stopped in front of the diner. Theo got out, wearing black jeans and a black sweater, with high heels and a black cashmere peacoat. She hadn't had time to change after her meetings, and had answered work emails and phone calls instead. She had washed her face and put on lipstick and brushed her dark hair until it shone. She smiled when she saw him waiting for her.

"You helped me impress my young designers. They thought I was very cool when I told them where I was having dinner. It sounds like fun," she said to him with a smile, as he looked at her. He felt as though someone had pulled all the bones out of his body and dumped them on the street. He'd had the same feeling the first time he saw her, hiding in the back room. "Thank you for inviting me," she said politely. They walked into the diner together, and she grinned when she saw the authentic décor. "I love it! Thank you for not taking me someplace fancy. I like this so much better." She thought how much Axel would have liked it as they sat down in their booth, but she didn't say it.

"Thank you for making the time to see me," he said, unable to take his eyes off her. Just knowing what she had been through and survived as a whole human being made him respect her more, and he wanted to protect her from anything like it ever happening again.

"What kind of law do you practice?" she asked him after they both ordered burgers with everything on them. He was about to say "criminal" but didn't want to scare her.

"Just business law. Tax, estate, labor issues. I'm more of a general practitioner, for select clients."

"That must be interesting," she said. There was something so gentle about his eyes, which she found unusual, as though he could speak to her without talking, and she'd understand him. He felt the same about her, they had an instant connection, as though he had known her forever, or in a past life, which he didn't really believe in. He was more pragmatic than that. But there was something very special about her. He could feel it every time she spoke.

"Sometimes it's interesting," he said about his real job. "I used to deal with some very exciting cases, but the higher you rise, the more sedate it gets. I don't always enjoy that. What you do with fashion seems like more fun."

"I used to love it," she admitted as a cloud of sadness crossed her eyes, "and I'm starting to again. I like L.A., and Dallas is always fun. I hadn't been there in a long time. I have more time to travel now." She said it simply. She didn't know if he knew her recent history, but she had the feeling he did, and she didn't want to explain it to him tonight and spoil the evening with such painful subjects. "Do you travel for work?"

"Sometimes. I have a client in Paris," he suddenly invented, in case an opportunity came to visit her at some point and he'd need an excuse to go there. "Do you miss living in the States?" he asked her, and she shook her head.

"No, not anymore. I've lived in Paris for fifteen years. I moved there when I got married, and it's home now. I don't have family here anymore." She no longer had family in Paris either. She kept bumping into delicate subjects she wanted to avoid, but he didn't pursue them. He was being careful too. He wanted her to have a nice time. He realized as they sat there that he hadn't been on a date in months. He didn't have time, and hadn't met anyone interesting lately. He felt out of practice and so did she. She hadn't been on a date in fifteen years. But she told herself it was just dinner with a new friend. Her wedding band was still very much in evidence as their burgers arrived and they both ate them. They were delicious, and she ate almost all of hers. He had ordered the large size and finished it off. They shared a plate of fries, and he had brought a roll of quarters, so they could play songs on the jukebox. They made their selections at the table and laughed at each other's choices. He liked country and western, and she played hit songs from the seventies and eighties.

He talked about being in the navy, and in Iraq.

"When did you go to law school?" she asked with interest.

"After the navy," he said, thinking of CIA training in Langley.

"I wanted to go to business school after college, but I never went. My business had already taken off by then, and I got married," she explained.

"It sounds like you managed fine without it." He smiled at her, and she grinned.

"That was the best cheeseburger I've ever eaten." The

waitress came to take their dessert order and Theo looked shy for a minute, then laughed. "I want a banana split, but I don't want you to think I'm a complete pig. I haven't had one since I was a kid, and I love them. I don't think I can finish it though. Do you want to share one?" She smiled and he ordered it.

It arrived minutes later, looking like a mountain of ice cream, whipped cream, strawberry, chocolate, and marshmallow sauces, with nuts and a cherry on top. They each dug in at opposite ends, and he laughed when she got a whipped cream mustache on her upper lip.

"You're laughing at me," she accused him, and he chuckled.

"Actually, yes, I am. I never figured you for a banana-split person."

She fed the jukebox again with his quarters and she looked happy. "Well, I am," she said proudly. "I used to love them when I was a little girl. You know what's funny? You don't look like a lawyer."

He was embarrassed to be lying to her. "I don't? Why not?"

"I don't know. You look like something bigger. Like a ship's captain, or a military person, someone you can count on who would keep you safe. Lawyer seems too tame for you."

"It's just my height."

"What did you do in the navy?"

"I flew fighter planes for a while, got a master's degree, and then I wound up in military intelligence."

"Was that interesting?" She was intrigued.

"Very." His eyes came alive as he said it. His intelligence shone brightly, as hers did. He was eleven years older than she was, but they felt the same age and had the same landmarks, or similar ones. "Maybe I should give up law and become a ship captain."

She laughed and they ate most of the banana split.

"It was a perfect dinner. Next time, if you invite me again, I want to try the southern-fried chicken or the meatloaf. But I think we should stick with the banana split." It was fun and nostalgic for her to be eating American food.

"Agreed. Do you come to New York often?" he asked hopefully.

"Not really. I run it all from Paris. It works very well. I haven't traveled in a while. I'm trying to get my bearings. This trip was good for me." She looked at him, and she could tell that he knew the reasons why she hadn't traveled. She was grateful she didn't need to tell him. She didn't want to spoil the evening. She had had fun with him. "Did you play football in college?" she asked. He looked like he might have.

"Yes, for Notre Dame."

"I thought so." She smiled at him. "All I did was study

my ass off. I spent four years in the library. I didn't have much fun. I was very serious then."

"I'm not sure I had fun either. I had a football scholarship for college and joined the navy for graduate school. I liked the navy better, while I was flying fighter planes. And working in military intelligence was exciting." They smiled at each other and he paid the check. He hated to have the evening end. There was so much more to learn about her. And even without words, they were comfortable. He put an arm around her shoulders lightly when they left the diner, and she didn't object. Mike was relieved to see her driver was still waiting outside.

"Do you have a driver in Paris?" he asked her seriously, and she looked embarrassed when she nodded.

"I do, and several bodyguards . . . It's an unfortunate necessity."

"Keep it that way, Theo. Be careful, please," he said gently but with urgency in his voice, and she looked up at him and nodded. She felt so many things with him, so much in common, and she felt so safe standing next to him. She felt protected, and there was a current running between them that she couldn't explain, like a kind of electricity from a powerful source beyond her control.

"Thank you for a wonderful evening," she said as he walked her to her car and opened the door.

"Come back soon," he said, bending down to her, his face close to hers. She was shocked to realize that she would have kissed him if he dared, but she was relieved that he didn't. It was just meant to be a simple dinner between new friends, but she wasn't sure what it was now. It had the potential to be something dangerous and wonderful. She wasn't ready for that and he knew it, and all the reasons why. "Take care of yourself," he said.

"I will. You too," she said. "Life can be dangerous, more than you know. Be careful, Mike. I'll be back for another banana split, and I want to find you here." She had a terror of people disappearing now.

"You will," he promised. He stood back from the car, and she waved as they pulled away from the curb. He hailed a cab and thought about her all the way back to his apartment. She was magical, and the evening with her had been amazing, and nothing like what he thought it would be. It was all so simple and easy because she was, and he suddenly believed what they said about soulmates. But how could that be? He was a senior CIA agent, and she was one of the richest women in Europe, and possibly the world. There was no way it could ever be more than what they'd just shared. Dinner at a diner, burgers and a banana split. He felt like a kid as he ran up the stairs to his apartment, three at a time. He hadn't done that in years.

Chapter 6

Theo flew back to Paris the morning after her dinner with Mike at the diner. She used the card he had given her the night they met for his email address, and sent him an email to thank him. She really had had a lovely time, maybe more than she should have. She felt guilty when she thought about it on the flight. She was so attracted to him, and felt such a strong connection between them. It felt like a betrayal of Matthieu each time she thought about Mike.

But she was also well aware now of what Matthieu had been up to in Moscow with the actress. She had only discovered it after his death, so they had never been able to talk about it. She was sure he would have told her that it didn't mean anything to him. It wasn't the first time it had happened. He wasn't a constant cheater, but he had had his forays into infidelity from time to time, and he was very French about it. As far as he was concerned, as long as he didn't love the girl, it didn't matter. But it did to Theo, and it mattered now. She still felt like a married woman, and wondered how long that would last. For five years or ten or a lifetime. Even after his death, she considered herself married. But she had never felt as powerful an attraction as she had to Mike. She wasn't even sure how much they had in common. They came from different backgrounds. He was a lawyer, an interesting, educated person with a varied history. He seemed very understanding about human foibles, and the vagaries of fate.

What she felt for Mike went beyond words and intelligent exchanges. It was a force of nature. She couldn't remember ever feeling that way before, even with Matthieu. He had taken over her life like a domineering father at first, but she had liked it—it made her feel loved and safe. It had begun to chafe with time, particularly as she gained more experience herself and a mind of her own. She ran her business the way she wanted to. She valued most of Matthieu's advice and disagreed on some points. They had almost always agreed on how to raise their son. But Matthieu still treated her like a child at times, and he respected and valued his own freedom and independence more than hers.

Matthieu was very old-fashioned about some things, particularly about her. He was old school, which she had found charming at first and annoying later on. He was brilliant about business, but less so about people. He prided himself on knowing her perfectly, but he didn't always. He said things that hurt her, and when he cheated on her, she found it hard to forgive him, but she always did. He was far less forgiving than she was but expected his transgressions to be forgiven every time. She was having trouble getting over the last one. After all she'd been through with his death and Axel's, it was a final blow to learn that he had had a mistress in Russia until shortly before he died. She was fifteen years younger than Theo, which hurt too, and forty years younger than Matthieu. Now she was feeling guilty for being attracted to a man. What would people think if she stopped mourning him one day? She knew she would never stop grieving for Axel, but Matthieu had been her husband, not her child. They'd only been gone a year. It seemed like minutes at times, or days. Was it long enough? Had she cried enough? She looked down at the wedding ring still on her finger, and after a simple dinner at a diner, it felt like a lie. She wasn't the grieving widow if she was smiling and laughing and having dinner with a man.

Mike was having the same qualms when he thought about her. He berated himself for being too forward and letting his attraction to her show. He had spent seventeen years using Becky as an excuse for not forming a serious attachment to any woman. His survivor guilt had convinced him that her death on their mission was his fault, despite the fact that agents died in the field every day, and she had been marked by an informant and would have been killed whether Mike was there or not. She was doomed by the informant, not by him. He knew that now, too late. Now he was edging closer to a woman who had already suffered too much and didn't deserve the risks that his job exposed him to. He vowed to himself that he would do everything he could to get the investigation of the kidnappers brought to the forefront again. It was the best thing he could do for her, and he had no right to be in her life in any other way. He was angry at himself for missing her when he hardly knew her. He wanted to send her flowers for her arrival in Paris but wouldn't allow himself to.

Theo was alone in first class on the trip home, which was a relief. No one was there to stare at her or recognize her. She sat lost in thought watching a movie she paid no attention to, thinking about Mike. Being drawn to him seemed completely unreasonable. She couldn't wait to get back to Paris and get to work in her office. She had meetings for Matthieu's company too. She was on the board and an advisor of the company, as she had been for the past ten years. Those responsibilities remained and were even heavier now, with Matthieu gone and unable to run the company himself. His remarkable CEO was doing a great job and consulted Theo on an ongoing, nearly daily basis. Everything she had learned through his company had served her well in her own. She had learned so much from Matthieu, and was grateful for it. He had been an excellent teacher, and a relatively good husband. Even the girl in Moscow didn't change that, although it tainted things for Theo. It made her question how much he really had loved her. He had never been an entirely one-woman man, even for her. He had never considered them equals, possibly because she was so much younger than he was. She accepted it, because there was no other choice, but it chafed now, as she thought about Mike and made a decision to be faithful to Matthieu's memory for as long as she could, out of love and respect for him and Axel. Matthieu would have expected that of her, even if he didn't hold himself to the same standard, and probably wouldn't have done it for her.

She didn't contact Mike again after her email thanking him for dinner, and he didn't respond, which startled her. She told herself that the attraction she felt had been her imagination, the reaction of a lonely woman who had no one to talk to or share a life with anymore. She was determined to get used to it. She couldn't imagine herself ever marrying again, and didn't want to. She had had fourteen years of marriage, and she was going to have other pursuits now to fill her time. She had a business to run, and Matthieu's empire. She told herself it would be enough. It had to be. She doubted she'd ever see Mike again, and tried to convince herself she didn't want to. He was a nice man, but he had his life to lead and she had hers, with an ocean between them.

Daniel, the bodyguard who had gone to New York with her, accompanied her to her apartment, and went off duty immediately. The three guards she had left in Paris took on their usual shifts, so that she was never alone, at home or in the office. There was a private security guard at the entrance to the building now because of her, and another at the door to the apartment. She had the first two floors of an elegant building in the sixteenth arrondissement. She liked the seventh better, but had never been able to talk Matthieu into it. He wanted to live where his family had lived before they lost everything, which had been two blocks away in a similar building. She loved the idea of buying a small hôtel particulier, a private house, in the seventh, on the Left Bank, but Matthieu thought it was dangerous and more vulnerable to intrusions and burglaries. He thought they were safer in an apartment building, but that made no difference in the end, since he and Axel were kidnapped at the château in the late afternoon on a Friday, when all the servants had left and father and son were alone. The kidnappers knew exactly which day to come, so someone knowledgeable had been paid to inform them. She changed all the staff afterwards, once they were all interrogated by the DGSI and the police, but it was too late to make a difference. She no longer went to the château now anyway. It was too painful for her to even visit, let alone stay there. The shutters were closed and she hadn't seen it in a year. She couldn't bear the thought of going back.

Theo got home at nine o'clock that night. The housekeeper had left the lights on for her on the first floor of the apartment, which was the second floor to Americans. There was an imposing marble entrance hall, and the large living room they had used to entertain. Matthieu loved giving grand parties, as he knew his grandparents had done in their days of grandeur. There were billowing satin drapes that framed the long French windows, high ceilings, and beautiful floors. There was a spectacular oval dining room with marble columns, where they could seat up to forty people for dinner, and a big, sunny highly efficient kitchen, an office for Matthieu, which he'd seldom used when he was at home. She used it for meetings of her own office staff occasionally.

Her office was next to his, lined with books and framed pieces that related to Theo.com, a big antique desk and red leather chairs. It was a room where she was comfortable and liked to work on new ideas she wanted to develop. She had spent many long nights there in the last year.

There was a large guest room next to her office that she had made her own in the last year. Their living quarters, and the magnificent bedroom Matthieu had had decorated to look like Marie-Antoinette's boudoir for her, was on the floor above. She hadn't used it since he died. She had a dressing room beside it full of the elegant clothes she no longer wore. She had worn her simplest plain black clothes for the last year, mostly black jeans and sweaters. There was a bathroom with a deep marble tub, and Matthieu's wood paneled dressing room, with Axel's bedroom beyond it, which was closed now, with all his belongings still there. There were six guest bedrooms on that floor, used by the bodyguards now, and Matthieu's gym. There was nothing on the second floor of the apartment that she needed, and she never went upstairs herself anymore. In addition, there was a pantry with a microwave, refrigerator, and small stove, which the bodyguards used, and a laundry room, a luggage room, and a suite for the housekeeper and maid.

In fact, she only used her office and newly adopted bedroom and the kitchen now. The rest was either out of sight upstairs, or the curtains were drawn as in the living and dining rooms that hadn't been used in over a year.

In the last few years, she was too busy to entertain on the grand scale Matthieu enjoyed. She had never really liked it. She marveled at times at how much the apartment looked like his grandparents' old apartment from photographs she'd seen. He had achieved just the effect he wanted long before Theo came along. She had always felt it was his home, or his family's, more than hers, but it didn't bother her.

The château was equally grand, and restored to exactly how it had looked when his grandparents were alive and owned it in their heyday, before the war that took everything from them because of their own bad judgment and the country they had betrayed. As a boy, he had frequently been reminded by people who knew that they had been collaborators. It was something no one had forgotten in France, even seventy-five years later. His family name was well known.

Theo walked into her office, set her bag down and looked around. She glanced at her mail and knew that her assistant had come from the office and taken all the urgent mail that had to be dealt with and paid the bills for her.

The bodyguard had set her suitcase down in her bedroom

before he left, and the next one on duty was in the kitchen, in case she needed him. Some of them were more pleasant than others, and she chatted with them occasionally in the car, but she was tired of never being alone anywhere anymore, not even in her own home. There was a coffee station in the pantry for the staff, and a refrigerator for their use, with a small sitting area and table, so she didn't have to run into them in the kitchen, and there was a small living room for them, used by the bodyguards and the two housekeeping women, with a TV. The bodyguards were always there now. Matthieu would have hated it. He had liked his privacy, and so did she, which was why they had dispensed with employees at the château on the weekends, and why Axel and Matthieu were so easily kidnapped. But with six armed, hooded men, their house staff at the château wouldn't have been able to stop them, and Matthieu had never felt the need for security.

Theo glanced out the windows at the familiar streetlamps and the trees. She liked the view from her windows. From the living room, they could see the Eiffel Tower when it sparkled on the hour. It looked like a lovely toy when it did. Axel had loved seeing it and so did she on nights when she couldn't sleep. She had been nocturnal for most of the past year and was getting back to normal hours now.

She unpacked her suitcase in the small guest room she

had taken over for racks of the plain black clothes she wore all the time now. She had worn black for all of the past year, and had only recently added some color. It was a relief to wear white again, and pastels. She had done what Matthieu would have expected of her and she felt herself. But the year anniversary had come almost a month ago, and she had taken a few colored clothes on her trip. They felt foreign to her now, as though they had belonged to someone else.

She looked into the refrigerator, didn't see anything she wanted to eat, poured herself a glass of juice, and went back to her office to set up the laptop she'd taken with her. It made her think of Mike again. There was no message from him, and she didn't expect there to be. He was just a nice person she had met on her trip. She had almost convinced herself of it by the time she had gone through all her mail, which was mostly invitations she wouldn't accept. She was surprised that people still invited her after a year. It was too painful to see their old friends and the pity in their eyes. It made her feel even worse. Solitude was easier.

The guest room had an impersonal feeling to it, which suited her now. It was where she slept for a few hours and then got up at night and went back to her office, which was where she felt most comfortable. There were photographs of Axel on her desk and the bookcase, a few of her with Matthieu, but the cleanest memories she had now were of her son. The longing she had for him was pure, without resentment or regrets. It was an easier love than what remained of what she'd felt for Matthieu. Once she knew about the young actress in Moscow, they had unfinished business that would never be resolved, and she would have to bury it with him in time. But she had fewer illusions about how much he'd loved her. He had done what he wanted, to the end.

The morning after Theo left, Mike made a decision, in line with the promise he'd made himself, to try and inspire the DGSE in Paris to put some life back in the Pasquier investigation again. He firmly believed that Theo would never be safe until they found the kidnappers, tried them, and put them in prison. He called Guy Thomas, who was surprised to hear from him again so soon.

"I have business in Paris," Mike told him, "and I'd like to come and meet you while I'm there, if you can spare the time. Maybe we can come up with some new ideas together. MI6 has more agents on the ground in Russia than we do, but maybe we can lend some technology to the operation that might make things easier for you." He tried to be as pleasant and uncritical as he could.

"I'd like that very much," Guy said enthusiastically. "We send a lot of our investigations to Microsoft for them to do the digital work for us. We don't have the equipment you do. I have some other cases you might be interested in." He clearly liked the idea of collaborating with the CIA, but the only case Mike was interested in was Theo's, and what he could do to move it along and get the agents involved interested in it again. They clearly needed a push in that direction. The case had hit a wall months before, and gone nowhere since.

They made an appointment for Friday morning, and after they hung up, Mike made a reservation at a small hotel he knew near the CIA office they had in France. It was as discreetly tucked away as their buildings in New York and faded into the urban landscape so as to blend in and disappear. There was a small CIA staff at the embassy as well, although Mike didn't currently know anyone there. It was a cushy job, but not one that had ever appealed to him. Other agents would have killed to work in Paris, but he wasn't one of them. He liked the hardcore problems they dealt with in New York, even if less glamorous than working at the embassy in Paris. But he was more interested in seeing the French authorities than the CIA while he was there.

He had five days off coming to him and had decided to use them for Theo's benefit. It was the best gift he could give her, instead of flirting with her, or putting her at risk in some way, or giving in to the feelings he had for her that he was sure wouldn't be welcome anyway. They had shared a fun evening, but it could never be more than that. After a long, sleepless night thinking about her—in ways that seemed wrong to him now, and were surely presumptuous and over-reaching on his part, given who she was—he had no intention of telling her how he felt about her. He had gone crazy for a minute, and he knew that now. It was a heady feeling just looking at her, with her huge blue eyes and vulnerability. He wanted to protect her, not add to her problems. She'd had more than enough pain for one lifetime.

Mike made a decision not to tell Theo he was coming to Paris until he was there. He would see Guy Thomas, which was the main purpose of his trip, and if she was free and willing to see him, he'd see Theo, and if not, he'd either enjoy the beauty of Paris, one of his favorite cities, or take the Eurostar to London to see Robert Richmond at MI6 if he wasn't too busy to meet up with him. He was flying Thursday night, arriving in Paris in the early morning, and planned to fly back on Monday, to use two weekdays off. Most of the time, he never took time off, and cashed it in instead, but this time he intended to put the days to good use for Theo. It was his way of thanking her for having dinner with him, even if she never knew about it. It was an angel mission on his part.

* * *

117

Theo was in her office early on her first morning back. She woke up at six, dressed, and left with her bodyguard for their offices near the Place Vendôme in the first arrondissement. It was near the Louvre and the Ritz, where she met people for lunch or drinks. She loved the location. Matthieu had a large building on the Avenue George V in the eighth arrondissement, which was a great location too, and where many of his luxury brands were on the Avenue Montaigne.

She stayed in the office and worked late that night, and the bodyguards switched when their shifts ended before she'd left work—something that happened often now she was back in the office, which she had been for a month. She didn't bother to eat dinner. She often existed only on black coffee and whatever she found in the office kitchen. Usually a yogurt or a piece of fruit, which was enough to get by on until she got home. It contributed to her slim figure. Matthieu had always complained that she didn't eat enough, but it didn't interest her a great deal. They had a cook more for him and Axel than for her, and she had let him go after the kidnapping, making do with small haphazard meals ever since. She was thinner than ever as a result, but it looked good on her.

Mike's meeting with Guy Thomas went well, better than he'd expected. Guy was younger than he sounded on the phone and they were about the same age. He interrogated Mike at length about the databases they used, and the specialized equipment that he had no access to in France. "You guys have money to burn on technology," he said enviously. "What we use here is from the dark ages."

Mike finally got him back on the subject that interested him, the Pasquier case, and Guy confirmed that they had no new information, and were hearing nothing about it from their intelligence sources in Russia.

"She won't be safe until you catch them, you know," Mike said seriously, and Guy looked at him mournfully.

"She will never be safe," he said. "She has too much money, she's too successful, and she's too well known. People are jealous, they want to hurt people like her and her late husband. They hurt her in the worst possible way they could when they killed her boy. They had to be heartless bastards to kill a thirteen-year-old child. They want what she has. They can't earn it, they'll never have it, so they want to take it however they can. There will always be someone willing to take the chance and go after her. She will have to be careful forever." Mike didn't disagree with him, but what he described was a terrible life sentence for Theo, and Mike's heart ached for her. At least the last set of criminals who had tried needed to be found. Guy Thomas made it seem hopeless, and he obviously felt it was.

"You'll keep me informed?" Mike asked him before he left, after three hours in Thomas's small, cluttered, airless office. Guy had been impressed with Mike, and liked him, which was what Mike had hoped—that they'd form a bond of some kind, and Guy would be inspired to try harder and shake the trees again until something fell out to help solve the case.

"Of course," he assured him. "I'll let you know if I hear anything. But I don't have much hope. The trail is very cold."

"Someone knows something somewhere. All it'll take is for one of them to talk and it will start to unravel. I assume you have DNA samples from the scene?"

Guy nodded. "We do." He liked Mike's enthusiasm and positive attitude, even if he was less optimistic than his American counterpart. But the CIA had such great resources to work with, the DGSE didn't. France just didn't have the budget the U.S. had. "By the way, be careful tomorrow. We're having 'manifestations,' protests, and a general strike. There could be violence. Our protests have been getting out of hand. They're our specialty, all the way back to the French Revolution. Don't go out if you don't have to, or at least stay away from the large crowds of protestors."

"I'm a big guy, I can take care of myself." Mike smiled at him. "I'm not going to let them spoil Paris for me."

Guy smiled at his new friend. Nothing seemed to deter him on any front, and his enthusiasm was contagious. Guy felt revitalized about the Pasquier case after talking to him for three hours and showing him some of the files. Mike's heart nearly broke at some of the photographs, and he hoped Theo had never seen them. Guy assured him she hadn't. It made it all the more real to Mike, and made his sympathy for her even deeper.

He called Theo after he left the DGSE offices on the Boulevard Mortier in the twentieth arrondissement. He was going to suggest a last-minute invitation to dinner, that night or on the weekend. He was going to tell her he was on a brief business trip that had come up suddenly, not that he had come to Paris to see her or Guy Thomas on her behalf. He wondered if she'd be out to lunch, but the receptionist put him through to her immediately and she answered her direct line herself.

"Mike Andrews?" she said when he spoke. "What are you doing here?" She didn't sound unhappy about it, and her heart took a leap as soon as she heard his voice, in spite of all her recriminations since they'd had dinner.

"I came to see my client here," he said, sounding pleased too, more than he wanted to. The chemistry between them seemed to work even over the phone, much to his dismay. He could feel his good resolutions sliding away, like Jell-O down the drain. "I'm here for the weekend," he told her. "Any chance you're free for lunch or dinner while I'm here?" He was braced for a refusal and told himself it would be all right if she declined.

"That sounds good to me," she said, smiling at her end. "What's good for you?" she asked him.

"Tonight?"

"Perfect."

"Your choice this time. Your city. Same rules. Simple dinner. I left my tux at home."

"How disappointing," she teased him. "Do you like French food? Like bistro food?"

"That sounds terrific. We'll have to find a substitute for the banana split."

"Profiteroles."

"Excellent."

"Why don't you come to the apartment for a drink first?" She gave him the address and told him where it was.

"I'll take a cab or an Uber."

"Casual. You don't need to wear a suit."

"I usually do," he said. It wasn't entirely true, but he liked dressing for her. She was always well dressed, or at least on the two occasions he'd seen her, and she had great style.

"Come at seven-thirty. I'll make an eight-thirty reservation."

He took a walk after that, and then went back to his hotel. He noticed on the way that there were police barricades being set up in various locations, a water cannon truck for crowd control, and two tanks with tear gas cannons, and he wondered if Guy was right and the demonstrations would get rough the next day, or if they were just being cautious. There were trucks marked "CRS," which he knew were riot police. But he was more excited about seeing Theo again that night. It had only been a few days since they left each other outside the diner. He was glad he'd made the trip, even if he only got to see her once. He was smiling, thinking about it as he walked into his hotel, with riot police parked out front.

Chapter 7

The cab driver had no trouble finding her address, and he could see why when he got there. It was a large, imposing elegant building more than a hundred years old, and he was pleased to see armed security outside when he walked in. He rang the intercom for her apartment, and was buzzed in. The security guard outside her front door nodded and Mike smiled at him. Theo opened the front door herself, and was wearing gray slacks and a blue sweater the color of her eyes. She smiled broadly and looked pleased to see him.

"What a nice surprise to see you here," she said warmly, and he followed her into the impressive front hall. She led him straight to her office instead of the living room, as though they were old friends. One of the bodyguards appeared and she asked Mike what he'd like to drink. He would have been happy with a scotch and water, but decided it was the wrong way to start the evening.

"What are you having?" he asked her.

"What about champagne to celebrate your trip to Paris?" That seemed the right tone, so he agreed, and she asked the bodyguard to bring it. He disappeared as she waved Mike to the big leather chairs in her office. He felt instantly at ease, although he'd been nervous on the drive from his hotel. He had wondered if she would be as easy to be with and as low-key as she had been at dinner in New York, and he could see that she was. She didn't have that frightened look she'd had at the opening party in New York. And despite the grand surroundings of her apartment, she seemed casual and relaxed with him. There was nothing snobbish or pretentious about her, which he admired. She was a very modest person, though she could easily have been otherwise with her wealth and success.

She asked him again what he was doing there, and he told her about his fictional client, mildly embarrassed to be lying to her. But he couldn't tell her the truth that he had come for her, to push the investigation back to life, and hopefully to see her if he was lucky. He felt very fortunate that night, sitting close to her in the comfortable chairs in her office, as he enjoyed the mixture of fine art and personal memorabilia on the walls, and her company. He noticed the photographs of her son all over the room and didn't comment.

"I thought I might never see you again," she said gently, after the bodyguard brought the champagne and poured it for them. She had thanked him, and he disappeared.

"Why would you think that?" Mike asked her.

"Because New York seems a long way from here, and I didn't imagine you'd have to come to Paris so soon. Did you know when I saw you?" she asked, curious that he hadn't mentioned it to her, except that he had a client in Paris, but not that he was coming to see him.

"It just came up midweek. He needed to see me about some investments."

"Will you have to work all weekend?"

"No, we finished today. It went faster than we expected. He left tonight for the weekend."

"How long are you here for?" she asked.

"Till Monday. I hear you're expecting protests and a strike tomorrow. I saw the police setting up today. It looks like they're anticipating some heavy action."

"People get crazy here."

"What are they protesting?"

"Low wages, high taxes, all the usual things. They're not wrong, but a bad element always infiltrates those protests and then they go nuts and start destroying property, burning cars, and looting stores. It's very disturbing, and it can get dangerous." She looked faintly concerned, but not too much so. It was a common occurrence there.

"Sounds like a good day to stay home," he suggested cautiously.

"I usually do. They close all the shops and restaurants anyway. If you get bored, you can come here and watch from my windows."

"Do they come to this neighborhood?" He was surprised.

"Sometimes. We have the guards, so I'm not worried. People won't get in, but they can throw rocks through the windows. If it gets too bad, I'll close the shutters." It seemed run-of-the-mill to her and he was pleased to see that she was well protected. They talked easily for an hour, and then they left to go to the restaurant. He caught a glimpse of the grand living room and a huge crystal chandelier in the dining room from the front hall where she put a coat on, then he followed her out of the apartment. One of the bodyguards came with them, and her driver was waiting downstairs in a discreet Mercedes.

"I used to like driving myself on an evening like this," she said wistfully. "They don't let me do that anymore, in case . . ." Her voice trailed off and he understood.

They drove to the Left Bank, and he saw that more barricades had been set up and there were police in the streets.

They reached the cheerful-looking bistro quickly. It had a terrace outside, and the inside was bustling with Parisians, people laughing and chatting at tables with red-and-white-checkered cloths, and waiters were rushing around with the menu on chalkboards. It was exactly what she'd promised: warm, friendly, and simple. He saw several people glance at her and recognize her immediately, but no one said anything. They were led to a corner table, where they wouldn't be jostled and she wasn't on view the moment people came through the door. She was definitely well known in Paris, even more than in New York.

She translated the menu for him, and when the food came it was as delicious as it had sounded. She had bouillabaisse and he had oysters, followed by a steak for Mike and chicken with mushrooms that smelled delicious for her. It all tasted as good as it looked.

"It's not as good or as much fun as the diner," she apologized. "And no jukebox. They really should put one in, it would be so much fun!"

"I think it's great as it is, and it feels authentically Parisian."

"It is. I love it here, and they're always nice to me. I used to eat dinner here all the time." Axel and Matthieu loved it.

"You will again." He smiled gently, and she told him what she'd been doing since she got back. She'd been busy, which seemed to be her normal style. He wanted to ask her what kind of security she had in her offices, but he didn't dare. She'd wonder why he was asking, since he was supposedly a lawyer, not an agent of the CIA. He couldn't say what he did anyway, it was all classified at a high clearance level, but he had to keep remembering to maintain his pretense of being a lawyer. She never questioned the story, and the evening sped by with good food, good wine, and good company. She looked relaxed and happy as they talked their way through dinner. She ordered profiteroles for them for dessert, which were filled with ice cream and drowned in chocolate sauce.

"Put this on our list of favorites, along with the banana splits," he said, grinning.

"Good, isn't it?" she agreed with him. "The banana split was better, but this is pretty good."

"I think I'd reverse that."

"I'd take you for my favorite ice cream tomorrow, but I think we'd better stay home. You can come to the apartment whenever you want. Just be careful. People can get really crazy and rock cars sometimes, or set fire to them."

"What about yours?"

"I keep it in a garage farther away when there are protests. It's sad that they get so out of hand. They even attack the monuments sometimes and put graffiti all over them or try to break them. It's terrible when they behave like that. The police use tear gas on them, so be careful tomorrow if you come over."

"I will, and you be sure to stay inside," he said seriously.

"I promise." She smiled at him. "I used to go away on weekends, especially if there were protests. But now I stay in the city." She didn't mention the château so he didn't either. He was careful to avoid the painful triggers of bad memories for her. Fortunately, he knew what most of them were.

They walked a little way after dinner, and then they got in her car, and she dropped him off at his hotel.

"See you tomorrow?" she asked, smiling.

"I will, and thank you for the invitation." He looked at her longingly, touched her cheek gently before he got out of the car, and she waved as he walked into the hotel.

She was smiling as she walked into the apartment and went to her office to answer emails, which was what she did at night, for lack of someone to talk to. She never went to bed until she was exhausted and had a better chance of sleeping. She sent Mike an email and thanked him again for dinner. He smiled when he saw it on his phone at the hotel. He had to remind himself that he had made a solemn vow to himself not to involve her in his life and the risks it entailed, but he could feel his resolve melting. All he had to do was see her, and he wanted to protect her, even from himself.

She went to bed late, as she always did, and woke in the morning when she heard the crowds start to gather under her windows. She peeked out and saw hundreds of protestors in the street and riot police standing by, biding their time, until they stepped in and began sending tear gas into the crowd.

She called Mike on his cellphone.

"Be careful when you come over," she warned him. "It's starting to look a little rough here, and they have the tear gas tanks set up on my street."

"It's not looking great here either," he said, glancing out the window at people milling around, many of them looked like students. The crowd seemed restless and angry, shouting slogans and kicking cars. "Thank God they don't use guns here, or they'd all be killing each other," Mike commented.

"It can get pretty nasty. There will be a lot of injuries and arrests if it gets bad," Theo added.

"I'll come over soon. Jeans okay?" he inquired. It seemed smarter not to attract attention under the circumstances.

"Of course, you can come in pajamas."

"Best offer I've had so far today," he said, and didn't tell her he didn't own any. He slept in the buff, but he wouldn't have said it to her.

"Just be careful. I don't want you to get hurt." She sounded worried, and he had a thought as he put on his jeans and a black sweater. He called the American embassy before he left the hotel. He asked for the duty officer at the CIA desk, and introduced himself with his CIA ID number, and said he had the proper credentials with him. They said they'd be ready for him when he arrived. They had no problem with his request.

When he got to the Rue du Faubourg Saint-Honoré, the street was closed to protect the British and American embassies, and the Élysée Palace, the French White House. They had set up a movable bulletproof wall and there were swarms of riot police on the street. All the shops were closed and many boarded up to discourage looters. It was the fanciest shopping street in Paris, full of jewelers and luxury stores. When he got to a police barricade, Mike showed his badge and credentials and pointed to the U.S. Embassy, and the policeman in charge waved him past the barriers. He wove his way through the riot police, gendarmes, and regular police, and entered the American embassy. A battalion of marines in combat uniforms were protecting the building, but inside, people were busy and grateful to be well protected. Mike asked for the CIA duty officer, who was expecting him, and they led him into a room where the agent was waiting.

"They get a little out of control here, sir." The CIA agent in charge smiled at him. "You're smart to pick up a loaner." It wasn't a large gun, but if anything untoward happened, he wanted to be able to protect Theo, and the weapon they were lending him would do the job. He felt better having it than not. He never traveled armed, unless absolutely necessary. It complicated things at the airport, and he hadn't expected to need a weapon in Paris, and was surprised by how extreme the preparations in the streets looked. He put it securely in his waistband at his back, which he thought Theo was less likely to notice. The guards in her employ were heavily armed, so it wouldn't be entirely unfamiliar to her, but surely a surprise that he was armed too. And hard to explain why he'd need a gun, as a lawyer.

"I'll get it back to you on Monday," he promised, after signing a slip for the loan, and then he loaded it with the bullets he'd been given. They gave him an embassy pass to go with it, in case he got stopped by police, which they said wasn't likely, and then offered him a bulletproof vest, which he declined. "I hate the damn things. I get so hot in them and I won't need it," he said confidently, and the agent nodded in agreement. All the agents complained of the same thing.

"Watch out for the tear gas, sir," the agent warned him.

Mike walked back down the street he'd come and, once past the bulletproof barricade, was lucky enough to find a cab. He headed straight to Theo's apartment.

He could tell the crowd was restless when he got there. People were shouting, throwing small random objects, and a few of the young men in the crowd were breaking car windows and starting to light fires when he got to her address. The cab driver motioned to him to go inside quickly, and Mike thanked him and wished him good luck. He rang the intercom, and her door guard buzzed him in, and he hurried up the stairs. Theo was waiting at the door seeming nervous, in a black sweater and jeans herself, her hair barely brushed, with no makeup, and he loved the way she looked, except for the worried expression.

"It seems like it's getting bad out there," Theo said. The security guards were closing the shutters, leaving one of each two open so they could see outside. The windows were all tightly closed so tear gas wouldn't enter the apartment, and they heard the first cannons go off, shooting tear gas into the crowd. Mike was shocked at what was happening, it looked like a war zone in the most civilized city in the world.

"They were starting to set fire to cars when I got here," he told her. He followed her into the kitchen, where she made coffee. It was only ten in the morning, and she turned the TV on so they could see what was happening on the various streets in Paris. Violence was erupting everywhere.

"Does this get them what they want?" he asked her, fascinated by it.

"No, they wind up hurt or in jail, but they do a hell of a lot of damage before that happens. It's pathetic—and a crime what they do to the city. They actually come from other cities during protests, just to loot and burn and vandalize and destroy property. The real protestors are usually peaceful, but it's the bad ones and the hoodlums who blend in with them who do all the damage. They shouldn't allow them to demonstrate anymore, it always turns into this now. People forget that this is a country that loves revolution, and the French think it's their civil right to protest about just anything. But this isn't protesting, it's mass destruction." She was angry, seeing the city she loved so torn apart and damaged. They could see that violence was breaking out on the streets all over Paris, mostly in public squares and in front of national monuments. And on the fancier streets of expensive stores, rioters were breaking store windows and rushing into shops to steal whatever they could, as the police followed, grossly outnumbered.

The air outside her apartment was thick with smoke from tear gas and burning cars. The rioters were building barricades on the streets with anything they could find, even tires they ripped off cars before setting fire to them. Streets were blocked and there were seething crowds everywhere. The riot police wearing helmets and shields turned the water cannons on them after that, which barely slowed them down. The regular rioters had gas masks to protect them from the tear gas. They had come prepared, with sledgehammers to destroy cars and bus stop shelters wherever they passed. The riot police were herding them away from her building, but Mike wasn't reassured by what he was seeing, and was glad he had picked up the gun at the embassy.

They peeked outside between the shutters again, and it was a madhouse on the street. Her security guards were alert and observing at the windows. People were digging cobble-stones out of the pavement and throwing them through windows, some of them wrapped in oil-soaked flaming rags to set fires in apartments once they landed. Theo's security had placed fire extinguishers next to each window.

"Let's stand back from the windows, Theo," Mike told her. They could hear rocks and cobblestones hitting the walls of the building, as rioters aimed at the windows. He was standing close to her in her study so they could both see between the shutters, and it was a narrow opening. As she turned away from the windows with him close behind her, she found herself in his arms, looking up at him, her body pressed against his. Closing his arms around her seemed like the most natural thing to both of them. Their resistance melted away and vanished in the same moment, as he kissed her, and felt so overwhelmed with desire for her, that he couldn't stop kissing her, and she felt as though she'd been starving for him all her life. They were both out of breath when they stopped, and they looked surprised. Neither of them had expected it to happen or wanted it to stop.

"Oh, Theo," he whispered to her, "I'm sorry, I shouldn't have done that." He had tried so hard to resist her and failed.

"Yes you should have." She held him tightly and she kissed him this time, and the floodgates opened all over again. They could both feel the dam breaking with all the pent-up emotions of years in his case, and longer than she had admitted to herself in hers. Matthieu's last escapade in Moscow had broken something in her that she suspected might never have repaired even if he had lived. All she knew now was that she had never been so overwhelmed by passion in her life. There were tear gas cannons exploding outside, and an explosion in their minds and bodies inside. He wanted her then and there, and knew he had to stop. He forced himself to pull away from her, and could barely do it. She had bewitched him body and soul.

"I don't want you to do something you'll regret later," he said in a low voice, rough with passion and new love for her.

"I won't regret it," she said with utter conviction, as she

looked into his eyes. "He's been gone a year. This is fair, more than you know." But Mike did know about the girl in Moscow, which he couldn't say.

"You don't know me," he said softly.

"I know enough. I've never felt this way for anyone." But he also knew that she was lonely and had been severely traumatized. And he didn't want to take advantage of her when she was vulnerable.

"Neither have I felt this way," he admitted, and kissed her gently this time with an insatiable thirst for her that only she could quench. He had never wanted a woman as badly in his life, and he knew so much more about her than she did about him. That didn't seem right to him. But they were kissing again and couldn't stop. When they finally did, one of the bodyguards appeared in the doorway to check on her.

"Are you all right, ma'am?" he asked respectfully.

"Yes, fine, Daniel, thank you."

"We've set fire extinguishers around the house in case we need them."

"Thank you," she said again, and he left. Mike was satisfied to see that they were doing their job. He looked at her sheepishly, and pulled her into one of the big leather chairs with him. There was room for both of them, with her half on his lap.

"You must think I'm a savage," he said unhappily. "I didn't want to do this. I don't want to complicate your life."

"You're not," she reassured him. "I don't have a life. My life ended more than a year ago, with Axel, not Matthieu. Don't I have a right to be happy now, just for a moment, an hour, a day?" There were tears in her eyes and he pulled her into his arms again.

"Oh my darling . . . oh God, I'm so sorry. You deserve so much more than this . . . than me . . ."

"Shut up," she said. "Stop talking." She got out of the chair and pulled him to his feet, and then led him into the bedroom next to her office. She closed the door and locked it. The other door leading to it was already locked, and without pausing she pulled her sweater over her head, unzipped her jeans, slipped out of her ballet flats, and stood in her black lace underwear in front of him. She was nearly naked in the wisps of black lace that made it impossible for him to resist her. He pulled off his shirt and his own jeans quickly. The black lace vanished somewhere with his underwear. He had dropped the gun discreetly with his jeans, and she noticed it on the floor, partially covered by his clothes, and she looked startled for an instant.

"You carry a gun?"

"We'll discuss it later," he said, and crushed his mouth onto hers, but not enough to hurt her. His own passion was evident, as she turned her attention to that and he moaned. They fell onto her bed in a tangle of bodies and sheets and desire, as passion overcame them, the riots outside ceased to exist, and they couldn't stop until it was over and they lay breathless in each other's arms.

"Oh my God," he said breathlessly, as he looked at her. He wasn't sure if he was in heaven or hell, but wherever it was, he never wanted to leave or to leave her again. "Theo, we're crazy. This shouldn't have happened." She lay in bed next to him, smiling like the mystery she was to him. And she looked incredibly beautiful with her dark hair falling around her.

"Yes, it should," she said, catching her breath. "It's the only thing right that has happened in my life in years." She ran a finger from his Adam's apple down the center of his body until it reached where she intended it to, and then bent down and kissed him and he groaned. She looked so gentle and demure but she was a wild woman in bed, which he hadn't expected.

"Okay, I give up, you own me," he said, moaning as she guided him into her again, and they forgot everything but each other for another round of ecstasy and passion. She lay totally sated in his arms afterwards, as he looked at her in amazement.

"You're better than a thousand banana splits," he whispered to her, and she laughed. "Make it a million."

"Tell me about the gun. Why do you wear it?" She turned to look into his eyes.

"I borrowed it this morning," he said truthfully. "In case I needed to protect you."

"Do you always wear a gun?" she asked, curious as she studied him carefully. She loved everything she saw and knew about him.

"Yes," he answered her question. "Usually, but not when I travel." She was looking at him carefully, as though she could see inside his mind. It didn't frighten him. He liked it. He liked everything about her. They were on even ground, which was a first for her.

"You're not a lawyer, are you?"

He shook his head slowly. "No, I'm not." She was too smart for her own good, but he loved that about her.

"What are you really? I mean, what do you do?"

"I work for the CIA. And that's all I can tell you. Like in the army: name, rank, and serial number. I'm a senior supervising agent, and run a branch in New York."

She was intrigued, then sat up on the bed and looked down at him. "Why did you come to the party at the store?" She was beginning to think that it wasn't an accident that she'd met him.

"For two reasons. We had someone under surveillance who went to the party, and I wanted to meet you. That's the whole truth. I didn't happen into the back room by accident. I was looking for you."

"Why?" She was puzzled by his answer.

"To be honest, I don't know. I just felt compelled to meet you, as though I had to, for reasons even I didn't understand. Now I know. The minute I saw you, I felt this incredible pull toward you, like a magnetic force I couldn't resist and didn't want to."

"I felt it too," she admitted softly. "I felt it at the diner too."

"So did I. Do you suppose we're both crazy?" He actually meant it when he said it. He had wondered in the last week, but he didn't think so.

"Maybe this was our destiny—it was meant to be," she said thoughtfully.

"It feels that way," he said, gently fondling her breast. "You make me happy, Theo. I don't mean just like this. You make me happy like I've never been happy before."

"Me too." She was smiling at him. "And I'm not sorry, just so you know. And a CIA agent sounds quite exotic."

He smiled at what she said. She was graceful and elegant, even naked.

"It's not. It's anything but, but it's a useful job. I've made a difference in people's lives here and there. That's why I signed up. It's a good feeling."

"You've made a difference in mine," she said softly.

"Maybe we needed each other and that's why we found each other. Maybe why doesn't matter. It just is. I just don't want you to regret it one day," he said seriously.

"I don't think I will," she said, and he leaned over and kissed her.

"I know I won't. And I never want you hurt again." It was an enormous gift to give her, and a tall order to deliver in an unpredictable world, and they both knew it.

"Thank you," she said and stood up next to the bed as he admired her. She was a beautiful woman and he felt like the luckiest man in the world. "I suppose we should dress and pretend to look normal. Do you think we can stay out of bed until the guards go to their rooms tonight?"

"It will be an interesting challenge," he said, grinning at her as he rolled out of bed and stood next to her, towering over her. She felt small and safe next to him, and then they put their clothes back on, and he tucked the gun into his waistband again. They wandered back into her office, trying to look as though they'd never left it. He leaned down and whispered to her.

"Your sweater is inside out," he said in an undertone, and she giggled.

"So is my heart," she answered, and he kissed her again.

"So is mine," he whispered back.

Chapter 8

The rioters went crazy in the streets for the rest of the day, with the CRS riot police battling to control them while stores were broken into, vandalized, and looted, particularly on the Champs-Élysées. Cars were burned, buildings defaced, and monuments destroyed. It was upsetting to see even on TV, and Mike was shocked by the degree of violence. It seemed like an excuse for vandals and thieves to ravage the city, masquerading under the banner of a good cause. They sang "La Marseillaise" as they set fire to cars. It made Theo feel sick as she listened, it was a travesty. Nothing justified the wanton destruction of property and violence. They sat watching the news reports on TV and it was depressing to see.

Theo made lunch for everyone in the apartment. Both

the housekeeper and maid were off, but three of the rotation of bodyguards were there, and Mike talked with them during lunch. Then Theo and Mike sat alone for a while at her kitchen table.

"So what do we tell people you do? That you're a lawyer?" she asked him.

"That's usually what I tell people. My sister knows, but that's as far as it goes. I tell people when I deal with other law enforcement agencies in whatever country I'm working with on an assignment, but I don't announce it at dinner parties." He smiled at her.

"Is what you do dangerous?" She looked worried.

"Sometimes. Not as dangerous as it used to be. I spent a number of years in South America working undercover. That has a fairly high mortality rate. It's why most agents don't get married or have kids. It's not a life you want to inflict on someone else. When you do undercover work, you can be gone for a year or two at a time, with no communication. It's tough on families. There's a number you can call to leave or receive messages, but sometimes you can't even do that, if it puts an operation at risk. They pulled me out eventually, at the right time. What I do now is a lot tamer, and involves a lot more deskwork. But there's always a certain degree of risk. That's why I didn't want to drag you into it. It's not fair to you."

"I don't feel like I have a choice." She looked at him with

wide-open, innocent eyes. It touched him deeply. "I don't know why or how, but we found each other, and I feel like I belong with you, in your life. I *want* to be here."

"So do I," he said. "But if you don't want to be, I'd understand."

"Is that why you never married?"

He nodded. "Yes. It's a life that suits me. I've always felt that I was doing the right thing. That's a good feeling. And it's interesting and challenging every day. You learn to trust your instincts."

"It's a lot more complicated than figuring out what fashions to put online." She smiled at him.

"What you do is complicated too. I don't have the head for business that you do." He had saved money over the years and made some good investments, and he would be comfortable when he retired, with a good pension. But her success was huge.

"What I do is harder now, because I have Matthieu's business to run too. Thank God he had some great people working for him. I couldn't do it without them." Until now, she had felt like she was drowning for the past year. "I might sell my own business one day. I'm not sure I want to do this forever, but it's worked well, and it's been good to me. I've done it for fifteen years." Nothing in her life had the meaning for her that it once did. Except Mike.

"I've been with the agency for nineteen. I could retire at fifty, after twenty years, but I wouldn't know what to do with myself," he said.

"That's how I feel too. Especially now, after . . ." He knew the rest of the sentence. She didn't have to finish it.

"I could organize private security, and have my own firm, but that's never appealed to me. I like bringing bad people to justice." He smiled at her, then took her hand in his and kissed it. "I don't know what I'm doing here, or why you want me." Like her, he was a modest person.

"I do. I can make a list for you if you like. You're a special person. I felt it immediately."

"That's how I feel about you," he said gently. It had all happened so fast, they were like magnets. They had both felt it. An irresistible force that nothing could pull apart, or at least not easily. And having made love to her, he wanted more of her, and was more sure than ever. She felt that way too.

They spent the rest of the day watching Paris burn on TV. The guards made their own dinner in the small kitchen upstairs, and Mike and Theo were left to their own devices. As soon as the bodyguards went upstairs, they went straight to her bedroom and locked the door again, and they were both hit by another tidal wave of passion that kept them in its grip for hours. It was like a strong current they couldn't escape and didn't want to until they washed up on shore, exhausted, four hours later, at one o'clock in the morning. Mike said he was starving, but they were too tired to move and go to the kitchen.

It was an experience Theo had never had before, un-bridled sex for hours, and neither had he. He finally got out of bed and stood naked in front of her.

"I'll make an omelet, or something else from whatever you've got left in the fridge," he said, and headed for the shower first.

"I think I'm too tired to eat," she said, barely moving in bed as he smiled at her from the bathroom doorway.

"I'll be back in a minute," he promised. But the sound of the shower running and knowing that he was in it roused her from the dead, and she followed him into the bathroom a few minutes later, and stood under the pelting hot water with him. It felt good on their bodies.

"I might be too old for this," she said to him, and he laughed.

"I can hardly stand up," he said, and they both laughed. "Nice way to die though." He leaned down and kissed her, and she fondled him. "If you touch me without feeding me first, I may just collapse here in the shower." They managed to get out of the shower without making love again. He put a towel around his waist, and she put on a robe, then they walked to the kitchen, feeling better after the shower. "The bodyguards won't walk in on us, will they?" he asked, concerned.

"One of them will come to sleep down here eventually, but they're probably eating or watching TV or playing cards. The night guy doesn't come down till later." He was beginning to realize what a burden it was for her to be constantly surrounded by people, but she was going to have to live with it for the rest of her life. She would be a target forever, and probably had been for longer than she'd realized. It was hard to live like that on a daily basis and accept the restrictions on all the things she could no longer do, like drive herself or go to the grocery store alone, or run through her house naked if she wanted to. She was solitary but never alone.

He made her an excellent omelet, and they found some roast chicken, which Mike devoured ravenously. They went back to bed after that and lay talking once they turned out the light. There was so much they wanted to say and learn about each other. She drifted off to sleep while she was still talking to him, and he kissed her gently and rolled over on his side. He liked the feeling of her lying next to him, which was something he'd never enjoyed much before. He preferred spending his nights alone, and usually left as soon as possible after spending time with a woman. But he hadn't loved any of them except Becky, and he did love Theo. Even after such a short time, he knew it.

He woke up before she did the next morning. It was a sunny day and the rioters had vanished in the night. He had heard sirens in the distance, until three A.M.—fire trucks and police cars and the riot police going back to their barracks, he assumed.

He looked out the window and there was burnt debris in the street. Cars were smashed and blackened, empty hulls, and there was a carpet of glass in the street. It looked like snow. It would cost millions or even billions to repair the damage that had been done. He saw the graffiti on the buildings. It seemed like sacrilege to him in a city like Paris. When he turned, he saw that Theo was awake and watching him. He smiled and came to sit next to her on the bed.

"They're gone, but they left a hell of a mess," he reported to her.

"That's what they do," she said, and stretched, smiling up at him. "Did I dream yesterday, or did it really happen?"

"Something tells me this is for real," he said with a serious expression.

"I think so too. What do you want to do today?" she asked him. He was going home the next day, and she wanted their last day together to be memorable. She didn't know when she'd see him again. He was about to disappear like a mirage, back to his life in New York.

"Can we take a walk? I love this city, although it looks badly beaten up today."

"We can go for a walk in the Bois de Boulogne, but I have to take one of the guards with me." He was relieved to see that she was good about it and accepted it as a necessity in her life.

They were both shocked by the damage they saw when they went out a little while later. There were already cleaning crews picking things up and throwing them into garbage trucks. They were driven to the Bois de Boulogne and had lunch at a neighborhood bistro afterwards, where they sat in the sun on the terrace. The air was cool, but the sun felt good on their faces, and then they went back to her apartment and made love again.

He checked out of his hotel late that afternoon, brought his things to her apartment, and spent his last night with her there. He had to leave for the airport at five to be there at six o'clock the next morning. She got up with him at four, made breakfast for him while he showered, and then sat with him while he ate it.

"What am I going to do without you now? I won't be able to sleep without you," she said wistfully. Having him there had begun to seem normal, in a surprisingly short time.

"I'll come back and see you soon, Theo," he promised. He could see the sadness of loss in her eyes again and it pained him for her. She had no one now, and was so alone. But it was the reality of their lives. She lived and worked in Paris, and he had a job in New York. Neither of them could give up their careers at this point, and they didn't want to. They would have to find a way to make it work, living in two cities three thousand miles apart. Others did it, and they could too. But he hated to leave her when he kissed her goodbye. What if she came to her senses after he left and never wanted to see him again? He didn't even dare voice the thought to her, for fear it might come true.

"You won't forget me?" she asked as he kissed her in the doorway, and he laughed.

"I was just thinking the same thing. And no, I won't forget you. I've never even seen a movie this good. I'll need two weeks to recover from my three days in Paris, but it was worth every minute of it." He kissed her again with his arms around her, and didn't want to leave.

"If you miss your flight, come back," she said hopefully, and he smiled and gave her one last kiss. The magic was still there. It had only gotten better after the discoveries they'd made and the secrets they'd shared. He had to stop at the embassy on his way out of town to return the gun he'd borrowed. He had removed the bullets first, and they would give it all back to the CIA duty officer later in the morning when he came in.

She waved as he walked down the stairs, and then gently closed the door and rushed to the window to wave to him again. He waved back and got into the car. She was sending him to the airport in a car driven by one of her guards, although Mike insisted she didn't have to, but he finally gave in.

She watched the car pull away and climbed back into the bed she had shared with him for two days and two whole nights. A page had turned, another chapter in her life had begun. She had no idea where it would lead them, but she hoped to a better place than she'd been for over a year, after the worst moments of her life. But Mike was here now, a different person, a different life. It all seemed unreal once he was gone, and she fell asleep. She found a note from him on her bathroom mirror when she woke up again.

It said only "See you soon. I love you, Mike." It was enough, more than enough. He had put balm on her severely wounded heart, and if it worked, they had much to look forward to. It was something to hold on to. She folded the note and put it in her pocket. His plane had taken off by then, and she had her own life to get back to, until she saw him again. She hoped it would be soon, just as his note said. It sounded like a promise.

*   *   *

She was in her office when Pierre de Vaumont called her that afternoon. She remembered seeing him on the plane, and knew he had gone to the opening party in New York, but she couldn't imagine why he was calling her. They weren't friends and never had been. She avoided people like him. She no longer moved in the circles he did, and had no desire to. She had given up her entire social life since Matthieu's death, and didn't miss it. They were all Matthieu's friends anyway. He'd dictated their social life, and most of the time she'd followed, to please him and keep him happy. Although she wondered if she would have been quite so willing to follow his lead after the girl in Moscow. That last escapade of his would have had an inevitable impact on their marriage, if the worst hadn't happened. It had subtly changed her feelings for him even after his death.

Pierre de Vaumont made meaningless chitchat for a few minutes and she was eager to get back to work. She didn't know why she had taken the call, just to be polite. He finally spat out what he wanted.

"There's going to be a fabulous party at Versailles next month, for a good cause, of course. I'm putting together a table, and I was hoping you would join me and host it with me."

She didn't know if he was asking her to pay for it, or pay half of it, or just be there as his date, or as a showpiece to enhance his social status, but whatever his motive, she had no desire whatsoever to go anywhere with him or be seen in public hosting a table with him, whatever the cause. She thought it an unsuitably bold request.

"I'm not going out yet," she said demurely. "I'm just not ready, but thank you so much. Very kind of you to ask me." She hustled him off the phone then. He seemed slimy to her, and he clearly had an ulterior motive. He was incredibly transparent, and she knew that Matthieu had never liked him either. He had a nose for phonies and users, and was practically allergic to them. Pierre de Vaumont was a prime specimen of the breed.

Mike called a little while later to say he had landed safely in New York and was on his way home to his apartment, which would be morbidly depressing without her.

"I had the creepiest call today," she said, filling him in on her day. "From a disgusting social climber. He was on my plane to New York and I gave him an invitation to the party at the store. He came, which was good for press coverage. He called to invite me to some big event at Versailles next month. I turned him down flat."

"Who is he?" Mike had an odd tone in his voice, and she wondered if he was jealous.

"You won't know him. He slinks around anyone with

money in Paris. I think he takes commissions on introductions and deals he puts together. His name is Pierre de Vaumont. I felt like I needed a bath after I talked to him." Mike didn't acknowledge knowing who he was, but after they ended the call, he wanted to call Guy Thomas and tell him. De Vaumont was definitely after Theo for money or social connections. He called Guy but only got voicemail, and he didn't want to leave the message on voicemail.

He was already worked up, and concerned about de Vaumont, when Robert Richmond called about half an hour after he got home.

"Hello, mate. Hope I'm not getting you at a bad time. I wanted to give you a heads-up about your friend de Vaumont. He seems to be stepping up his game and moving in more dangerous circles. You're right. He bears watching."

"He's no longer in my jurisdiction. He's back in Paris," Mike said, annoyed to hear his name again. Mike still thought he was trouble, even if Guy Thomas didn't.

"He was in London this week and met with a Chinese arms dealer we know about and keep an eye on. He introduced him to a Russian 'friend' of his, who's actually a double agent we know all about. The Russian was poisoned and died yesterday."

"He's trying to crawl up on Theo Morgan too," Mike told him. "He is definitely broadening his circle. How does the

Russian double agent figure into this, and the Chinese arms dealer?"

"Just bigger commissions, I suspect. But he's playing in the big leagues now, or trying to. Those are both dangerous men, as witnessed by the poisoning of the Russian. He's been playing a double game for a while and it seems to have caught up with him. If de Vaumont falls in with that crowd and gets on their wrong side, they won't screw around, they'll kill him," Robert said bluntly.

"I'll pass the intel on to Guy Thomas in Paris," Mike said to Robert.

"That sounds like a good idea. You never know who these connectors and dealmakers will fall in with."

Mike thanked him, hung up, and called Guy Thomas again, this time on his personal cell, but still didn't get him. He was anxious to share the info on de Vaumont with him.

Guy called him back at seven A.M. in Paris when he got up. It was one A.M. for Mike, but he was still awake, at his computer.

"Something important?" he asked with his heavy French accent, and Mike reported to him what Robert Richmond had told him about the meeting and the Russian double agent being poisoned.

"I still think de Vaumont's a small-time bullshitter, and relatively harmless." Guy Thomas held firm to his position.

"His friends aren't harmless," Mike pointed out to him. "And he's chasing after Theo Morgan now, with social invitations. I think you need to keep an eye on him."

"I have a better idea," Guy volunteered, "for your peace of mind and mine. I'm going to put a tail on Theo Morgan Pasquier. I won't tell her. He'll be discreet. It's more important that we keep her safe and see who approaches her, than worrying about a little piece of garbage like de Vaumont. He's a waste of time."

"Maybe less and less so. I think we need to keep a vigilant eye on him." But he did like the idea of protecting Theo. "I think that's an excellent idea about a tail for Theo Morgan. How soon can you start?"

"Later today. I promise." Guy Thomas was surer than ever that Mike had some kind of personal interest in the Pasquier case, but whatever it was, he didn't need to know it. Theo was the one at risk, not the people who knew her.

"Thanks, Guy, I appreciate it," Mike said.

"I think it's the right thing to do," Guy responded. "And maybe we'll get lucky and catch a bigger fish in our net. I just hope it's a bigger fish than de Vaumont."

Mike fervently agreed with him. He slept better that night, knowing that by the next day Theo would have an agent assigned to her as a protective tail at all times. She wouldn't even be aware of it, but he'd be there. Mike thought they should have been doing it for the last year, but better late than never. He could tell that Guy was already more alert and interested in the case. They had to find her husband's killers. Theo would be even more at risk than usual until they did. Mike's worst fear was that the same men would return for the rest of the money, and they'd kill Theo this time. He wanted to do all he could to prevent it from happening, whatever it took, and whatever he had to do to help.

Chapter 9

During the week after Mike left Paris, Theo felt as though she had been running from one meeting to the next. Meetings in Matthieu's old offices, meetings at Theo.com. She hardly had a minute to breathe, and Pierre de Vaumont called her again. The call came through her assistant, and she told her bluntly she didn't have time. She wasn't interested in his social invitations or his attempts to become friends. He didn't have a chance of that happening, and she was even more annoyed when he called again the next day, twice. He was persistent, if nothing else. She had been happy to invite him to the party at the pop-up in New York for the press he'd attract, but that was as far as it went. She had two mammoth businesses to run, and no time to waste on him.

On his third call, she finally picked it up and sounded somewhat exasperated when she said hello. As usual, she hadn't had time for lunch. They were revising all their merchandise on Theo.com for the fall, and she had to approve every item they put on the site.

"Oh, I'm so sorry," Pierre said when she answered. "Is this a bad time? I'm sorry to disturb you, Theo," he said as though they were pals.

"I'm running between meetings. What can I do for you?" she said coldly. She didn't want to encourage him or be a regular on his list of calls.

"I hope this isn't inappropriate, but I have a dear friend from Moscow arriving at the end of the week. He's desperate to find a home here, and he wants a château not too far out of the city. He has a wife and three small children, with full staff of course. You have such exquisite taste, and I have no idea if you'd be interested in selling your château, after . . . well, you know. It must be painful for you there now. My friend would even be willing to rent it fully furnished until you make up your mind. I wouldn't have bothered you, but he'll only be here for a few days, and he has to find something before his wife and children arrive." He sounded obsequious and apologetic, and just as slimy as before to her. Possibly even more so.

"Well, I certainly couldn't move that quickly. I haven't

thought about it. I have no idea if I'll want to sell it one day, and I'm not interested in selling it now." But he was right, she thought. It was unbearable going there now. She hadn't braved it yet, and she dreaded it. She'd been meaning to go in the next few weeks to bring back some of her fall clothes. "If I do sell it, it will be through a realtor," she said pointedly. He could smell a fat commission if he could convince her to sell or even rent it. And he suspected she'd be more likely to rent or sell to someone she knew than someone she didn't.

Matthieu's family château, which he had repurchased, was an extraordinary showplace he had lovingly restored and redecorated with the help of one of the best decorators in France. It looked like a smaller version of Versailles, and the gardens had originally been designed by Le Nôtre, who designed the Versailles gardens. The place had meant so much to him that she felt guilty selling it, but going there to stay again was impossible for her, knowing that Matthieu and Axel had been kidnapped from there. "I just don't know," she said vaguely, upset by the question, and even having to think about it. "I'm sorry, I can't tell you now. And I'm late for a meeting. If I put it on the market, I'll let you know."

"Could I go and visit it sometime, so I can describe it to him, and tell him if it would work for him? I've actually never been there myself." Of course not, she thought.

Matthieu would never have let him in the front door, given the slimy little opportunist he was.

"I have to pick some things up there myself in the next week or two, but I don't know when."

"Of course, I understand. You're so busy, and I hate to disturb you. I don't mind seeing it with a member of the staff."

"That won't be possible," she said coldly.

"May I call you at the end of the week and see if you might be going? I promise I wouldn't stay long."

She wanted to say no but she didn't, and she didn't know why. He had a way of worming his way in that was very effective, no matter how much he revolted her. But maybe his "friend" would actually buy the château if she decided to sell, which she thought she eventually might. She couldn't imagine staying there again or being happy there. She just hadn't decided yet. The decision was painful for her.

"All right, fine," she said, and could have kicked herself when she hung up. He was harmless, but he was such a little weasel. And then she forgot about him as she rushed to another meeting at Matthieu's offices, in preparation for a board meeting.

The rest of the week moved just as fast. She hardly had time to talk to Mike and forgot to mention de Vaumont's subsequent calls when she did. He had gotten so upset the

163

last time she mentioned him, about the party at Versailles that she'd declined, that she wasn't sure she'd tell him anyway.

Mike had been busy too. He never told her what he was working on, but she had learned to detect the stress level in his voice, or when things were going smoothly. Even long distance, they were learning each other's ways and inflections. She loved talking to him and hated that she had so little spare time at the moment. Things didn't slow down for her until late at night, and by then she was tired, but happy to hear him at the end of her day. He was usually still at the office then and getting ready to go home. He was working on finding a long weekend when he could come back to see her, but hadn't found the free time yet. They might have to wait another month, until Thanksgiving, when he could take a week off, but it wasn't a holiday for her in France, since it was an American holiday they didn't celebrate.

True to form, Pierre de Vaumont called her on Friday afternoon, but he called during a lull when she was a little less rushed and slightly more pleasant to him.

"Do you think you'll be going to the château this weekend?" he asked her. "My friend's trip has been delayed, but he has authorized me to look at a number of châteaux for him. Yours, of course, would be the most beautiful, and his first choice, and certainly mine."

"I haven't made any set plans, but I do need to pick up some clothes." There were several coats and a lot of sweaters she wanted to bring back, and there was no point leaving them since she knew she wouldn't be spending time there. He was so pushy that it was easier to say yes than continue to fob him off. He was very artful at what he did, and persistence usually got him what he wanted. "I suppose I could go tomorrow, around noon." She made the decision while she spoke to him. It couldn't do any harm. He was annoying, but maybe he really would pull off a simple advantageous sale, since he knew plenty of rich people who could afford a château. And then she wouldn't have to deal with realtors, strangers, and a curious press. She could see how he made his deals, all "among friends."

"I won't stay long. I don't want to intrude. I just need to see enough to give my friend an idea. May I take a few photographs while I'm there with my phone?"

"I'd rather you didn't," she said bluntly. "It's our home, and it's not on the market." And it had a shocking history now that the tabloid press was always hungry to exploit.

"Of course, I understand. See you tomorrow at noon," he said quickly, and hung up before she could change her mind.

* * *

The next morning, Theo overslept by half an hour, which was unusual for her. She got three important emails from Matthieu's CEO, which she had to respond to, so she got in her car a little later than planned. One of the bodyguards, Daniel, was going to drive her, and she'd given her driver the day off. Daniel was driving a station wagon they always used on the weekends. She could almost see Axel in the back seat when she got into the front passenger seat. She usually sat in the back seat with him, and Matthieu in the front seat where she sat now, with their driver at the wheel. Or sometimes she drove there alone with Axel, and Matthieu drove up on his own. She tried not to let the past surge into her head. There were so many good memories associated with the château, before the last bad ones replaced them. It was all a jumble in her mind now as she watched the familiar landmarks begin to slide by. It was only a little over an hour from the city, and it looked like real country, not a suburb. Matthieu had bought back a lot of land around it, which was planted in orchards and surrounded by farms.

She noticed that it was twelve-thirty when they reached the driveway and turned in. She could see Pierre de Vaumont waiting for them, and she wished she had gotten there slightly early as she had planned.

Minutes after they arrived, a man walked onto the grounds carrying a shovel and a watering can. He was clearly one of the gardeners, but she didn't recognize him. He began shoveling dirt under some bushes. She hadn't been there in over a year, so it didn't surprise her to see a new face on the grounds. He respectfully touched his cap as she got out of the car and walked toward Pierre with a quick step, then shook his hand. He was wearing brown leather Hermès gloves and was very chic in a dark brown suede jacket, gray turtleneck sweater, crisply pressed jeans, and brown suede low boots. He looked like the cover of a men's magazine.

"I'm so sorry, I got delayed," she apologized, and he smiled. She studied his face as he did and noticed again how handsome he was. She didn't know why she had such a viscerally negative reaction to him, but it was the oily way he always seemed on the make for what he could get out of a situation. There was nothing real or natural about him. It really seemed too bad. He was very good-looking and painfully polite, which made him socially acceptable, along with his aristocratic name, although she was sure he had no money other than what he made on his deals.

She pointed out the gardens and orchards to him and said that they were designed by Le Nôtre, who had done the gardens at Versailles. Everything was in immaculate condition, and it tugged at her heart to see the place again and remember how much Matthieu had loved it, and why.

It brought back tender memories for her too, of their happy times and watching Axel grow up there. They had gone faithfully almost every weekend.

The château had been Matthieu's first step back to restoring his family's property and fortune, and it had been deeply symbolic for him. He had been so eager to pass it on to Axel one day, and always made Axel walk the property with him, telling his son all about it. Inevitably one day Axel would have learned of the family's strong Nazi connections too, and that they'd lost everything they had as a result.

"Do you mind if I take a brief look in the house?" Pierre asked politely, and she nodded.

"Of course." She led the way and asked Daniel to bring in two suitcases she had brought with her for her clothes, and the two men followed her up the front steps. She had given the inside staff the afternoon off. She didn't want anyone around for her first visit back since the kidnapping. She wanted to be alone with her painful memories without anyone watching her. It was hard enough having de Vaumont there.

The new gardener continued shoveling dirt as she unlocked the front door, turned the large brass knob and switched off the alarm. Daniel and de Vaumont followed her in, and she closed the door behind them. She told Daniel where to leave the valises in her dressing room and gave

Pierre a brief tour of the main floor. Everything was in perfect order and of the highest quality: beautiful paintings, lovely antiques, fifteenth-century tapestries covering some of the walls, antique rugs. It really was easy to see why Matthieu had loved it, and she had too. But she no longer did. She didn't want to stay long enough for it to seriously upset her. De Vaumont could see that she was eager to leave. She showed him the large, extremely functional modern kitchen, and offered to run him upstairs quickly.

"You don't really need to. I don't want to overstay. It's a magnificent home, and a piece of history. I'm sure it has enough bedrooms." But she felt he should see it all and took him upstairs, where she carefully avoided Axel's room. She was grateful the door was closed.

"There are sixteen bedrooms, including the master suite," she explained. "Fourteen baths, and the entire top floor has been redone for nannies and house staff, and a nursery I put in when my son was born." Just saying it almost made her wince from the pain. The château was still an open wound for her, one she knew she wouldn't recover from.

"My friends would be fortunate if you ever decide to sell or rent to them," he said in respectful, hushed tones, as if visiting a church or a sacred monument, which it was to her.

"I'll let you know what I decide when I'm ready," she said

a little stiffly. It was hard being there, which made it difficult to talk to him.

"Thank you for letting me drop by. I'm afraid anything else I see will suffer by comparison."

She followed him out and walked the gardens with him, which were spectacular. She spent an hour with him and had a headache by the time he left. She went back upstairs to her dressing room and sat down for a minute. Being there upset her even more than she'd expected. She felt dizzy and lightheaded, and then got up, opened her drawers, and put stacks of sweaters on the bed. It took longer than she planned. She packed the sweaters neatly to take back to the city, as well as several coats she could wear with jeans on weekends. She went through her boots and decided that they were all rough heavy boots for walking on muddy country roads and not for the city. She stood up after packing for an hour and was perspiring from the effort. Her face felt damp and she felt dizzy again. It was too hard being there and she wanted to leave as soon as she could. It was too emotional. She took out another stack of heavy sweaters, held them in her arms, and walked down the stairs with them, feeling disoriented. She was confused for a minute and then reminded herself that she had come to take her sweaters home. For a minute she wondered where Axel was and thought he was upstairs, then remembered that he wasn't there.

She let herself out of the house, walked down the outer steps, and headed across the lawn holding her sweaters, walking past Daniel as she did. He was startled when he saw her, and she looked very pale.

"Can I help you, ma'am?" he offered.

"No, I'm taking these to Paris," she said with a determined look, and walked right past the station wagon with them toward the driveway. The gardener was staring at her too. Her bodyguard wasn't sure whether to interfere or not, or if the visit had been too much for her and snapped something in her mind. The gardener was watching her closely as Daniel followed her discreetly. She was standing in the driveway, looking confused. She gazed up at him when he reached her.

"I can't find my suitcase. It was here a minute ago. Did you bring it down?" she asked him.

"Not yet. It was in your dressing room, ma'am, when the gentleman left. I put your valises in your dressing room two hours ago."

"What gentleman? Was someone here?" He could see that her face was glistening with sweat, and she looked like she needed to sit down. He took the sweaters from her and walked her back to the front steps. She sat down and glanced up at him again. "I think I feel a little sick." As she said it, the gardener dropped his shovel and approached, and spoke in a smooth even voice to the bodyguard.

"I'm a paramedic," he said quietly as he reached for Theo's wrist and took her pulse. It was unusually slow and he glanced up at the bodyguard. "Does she take medication for low blood pressure?"

"No, I don't," she answered for herself, "but I'm feeling sick. Maybe I have the flu. I have a terrible headache." The gardener-turned-paramedic looked into her eyes and saw that her pupils were constricted. He stepped away and Daniel followed.

"She's been drugged, or drugged herself, an overdose of some kind. I'm calling an ambulance now." He took something out of his pocket then that appeared to be a wallet, and Daniel hoped it wasn't a gun, since he wasn't armed himself. The gardener flipped it open and it was a badge.

"I'm DGSE, assigned to Mrs. Pasquier. We need to get her to a hospital fast." He took out a cellphone and walked away to make the call for an ambulance, and as Daniel turned to check on Theo, she had her cellphone in her hand. She was calling Mike in New York. It was almost nine in the morning for him. She couldn't figure out the time difference, but she knew that something was wrong. She was groggy and dizzy, and felt confused. She was nauseous and her head was pounding and spinning. Mike had been doing his morning exercises and answered when he saw her name come up on his phone.

"Good morning, sunshine," he said in his deep morning voice that she knew now.

"Mike," she said, sounding breathless, "I think I'm sick."

"What kind of sick?"

"I'm sick to my stomach, and my head is pounding. I'm dizzy. And I keep forgetting what I was going to do. I'm at the château. I came to get something, but I can't remember what."

"Are you upset about being there?" His own heart was beating fast now too.

"Yes. No. It's sad, but I knew they wouldn't be here. I thought Axel was here, but he's not." She did remember that. "I think I came to get a coat," she said, sounding vague again.

"Who's with you?" he said, trying to sound calmer than he felt.

"Daniel and the gardener. They've been very nice, but I don't think I'm all right. That's why I called you. I keep getting mixed up like I'm half asleep. And Pierre de Vaumont was here, I think, but I'm not sure. I think he wants to buy the house or something."

"Theo, let me talk to Daniel," he said quietly. She didn't answer but handed him the phone. Mike had his official voice on the moment he spoke to the bodyguard. "Daniel, there should be someone in plainclothes in the vicinity. Look around and see if you notice anyone."

The bodyguard turned away so Theo couldn't hear him. "There's a gardener who says he's DGSE and a paramedic. I saw his badge. He called an ambulance."

"That's the one. How does she look?"

"Not well. She says she doesn't feel well, she's perspiring, and the gardener, the paramedic, says her pupils are constricted and her pulse is slow. He thinks she may have had an overdose of something, a medication maybe."

"Get her to a hospital as fast as you can. She may have been poisoned. I'm going to call his boss and see what we do now. Tell the ambulance when they arrive that it may be poison. I'll call you back."

Mike hung up, and called Guy Thomas on his personal cellphone. He picked up immediately when he recognized Mike's number.

"Theo's at the château and I think she may have been poisoned. De Vaumont was there with her."

"Christ, this is all we need. Is my guy with her?"

"Yes, he called an ambulance and identified himself. He was posing as a gardener," Mike told him rapidly.

"He has medical training. I'll call him right away. I want her taken to the nearest hospital, and if they let her, I'd like to have her at a hospital in the city, so our people can keep an eye on her if she's been poisoned. And I want all her lab work sent to one of our facilities. They know what to look for." As he said it, he was praying that no one had administered one of the Russian nerve agents, which would be disastrous. Even the château would have to be decontaminated, if that was the case. "I'll send someone to get the keys to the château from her," Guy said to Mike. "I want a forensics team out there immediately to comb the place and see what they find. How bad is she?"

"I can't tell. She doesn't sound good, and she knows something's wrong, but she knew enough to call me. She says she's confused, and she sounds it."

"Let's hope it's not too bad. I'm on it, Mike. I'll get things moving."

"Thanks, Guy," he said, then hung up and called Robert.

"I think Theo's been poisoned. I could be wrong, but it sounds like it could be. And I have no idea why, but de Vaumont was with her. Something about buying her house."

"Is he still there?"

"No, I think he left."

"If you're right, have them tell the hospital to give her atropine immediately. It won't cure her, but it will stop the action of the poison and restore her functions to normal. And they have to give her oximes. They're the only antidote, if it's a nerve agent. The fucking Russians love them and use them on each other all the time. Some are stronger than others. Let's hope this is a mild one. This is serious, Mike. It could be fatal."

"Why on her?" Mike said through clenched teeth.

"For a lot of reasons we can figure out later. Let's make sure she's going to be okay first. They don't want to kill her, they want to scare her. We've been hearing echoes in Russia this week that they want their other fifty million. They're finally coming out of the woodwork, and if they kill her, they won't get it. They're smart enough to know that. Where are you, by the way?"

"I'm in New York, she's outside Paris, at the château. Guy Thomas at the DGSE is going to get her taken to the right hospital and do a forensic search at the château."

"He's a good man, even if a little slow to react sometimes."

"He had a protective tail on her and his guy is with her now. He's a paramedic and works for the DGSE. He said it looks like some kind of overdose."

"That's about right. Tell them about the atropine and oximes, and keep me posted."

"Thanks, Robert," Mike said, distracted and worried about Theo.

Mike called back to her cellphone and Daniel answered. "What's happening?" Mike asked him quickly.

"The ambulance just got here, they're putting her in now. They're going to take her to a hospital here to check her out and see if she can go to the city. She's a little more confused and she says she's dizzy. I'm going to lock up here and follow in the car."

"Tell them it may be a nerve agent of some kind, and to use atropine to stop the action of the poison, and oximes are the only antidote. I hope to hell they know what they're doing."

"She was having a little trouble breathing and they gave her oxygen. I'll run in and lock up now," Daniel told him.

"Call me from the hospital when you know what's going on."

"Yes, sir." He ran into the house then, forgetting about her suitcases upstairs. They could come back for them another time. He picked up her purse from the hall table, pulled the front door firmly shut by the big antique brass knob, and rushed out to the car. The DGSE agent was in the ambulance with Theo, and Daniel rushed to start the station wagon to follow them.

They took her to a local hospital ten miles away. It was small, clean, and efficient, and Daniel relayed all of Mike's messages to them. The attending physician looked startled when Daniel suggested it might be a nerve agent, and what medications to administer. He looked it up on his computer and saw that her symptoms matched those of a possible nerve agent, and he administered the medications Robert had recommended. Within twenty minutes the symptoms had stopped, but the danger, if it was a nerve agent, was permanent nerve damage. They suspected that she'd had an infinitesimal dose, but enough to cause considerable disturbance. Any more would have had a much more severe reaction. A poison called Novichok was the most dangerous one, in which case she would be severely disabled or die. She needed bloodwork to determine if, in fact, she had been poisoned, and with what substance. The DGSE agent had taken over communicating with the doctor once they were in the hospital, and the doctor felt that she was well enough to be moved to the city, to a hospital where they could test her to find out what had been administered and how extensive the effects were.

They were getting ready to move her back to the ambulance when Daniel stumbled into the room and said he was feeling ill too. They examined him immediately and his symptoms were identical to hers. They waited another fifteen minutes and put him in the ambulance with her. The DGSE agent drove the car home for them, and they reached the Pitié-Salpêtrière Hospital in Paris forty-five minutes later, with the siren blaring, the lights flashing, and the DGSE agent driving right behind them.

Guy Thomas and one of his assistants were waiting for them there. He spoke briefly to Theo and reassured her that they would take good care of her. He got the keys to the château from her bodyguard and dispatched a forensics team within half an hour. Theo described where she had gone in the house and what she might have touched as best she could, and Daniel did the same. With the atropine, their symptoms had abated, and oximes had been administered as a precautionary antidote. Their bloodwork was on the way to the DGSE lab.

By midnight the first reports were back from the lab. They had been poisoned with a minute quantity of a new nerve agent that mimicked the much more dangerous Novichok nerve agent, and the weaker substance caused far less damage. Oximes were effective as an antidote, and Theo and Daniel were lucky it wasn't worse.

The DGSE forensics team found traces of it on the brass doorknob of the château. It could be inhaled or ingested or absorbed through the skin. It was odorless and slow to deteriorate. It acted by blocking the messages from the nerves to the muscles, causing a collapse of bodily functions, and when given in large enough doses, it could cause lasting nerve damage, permanent disablement, or death. The substance would not wear off the surfaces where it was applied, so the DGSE anti-poison team had had to remove the brass doorknob where it had been applied and it would have to be replaced. It couldn't be decontaminated.

Guy Thomas called Mike with all their findings at one A.M., which was seven P.M. in New York. Mike had been worried sick about Theo all day, but at least he knew she was in good hands.

"How is she?" he asked with deep concern in his voice.

"I think she and the bodyguard are feeling slightly better. Our friend at MI6 recommended the right substances to arrest the action of the poison and provide the antidote. The atropine stops the effects, and the oximes will counter it. Apparently confusion and dizziness set in very quickly. It's a fast-acting poison, but the effect is far less severe than other nerve agents used in Russia. They're both going to be okay. They'll be kept in the hospital for a week of observation. They were lucky it wasn't worse."

"Why would de Vaumont do that, if he did?"

"Apparently he wanted to help one of his clients buy the château. It's worth a fortune and probably represents a huge commission to him. I think the intention may have been very subtle. If she thought that she was so upset when she went there to the point that she felt ill, she might sell to him more quickly, and at any price. It's one way to close a deal, *if* it was him. I took a statement from her and the bodyguard myself, and they both mentioned that he was wearing gloves. He may have applied the poison to the doorknob himself, or someone else did. It could have been a very convincing tactic, if you hadn't figured out immediately what it was."

"Robert Richmond at MI6 had given me some of the information before and it rang a bell," Mike said simply.

"The Russians use a lot of those nerve agents. They can be brutal. With the stronger ones like Novichok, most of the victims die, or are severely impaired for years or for life," Guy said.

"I've read a lot about it lately in *The New York Times*. We haven't seen any of that here," Mike said, deeply troubled by what had happened.

"I think we should arrange a conference call between you, me, and Richmond this week," Guy suggested.

"That's fine. He said he'd be willing to come to Paris if you want. He's been hearing vague rumors from informants in the Russian underworld that the original kidnappers want to come back to collect the other fifty million. That means you'll have to watch Mrs. Pasquier like a hawk. These people will stop at nothing."

"We will be watching her closely from now on, even more closely than we have been. We want to catch them this time, once and for all," Guy said, angry at what had just happened to her.

"Yeah. Me too. What are you going to do about de Vaumont?" Mike was anxious to know.

"I think we'll bring him in for a little visit. We'll tell him how concerned we are about him, that he may have come in contact with it too during his brief visit, and we want to test him, for his own sake, to make sure he wasn't exposed. We'll see if we find traces, but he may be knowledgeable about how to handle it. It's a long-lasting agent, so we may find traces. I'm sure he threw away the gloves."

"What a sonofabitch," Mike said in a fury.

"You were right," Guy admitted. "He's worse than I thought, and not as small-time as I believed he was. Or maybe his friends are teaching him new tricks. He bears watching, very closely. Apparently he's willing to do anything for a price. Who knows, he may have supplied information to the kidnappers a year ago. Maybe he talked to a gardener or a maid to learn their habits. Anything is possible. If he did, we'll find out eventually, even if it takes time. Someone always talks."

"I hope so," Mike said, shaken by the experience of the day. He thanked Guy for his rapid action, and the very efficient agent he had assigned to Theo, who had moved quickly and effectively to get her medical help.

He called Robert after that and thanked him too.

"De Vaumont is a rotten piece of work. I didn't think so at first. I thought he was a lightweight," Robert said apologetically. "I question that now."

"We all did, but I had a bad feeling about him," Mike said. "I think now that he's worse than we believed. A lot worse. He'll stop at nothing to cash in on any situation. I wonder what they paid him to poison Theo today, or maybe it was his idea to speed along the sale of the château. Pretty heavy-handed."

"Thank God it was a small dose of a less lethal substance. We deal with these things all the time. If it's bad enough, they don't recover. They die within a few months because nothing can reverse the damage. I hope she'll be all right," Robert said.

"It sounds like she will." Mike had already booked a flight and was taking Thursday and Friday off to be there through the weekend. She was expected to be out of the hospital by then, if all went well.

Mike had spoken to Theo that night before she went to sleep. They had given her something to relax her, so she was drowsy but she made sense. She had had a long, traumatic day. She still felt ill from the poison, but not extremely so, and she had been exposed to so little of it that they thought she'd make a full recovery, but it was very upsetting anyway.

"Do you really think de Vaumont would do that to me to make me sell?" she asked him, still somewhat incredulous

183

about everything that had happened, and the theories that had been proffered.

"I don't know," he said, "but it's possible. He sounds like a very greedy guy with some dangerous connections." He didn't discuss the kidnapping with her. He didn't want to upset her. "Just rest and get well this week, till it gets out of your system. Leave the bad guys to the agencies who are there to take care of that."

"I feel bad about Daniel. The poor guy was sicker than I was. But they said we were both lucky it was on a door-knob and not some other place. Apparently your palms are more resistant than other parts of the body, so it couldn't penetrate as easily." They had learned more about poison that day than they ever wanted to know.

"I'm just glad they got you to the hospital quickly, and it was a small dose of a less dangerous substance than some of what's out there." He wondered how they were going to keep her safe from people who used such lethal and creative methods to destroy their victims.

"I really need to get to the office," she complained, sounding anxious. "And I miss you," she said in a small voice.

"I miss you too. I wish I were there to protect you myself." He had thought a lot about it, and he wanted to review all her security measures and tighten them when he came back. It would be a big project, but it was necessary, particularly if the kidnappers had surfaced and were restless. "I want you to be very, very careful. The DGSE is going to give you some extra coverage for a while." She yawned as the medicine started to take effect, and he smiled when he remembered how she had looked sleeping next to him. He couldn't wait until he'd see her again. But she had to get well. And de Vaumont had to be stopped.

Chapter 10

A senior agent of the DGSE called Pierre de Vaumont on Monday, explained that there had been an unfortunate incident at the Château Pasquier on Saturday, and said they wanted to discuss it with him and have him examined to make sure it hadn't affected him too. He assured them that he was fine, but they were adamant and refused to be put off.

Guy Thomas was in the interview with him. Pierre was very smooth on the surface, but Guy thought he looked nervous.

They explained that Theo Morgan Pasquier had been poisoned with a Russian nerve agent, as had her bodyguard, and they wanted to be assured that there were no traces in Pierre's bloodstream. They insisted on taking blood to be examined, and at the end of the interview, Guy asked him casually if he would mind bringing them the gloves he had worn to the château to be tested. He suggested delivering them in a plastic bag, and Pierre had a quick answer. He explained that he had gone to several châteaux over the weekend for his client, and had lost the gloves. He had already called around, as he liked the gloves, and no one had found them or turned them in.

"That is unfortunate, isn't it?" Guy said, looking him in the eye.

"It is," Pierre said innocently, "and I just got them at Hermès."

His bloodwork showed no trace of the nerve agent, not surprisingly since he clearly knew how to apply it. It had been put on the doorknob in a liquid form, which had neither color nor odor. And the gloves that might have shown traces of it had vanished. Guy surmised that he had arrived that day before the appointed hour so he had time to apply it. Theo would be exposed as soon as she touched the doorknob. Lucky for him, she had been half an hour late so he had even more time. He was wily.

Guy, Mike, and Robert had the promised conference call on Tuesday. It was entirely about how to protect Theo if the kidnappers came back to Paris and tried to kidnap her this time, or if another group came along with the same idea. Guy vowed to put more of his agents on the detail following her, until some new evidence appeared suggesting that she was no longer in danger. None of them felt that was likely to happen. She was undeniably a highly desirable target. Mike trusted both men, but was uneasy about what might happen, especially given the rumors Robert had heard, and the recent poisoning.

By Wednesday, Theo felt well again, and was due to go home on Friday. So was Daniel. They had both been extremely lucky, given the possibilities from the substance used to poison them, or if a worse one had been used instead. It seemed likely that it had been applied in order to give her a dread of the château so she would sell. It was not supposed to disable or kill her, or the château would have been tied up in her estate.

On Thursday morning, Mike landed at CDG, dropped his small bag off at Theo's apartment with one of the body-guards, and was at the hospital at nine A.M. Her face lit up the moment she saw him.

He spent the day with her and on Friday, she had to wait until noon to be discharged, after her last blood tests were in, and then she could go home. Mike waited with her and dozed in the chair in her room. He was relieved to see her looking well. They had said that she might feel dizzy occasionally, or have headaches, for another week or two, but it would dissipate after that. It made Mike angry just thinking about it. This wasn't his case, and he was there unofficially. All he had to contribute was his own expertise and his deep feelings for Theo, but both Guy and Robert were grateful for his input. Having a high-ranking, highly experienced CIA senior agent was an asset to any investigation, although he had far less knowledge of the Russians and their practices than either Guy or Robert and their respective agencies. Mike's expertise was with the drug lords in South America.

He had his own problems with the cartels in Central and South America, whose men regularly tried to enter U.S. territory to do business. He was currently working on a big case, which he couldn't discuss with Theo, but he had with Robert. They each had their own criminal element to deal with, and their own challenges.

He woke up after a half-hour nap on Theo's bed while they waited for her test results, on Friday morning. He couldn't wait to get home and be alone with her. He didn't like the reason he had come, but he was happy to see her.

They talked about de Vaumont and the poisoning. She said she had decided to sell the château.

"I had almost forgotten how beautiful it is. It broke my

heart to see it again, but I could never stay there now. I just couldn't do it. And it was always Matthieu's, not mine or ours. It was such a loaded subject for him, and so meaningful. I never really felt at home there. I think it's best to sell it. I'm going to list it with a realtor." She looked sad as she said it, but it sounded right to him too, given what had happened there.

"Do you think de Vaumont and his client will try to snap it up the minute you list it?" he asked her.

"I doubt it. He was very eager to see it before I listed it. His client may not be respectable at all, and Pierre doesn't want to lose part of his commission to a realtor. He wants it all for him. For Matthieu's sake, I hope someone buys it who treats it well and loves it. I would never sell it to de Vaumont and his client now."

They lay in the bed side by side, talking quietly until the doctor came in at almost noon and told her that her blood-work was satisfactory and she could leave. She already had her little bag packed, and her car and driver were waiting outside. Daniel was due to be discharged an hour or two later. His girlfriend was picking him up, and he was coming back to work after the weekend.

She and Mike drove home to her apartment, and they retreated to her bedroom. He was gentle with her, not wanting to wear her out since she'd been sick, but their lovemaking escalated rapidly to what it had been when he last saw her. They couldn't resist each other.

"What do you suppose it is with us?" she asked as she lay in his arms after they made love, feeling sleepy and sated and alive again. It was as though they shared their life force with each other and became more by being together.

He laughed at the question. "I think they call that lust. Pure raw passion."

"I've never had anything like that before, with anyone." He was an extraordinary lover, and he thought the same of her.

"Never?" he asked her. She shook her head. Matthieu had been Mike's age when she married him, and he had never had the wild abandon or sexual skills that Mike did. Or maybe she had been different then. Mike brought out something very different in her. She had been a young girl with Matthieu, and then a mother. Mike made her feel like a woman. She loved how powerful and manly he was. It pained her at times now that she was no longer a mother—she had lost a major part of her identity, as Matthieu's wife and Axel's mother—but she was growing into it with Mike, being "just" a woman. It was a new role for her, and there were things she liked about it, aside from the losses, which were devastating.

They went out that afternoon for a walk and stopped by

her office. Everyone was relieved to see her. No one knew the details of the poisoning, and she had decided they didn't need to. They only knew that she'd been ill with a severe flu. And Daniel had caught it too.

She introduced Mike to her assistants and some of the key people in her operation, then showed him their full offering online. He was surprised by how many employees she had, that she had started the business at twenty-two, and how much it had grown in fifteen years.

"How sophisticated is your security here? To keep the wrong people out of the building?"

"It's probably not tight enough," she admitted, "but we've never had a problem."

"That's the trouble in security. You don't have a problem until you have a problem and then it's too late. With all the crime that happens in Paris, and the trouble in Europe these days, it sounds like you need a better system and proced-ures. You have a lot of people working here. You need to protect against a hostage situation run by some nutcase. I've been thinking about that a lot lately, and your systems at home. What you have relies more on humans than on technology. Sometimes technology is more reliable. I want to give you some suggestions, but I haven't had time to work on it. We've been a little crazy at the office." She knew he wouldn't tell her why, so she didn't ask.

"And I've been driving you crazy too, getting poisoned by a doorknob," she said with a laugh. She had gotten over the shock and felt fine again. She had read up on the Novichok nerve agents, and related poisons, while she was in the hospital. "Do you know that one of the guys who invented them actually poisoned himself by mistake and died from it? It took five years for it to kill him, but it did. That stuff is nothing to mess around with. The first thing it did was confuse me so much I couldn't think straight."

Mike kissed her neck and then held her. "That's what happens to me when I'm anywhere near you. I can't think straight," he said, and she laughed.

"You're just a sex addict," she teased him, and he looked at her.

"Is that a compliment or a complaint?" he asked her.

"A compliment of course. You've turned me into one too."

"That's the best news of all. And you've made my life more glamorous. I spend my weekends in Paris now. Me, a poor boy from Boston." But he wasn't that anymore, and he was way more sophisticated than that. Enough so to fit perfectly into her life. He had his own field of expertise. "Theo, do you ever think of moving your business back to the States?" He had been thinking about that a lot lately, about how they could be together more, and even live in the same city.

"Never," she said simply. "This works. I have access to great talent for my business. People with terrific experience. I love living here. This really works well for me, and for the business. And I have Matthieu's business to take care of now too, even though I don't work on it full time. If I moved Theo.com to New York, I'd be on a plane every five minutes to deal with his business. It's hard enough having both offices in two separate locations in the same city, let alone three thousand miles apart."

"I didn't think of that," he said, obviously disappointed. But so far, in a short time, long distance was working for them, although they both knew it might not forever. Theo didn't want to think about that now. This was only the beginning of something very beautiful, for both of them.

After they left her office, she took him to Berthillon to buy ice cream, and he agreed that it was the best ice cream he'd ever eaten. She liked walking down the street with him and feeling like a couple.

They had dinner at home that night, and on Saturday they made a reservation at an Italian restaurant she knew he'd like that served homemade pasta and delicious food prepared by the grandmother in the kitchen. It had a family atmosphere. And she was right, he loved it.

"You're such a contradiction, Theo," he said to her over dinner. "With everything you have, you could do whatever you want, and you never show off. The simplest things give you pleasure."

"Like making love with you day and night," she whispered and kissed him, and he grinned.

"You know what I mean. Will you miss having the château if you sell it?"

"Probably. A little. It was a wonderful place to spend time as a family. It was built as a magnificent showcase, but we didn't use it that way." That was her style. Her apartment was beautiful, but it was cozy and felt like a home at the same time. She created warmth and good feelings wherever she was. She was changing his life too. His apartment in New York seemed unbearable to him now. The bare walls and ugly furniture were so depressing. The only décor were his computers and his gym equipment. It was a little too basic, industrial, and masculine even for him. His apartment had no charm whatsoever. He couldn't imagine her staying there if she came to see him. He had thought about it and decided they should go to a hotel where she'd at least be comfortable. His apartment was more like a bare-bones office with a bed in it. There was nothing homey about it. It had taken him ten years to notice. He hadn't even unpacked his books and trophies from his old apartment. He knew where they were if he ever wanted to see the trophies or read a book. The contrast between their two homes was astounding. He was so comfortable in hers, he never wanted to leave it.

They spent a quiet Sunday at home, in and out of bed before he left again. She hated to see him go when he was dressing to leave, and he looked as sad as she did.

"Will you be okay?" he asked her. She had that air of an abandoned child as she watched him. It tugged at his heart.

"I will. What about you? Will you be okay? It's weird not being able to talk about your work. I never know what you're working on. Is everything going well for you?" she asked, and he smiled.

"Everything goes well for me, perfectly in fact, the minute I see you." They had just shared another beautiful weekend. He had to be at the airport at eight P.M. for a ten o'clock flight that would land at JFK before one A.M. local time, and he was due in the office the next morning. He knew he'd be thinking of her most of the way home, when he wasn't sleeping. He flew business class because he was just too tall and powerfully built to travel coach and be able to function the next day. He wasn't traveling on the government's dime, but on his own.

She and her bodyguards went with him to the airport. She left him at security, which was as far as she could go with him since she wasn't flying herself. She wished she was. She was going to miss him terribly. They grew more attached every time they saw each other, and so far there had been no bad moments between them. They were both easygoing people.

He kissed her one last time before he got into the security line.

He could see the DGSE agent assigned to her now, out of the corner of his eye, and was glad he'd be with her. There were too many evil forces focused on her now, the original kidnappers lost somewhere in Russia, Pierre de Vaumont poisoning her to chase her out of her château, unknown people who were envious of her, or being paid to harm her, or take advantage of her. He hated not being with her to protect her, but at least other professionals would. He saw her leave the terminal, with the plainclothes agent close behind her, glancing left and right, aware of his surroundings and the unseen threats, which hovered near her, out of sight but never gone. She was a brave woman.

She got in her car with one bodyguard driving and the other in the front seat. She sat silently in the back, thinking of Mike and the happy times they shared. She missed him already, and she no longer felt as safe when he wasn't there. No one protected her as he did.

Chapter 11

There was an odd article in the newspaper the next day. Theo saw it over breakfast. It said that socialite and entrepreneur Pierre de Vaumont had disappeared. He had failed to show up at a weekend house party where he was expected, and the hosts were concerned. They called his cellphone and got no answer, then went to his home on Sunday. The concierge in his building said he had left with two men in a black Mercedes on Friday night around midnight, and he hadn't returned since. The concierge didn't know if he was traveling abroad, as he often did, or away for the weekend. She couldn't recall his taking any luggage when he left with the two men, and he hadn't been seen again. She said he always kept odd hours and stayed out late. She thought he had many friends, although he never entertained at the apartment and was a quiet tenant. His friends had reported his disappearance to the police, and foul play had not been ruled out.

There was still no sign of him by late Sunday night, and he had never called the people where he was meant to spend the weekend, which was unlike him. That was all it said. Theo reported it to Mike when he called her after he got up at seven, which was lunchtime for her. As usual, she was eating a yogurt and an apple at her desk, with new merchandise samples to choose all around her in the room. Mike teased her that she kept her slim figure because she never had time to eat. She wondered what had happened to Pierre, and Mike was curious about it too.

"With someone like him, anything could happen. He could be in Russia by now—with two goons dragging him there—or dead, poisoned like he tried to do to you. It sounds like he has too many irons in the fire these days, with some very dicey people. And the people he's making deals with don't play games."

"Maybe he'll just turn up, and went to a party at the last minute in Dubai. Or someone sent a plane for him. I think he's capable of that too. He goes where the money is. His friends probably don't realize who he does business with."

"You're probably right. But he's one guy I won't worry about. He's a social butterfly, and he's dangerous and ruthless if he's the one who poisoned you. That's a very heavy-handed sales pitch."

She didn't disagree, and as the day went on, she forgot about de Vaumont. That afternoon she called the realtor she wanted to use and listed the château, as she said she would. She had a pang when she did it, but she'd thought about it, and she knew it was the right thing for her. She was never going to use it again after what had happened there, and it made no sense to keep it.

The listing went up on the real estate agency's website the next day, with a few photographs she provided them. The price was listed as "upon request," which suggested it was very high. She was shocked when, two days later, there were four requests to see it. Things were moving faster than she'd expected, or maybe even wanted them to. She had put a huge price tag on it, but it was worth it. She had one price to sell it furnished, minus some of the art she wanted to sell separately or keep, and another price to sell it empty. Either way she was going to make a lot of money if the château sold.

The realtor had made appointments for all of the potential buyers to see it, and told Theo that there were two Americans, a Russian, and a Chinese man scheduled for visits by the end of the week. She wondered if the Russian was Pierre de Vaumont's client, but she had no way to know.

Her bodyguard Daniel came back to work that day, and

she was happy to see him when she got home. He said he was feeling better. He'd had one dizzy spell that weekend, but since then he'd been fine.

She had brought home some work that night, and waited for Mike to call her after midnight, as he always did now, at the end of his workday. He sounded tired and distracted when he called, and she told him about the four prospective buyers set to look at the château. She was sending a body-guard to protect the house, to each appointment, so no one damaged anything or stole something as a souvenir.

"I hope you sell it if that's what you want, Theo," he said, tired but happy to hear her.

"I think it is." She sounded quiet.

"Did you take one of the DGSE guys with you to work today?" he asked her.

"Yes, he sat outside my office and made everyone nervous." There was a feeling of tension having him there, as though they were expecting an attack any minute. There was the heavy sense of waiting for the other shoe to drop. It reminded her of when they were waiting to pay the ransom a year before, and every minute felt like an hour. She tried not to think about it after she and Mike hung up. The nights seemed empty without him after he left. She was used to filling her life with work, but now it no longer seemed like enough.

They were going to open pop-up stores in Paris and

London before Christmas, and she had plenty to do, making plans for them. To make it exciting, they had rented a fabulous private house in London, and a big space that had just opened up on the Avenue Montaigne after being vacated by a store that had closed. They were hoping to catch the wave of Christmas sales, people wanting clothes for parties and as gifts. It was fun working on it, and made her miss him less, and filled her nights when she couldn't sleep. But she was sleeping better now since Mike had come into her life.

What she had to get used to was no longer having a family, no husband to take care of, no child. It had left an enormous void in her life that she still didn't know how to fill except with work.

Mike was like a shooting star in her life, a comet across her skies. His visits had been brief and very bright. But he couldn't get away as often as she would have liked. He had only been in her life for a month, and it already felt as though he had been there forever, but in fact it was all very new, and they hadn't figured out how to spend time together yet, with both their jobs. His was even harder to get away from than hers. He'd managed to come to Paris twice in the last month. He wanted her to come to New York, but she hadn't been able to figure out when yet, and she was busier than ever at the office, since she had spent a week in the hospital. She hadn't been able to work at full speed while she was there. The remnants of the poison in her system had made it hard to concentrate, which was one of its effects.

It was almost Thanksgiving when she got the first offer on the château. The Russian had dropped out when he learned that her price was firm, and she had no financial need to sell it. He had tried to get the realtor to cut his commission, and he refused, so the Russian never made an offer. One of the Americans thought it was too pricey too. It became a bidding war between the remaining American and the Chinese buyer. The American was from Houston and wanted to buy it as a gift for his wife. She had always wanted a château in France and he wanted to make her dream come true, while the Chinese man was single and wanted it for himself, for his visits to Paris.

Mike was coming to see her for four days over the holiday. She hadn't seen him in three weeks. He checked in with Guy Thomas and Robert Richmond in London regularly, and there was no news. The rumors from Russia had gone dead again. And interestingly, Guy had told him that Pierre de Vaumont was still missing. There was no underground information on that either. No one seemed to know anything about his disappearance, and none of their usual informants had heard anything either. He had vanished without a trace.

There was another brief mention of it in the paper, and he was listed as a missing person.

Theo had a mountain of work to do before Mike arrived. She was taking two days off to be with him, which was even harder because they were opening the two pop-up stores the following week, and she had all the final details to approve. She visited the space on the Avenue Montaigne regularly, and it was looking fabulous. They were turning it into a winter wonderland, all done in sparkling white, with ice sculptures and a bar made of ice for the opening party. She was tempted to go this time, but she didn't want to deal with the press, and have all eyes on her. She was feeling more gregarious since Mike had come into her life, and she was beginning to miss having a social life after fifteen months of solitude. If he had been in town, she would have gone with him, but he was going to be back in New York by then, and she didn't want to face the press alone. She didn't know what the press would have made of him. He was a mystery man to the Paris press. She liked it better that way than if she had appeared with some well-known bachelor on the Paris scene. Mike suited her better, he had been in her life for two months by then, and he made her happy.

She had oysters and champagne and caviar waiting for him when he arrived the night before Thanksgiving. She'd ordered a full turkey dinner from the Ritz for them at home on Thanksgiving Day. She was thrilled to see him. He looked tired, as though work had been stressful since she'd seen him last. He never complained when they talked. It wasn't in his nature, he was always upbeat and wanted to know what she was doing.

"Was your sister upset that you came here for Thanksgiving?" she asked him as he undressed for bed. He looked dead tired after the trip.

"No, she hates holidays and never celebrates them. I always spend it with friends. I want you to meet her when you come to New York. She's eccentric as hell, but she's a good soul." He smiled as he said it, thinking about her. Theo knew only that her name was Fiona and she was an artist.

"She never married?"

He shook his head. "I guess my parents didn't inspire much faith in the institution." He grinned sheepishly. "It's never been a priority for me either, especially with my job."

She nodded and smiled. She had no desire to remarry either. What she had with Mike was enough for now, although she wished they could see each other more often.

She took him to see the location for the pop up store, and he was stunned by how beautiful it was. He was constantly impressed by how creative and talented and full of innovative ideas she was. She had endless energy, even after the poisoning a month before. She had no ill effects from it, nor did Daniel, which seemed like a miracle to them both after reading about the nerve agents that were currently in use among Russian spies, including the one used on them. Most people died from it, which was usually the intention.

After Theo showed Mike the pop-up store, still in progress, they went to L'Avenue for lunch, and he handed her a thick folder, with a look of pride and excitement.

"What's this?" she asked him.

"Some security ideas I had for you, for office and home. I told you I'd think about it. I didn't have a lot of spare time in the last few weeks, but it's a good start. See what you think." They were enjoying the lively restaurant, where models and actresses and hookers arrived every few minutes in stunningly sexy outfits, with alligator bags in rainbow colors, fabulous shoes, and exotic furs, and were with men who had paid for them. It was a racy, dazzling crowd and Mike loved it. It was like watching a movie or some kind of show.

Theo looked through the folder and was impressed at the detail he'd gone into. There were drawings and diagrams and explanations, and information on the equipment he suggested, and the number of fail-safe procedures and security men he thought she should have, including an armored safe room. Some of it was already in place, but a lot of it wasn't.

"Thank you, Mike. I want to read it carefully when I get home. How complicated would it be to implement all that?"

"Not so complicated. Some of the technology and equipment is expensive, but worth the investment. It would protect you and the staff, in your offices, home, and Matthieu's offices too." They both agreed that she was a long-term security risk and needed to plan accordingly. The problem wasn't going to go away. She put the folder in her big black Birkin bag, and he was pleased that she seemed to take it seriously. She was a reasonable person and appreciated the effort he'd put into it.

They did a little shopping on the Avenue Montaigne after lunch, and then went home and made love as they had that morning. Their lovemaking had the benefit of knowing each other well now, and the excitement hadn't worn off. Their time in bed together was a lovefest of tenderness and passion, and everything they felt for each other just kept growing and getting better.

Their dinner that night, catered by the Ritz, was a perfect Thanksgiving meal, with a few French touches, like delicate Grand Marnier soufflé for dessert, black truffles on the turkey, and foie gras in the stuffing.

"I have never had a Thanksgiving meal like that," he said,

looking dazed and sleepy by the end of it. "It was superb. You spoil me while I'm here, Theo. It gets harder and harder to go back to my awful apartment."

"Should you cheer it up a little? Can I do anything to help?" she asked him, happy and relaxed to be with him.

"I suspect that burning it down would make more sense. It's pretty grim. I have to do something about it, but I never have time." He hadn't had the interest to either, until now, in case she saw it one day when she came to New York.

She had no sense of what he did at work since he couldn't talk about it, but she could tell that he was stressed at times when a case wasn't going well. He had a lot on his shoulders—saving lives was the goal, but losing them was at times the reality when a mission failed. It mattered to him to his very core to prevent loss of life among his teams, and the victims.

She had no idea that he wore a bulletproof vest when he went to work on most days, since he never told her. It would have frightened her if she knew. She didn't know if he was on the front line at times or mostly in the office.

They ended their Thanksgiving in bed making love. It was a perfect end to a perfect evening, and they were asleep by midnight in each other's arms. She realized that she had much to be thankful for, despite the terrible losses of the year before. Mike couldn't replace Matthieu and Axel, and never would, but he had put joy in her life again, which she never thought possible.

The morning after Thanksgiving, she got a call from the realtor about the château. The Chinese potential buyer had given up, and the man from Houston who wanted to buy the château for his wife had won. He was going to pay way over her asking price, and wanted to buy it fully furnished, minus the items she had specified. It was better for her that way, and easier for the buyer. He was planning to hand his wife the keys on Christmas, and she would have nothing to do except pack and arrive. Theo was giving them all the linens, and the practical items too, like everything in the kitchen, none of which she needed in the city.

The price the buyer was paying was astronomical, and she couldn't believe she had gotten her price and more. He wanted a thirty-day closing, which was very fast, and very few inspections, just the most basic ones, which meant that by Christmas, if they signed the preliminary paperwork soon, the château would be his and out of Theo's hands. She was both happy and sad about it. It was bittersweet.

She walked into the kitchen to tell Mike, who was reading the newspaper, and he was happy for her. She didn't tell him the dollar amount, which seemed indiscreet and was embarrassing. But she said she was very pleased and had gotten more than her asking, and much more than she'd hoped for.

"That must be some place," he said admiringly.

"It is. But it was never mine. I never minded. And now I'm going to have to run like crazy to get all our clothes out and the art that I'm keeping, or selling at Sotheby's." She knew it would be a painful mission, especially when she got to Axel's room, which she hadn't dealt with at all. She had never gone there to pack up Matthieu's clothes either, and now she had all of it to do, as soon as she could manage it.

She called her office to ask her assistant to hire an art packer, and the rest was just clothes. She was lucky she didn't have to pack and move all the furniture, and everything else. The curtains alone would have been a massive project to take down. They were antique and beautiful, originally purchased from another château. The new owner was wise to keep them. From that moment on, she felt as though it was the buyer's château and not hers, or even Matthieu's. It was time for it to be passed into other hands, honorably this time.

Over the weekend with Mike, she didn't feel sad about it. She felt as though she'd done the right thing with the château. It deserved a life with people who would use it and love it, and she could never have done that again.

She told Mike on Friday night that maybe she should buy a little country house in Normandy, where she could spend the weekends. She hadn't thought of it until now, but she liked the idea.

"With a big house next to it for your security guards, I hope. You can't be in the country alone," he reminded her. It wasn't a pleasant thought for her. She no longer had the freedoms she had once enjoyed, despite the many comforts in her life now.

He'd never been to Normandy, so they drove to Deauville the next day, with the ocean and the beach, the quaint shops, two big old-fashioned hotels, and the ancient Norman houses that were very picturesque. Finding a house for herself there appealed to her, and worried Mike.

"I'd feel better with you in your apartment in the city, with good security all around you, and plenty of alarms, and panic buttons." She knew he wasn't exaggerating. He saw dangers for her everywhere.

"I can't live like that forever, Mike," she said as they ate lunch at a little bistro. She was having onion soup and he was having a wonderful bouillabaisse, chock-full of local seafood and rouille to add to it.

"You have to, Theo. You can't avoid it."

"The whole world isn't going to try to kidnap me," she insisted.

"It just takes one who succeeds, or a group of them," he said unhappily.

"I miss driving, and living like a normal person," she said wistfully. "I used to drive myself to the château on the weekends."

"You're not a normal person. You're an exceptional, remarkable one that people are jealous of, which makes you a target. And there are dangerous people in the world." He was adamant on the subject. She hated the thought of it and didn't want to think about it. She was quiet for the rest of lunch, and they went for a long walk on the beach, past the little old-fashioned cabanas with stars' names on them lining the boardwalk, before they drove back to the city.

She was totally relaxed as they drove home and she dozed off for a little while. He smiled over at her. It was the best Thanksgiving of his life, and she was the best woman.

When she woke, she smiled at him. She liked seeing him next to her, and not a driver. The DGSE tail had followed them in a separate car, but Mike had driven them without a bodyguard in the car. "Did I snore?" she asked him, and he laughed.

"Like an old man, a chorus of them!"

"I did?" She looked embarrassed and he grinned.

"No, you didn't." She was glad he was coming back at Christmas, but it was a month away. He had asked her about going skiing, but she hadn't skied in years. Axel had gotten too good for her by the time he was ten, so she finally gave up, since she couldn't keep up with him. Matthieu had been an outstanding skier too. She didn't veto Mike's suggestion, but they didn't organize it yet. And Courchevel was full of Russians, with their mistresses and hookers, and so were most of the snow towns, and they would be mobbed at Christmas. She was thinking maybe they should go someplace else, like someplace warm.

They stayed in bed on Sunday until he had to leave for the airport, and she had brought him breakfast on a tray.

"You ruin me for real life, Theo. My breakfast is usually a granola bar on the subway on the way to work." The reality of his life was very different from hers, she knew it but hadn't seen it yet. She hoped she would one day.

"Stick around," she said, smiling at him, "the service is pretty good." She had made fresh-squeezed orange juice and bacon and eggs the way he liked them. She knew that about him now. And coffee with a tiny splash of milk. "I'm going to have so much to do, getting my stuff out of the château," she said while he ate, almost cringing as she said it. "And I have to get it all out in the next three weeks."

"It's too bad you can't wait till I'm here over Christmas," he said thoughtfully. "I could help you pack up."

"The new owner is planning to come with his wife the day after Christmas, so she can see her new château. I hope she loves it. It would be hard not to."

"Just be careful who you hire to do the move. Moving companies aren't always the most respectable, they use a lot of temporary help. Make sure you use a reliable firm."

He left a few hours later, after they'd made love. They could barely force themselves to get out of bed, savoring every moment.

"I'll be back in a few weeks," he reminded her and smiled after he kissed her at the airport, lingering for a minute. "Thank you for a beautiful Thanksgiving."

"Thank you for everything," she said, and she left the airport after Mike had gone through security and disappeared.

All she could think about was how much she had to do. Now that the château was sold, she wanted to get her things packed up and moved, and Matthieu's and Axel's, and turn the page. She was going to be busy every minute of the day while Mike was in New York. Then he'd be back for Christmas and the magic would start again. He had given her back something to live for, which she had thought she would never find again.

Chapter 12

The opening of the pop-up store on the Avenue Montaigne was a huge success, like everything Theo did relating to her business. She had an unfailing eye and instinct. All of fashionable Paris came and crowded into the glamorous space she had created. All dazzling white, it looked like the inside of a giant snowflake. The ice sculptures and bar were fabulous. The press loved it. Lots of movie stars, socialites, and famous people attended.

She made a brief appearance at the party, for the first time in over a year. She felt anxious about it at first, but was pleased to see familiar faces and all of the fashion editors she knew. She wore a soft white cashmere dress from their own line. It draped over her body, showing off her dark hair down her back and tall black suede high-heeled boots to

Danielle Steel

her thighs. She was the chicest woman in the room, and as soon as the photographers realized she was there, they thronged her, and told her how glad they were to see her. Everyone knew what she'd been through, and no one had seen her publicly in fifteen months. She was surprised by how warm their greetings were, and how comforting it was to feel their support.

"Fabulous place, Theo . . . gorgeous . . . love the ice sculptures . . . so nice to see you back, we missed you," was what she heard from everyone.

She only stayed for half an hour, and then went home and told Mike about it that night.

"The store looks fantastic," she told him.

"I'm sure you did too. Send me pictures." He missed her and wished he could have been with her. The party in New York had been beautifully done, but the sparkling white ultra-modern space for the one in Paris was spectacular. And the one that opened in London the next day was just as big a hit and received accolades from the British fashion press. They said she had a magic touch and hadn't lost it in her long seclusion. Everyone who was anyone in London had been there, including several royals.

Mike was still in constant touch with Robert Richmond at MI6, and they were both in touch with Guy Thomas. Mike had an uneasy feeling about the vague, intermittent rumors Robert was hearing from Moscow. There was no specific threat to Theo. But Matthieu's disgruntled Russian investor, Dmitri Aleksandr, had reared his ugly head again, complaining about how much money he had lost when Matthieu did an about-face and refused to open the two stores in Russia. He came within a hair of calling Matthieu a crook, according to one informant, and said he still hadn't recouped his losses or recovered from it, which Robert was sure wasn't true. He was one of the richest men in Russia, with countless illegal businesses and a few legal ones that were highly profitable. Both men had been able to afford to lose the money, and Theo knew Matthieu had never regretted backing out on the deal when he saw the degree of corruption he had to contend with in Russia. Theo had been relieved when he got out of it. She had never liked the smell of it, or the people she saw him meeting with, and she hadn't even known about the young actress then, but he was in Moscow constantly while trying to get the stores finished, which never happened.

It would have taken several more years and a lot more bribes to do it than he was willing to put up with. His angry partner in the deal had come to meet with him at the château several times and he had made Theo's skin crawl. He looked like a gangster and the men with him looked like thugs. And worse than the money Matthieu had lost, he had lost his life and their son's. Too high a price to pay for any deal.

The memories came back to her in a rush when she got to the château to begin packing her belongings. When she arrived, Theo took a long quiet walk through the château, making note of the paintings she was keeping and taking photos with her phone for reference. There were several paintings she was going to sell at Sotheby's. They were too valuable to include in a house sale. She felt somewhat guilty now, knowing how much Matthieu had loved the place and how hard he had worked to earn the money to buy it back. It had been in terrible shape when he got it, long before she met him, and he had so lovingly restored it. But the heartbreak was woven into its history now for her. Just being there took her breath away, remembering the day he and Axel had been kidnapped, and the day they had been found buried nearby.

Her eyes filled with tears as she walked through the house, trying to be practical about it. She clung to thoughts of Mike to give her strength. She wanted to call him, but felt too emotional to do so. She had decided not to bring an assistant with her. She wanted to be alone in her final hours in the house and not have to talk to anyone. She had brought her driver and one of her bodyguards to help her carry things that were too heavy for her. The DGSE agent assigned to her had followed them in a chase car, as they always did now, since Mike had convinced Guy Thomas to provide protection for her. The poisoning had proven him right. There was no question about it now. It made her wonder again what had happened to Pierre de Vaumont and where he was hiding, and from whom. He had been noticeably absent from the Paris social scene for over a month now. Guy Thomas had said several times that he could be dead, and Robert Richmond didn't disagree with him, but Theo thought it unlikely. He was probably just hiding somewhere, maybe afraid he'd be blamed for poisoning her, and he was waiting for the storm to blow over.

The movers arrived an hour after she got there. She got them started, and told them which paintings to take down. She scolded them immediately when they began doing it without gloves. They were professional movers and she told them they should have known better. One of them rolled his eyes, and the others did as they were told. She was removing nineteen paintings from the walls, and got her bodyguard to rehang some others, so the rooms didn't look odd with empty spaces on the walls. The paintings she was taking were on a list as "excluded from the sale." She wanted everything to look perfect when the new owner showed it to his wife for the first time. She had even bought new kitchen towels and a few things to replace the old ones. She had tried to think of everything, to help prepare the gift.

She had marked with stickers and colored dots each of the paintings that were going, and the movers began putting them into wooden crates, as she walked slowly up the stairs to the bedrooms. That would be the hardest part for her.

She walked into her dressing room. The piles of sweaters and the coats she had left when she had first felt the effects of the poison were still sitting on the bed with her two valises standing by. Nothing had been touched since then. She called her bodyguard and asked the movers to bring her wardrobe boxes, which they did a few minutes later and set them up for her. Her bodyguard helped her unload her closets into them. She had fifteen years of country clothes there, and she was going to give some of it away. This was where she kept old, comfortable things to wear on their weekends in the country, a few summer dresses, and bathing suits. She had a stack of summer hats, most of them fairly tired and nothing fashionable. It took eight wardrobe boxes, half a dozen suitcases, and a big box of rough boots, to empty her closets.

It actually took her less time than expected. The bodyguard emptied the contents of her bathroom cupboards into boxes, and then did the same in Matthieu's bathroom.

She stopped when she walked into his closet. Everything was there as though he was coming home to dress or was about to arrive from the city any minute. She could still smell the faint pungent smell of the cologne he wore, which brought tears to her eyes. She wondered if he had worn it with the Russian girl too. But it didn't matter now. She was dead, and so was he. She knew he had loved her in his own way, even if fidelity wasn't his strong suit. She was his wife and the mother of his only child, which was a revered position to him, and he treated her accordingly, and had always been very kind and generous with her.

Martine, her assistant, had already removed Theo's jewelry from the safe a year before. She had nothing of value there, just memories, the important paintings, and the château itself. Matthieu would have been pleased by how much the man from Houston had paid for it, since he was a businessman above all else, but family was important to him too.

Theo had the bodyguard empty Matthieu's closets into the wardrobe boxes, so she didn't have to do it herself. She took a handful of boxes and walked upstairs to the top floor, to the servants' rooms, and where Axel's nursery had been when he was a baby, when she didn't keep him in her room with her while she was nursing him. Two of the rooms were still occupied, and the new owner was taking over their staff, and bringing some of his own. It took an army to run the château efficiently.

The nursery still had some of Axel's baby things in it, favorite blankets and some baby toys, which she carefully put into the boxes to take downstairs, and she left the rest, the contents of the linen closets, which were part of the sale, and she walked down a floor to the room she had been avoiding and dreaded most, Axel's room. She opened the door, the shades were drawn, and she could almost sense him fly into her arms when she walked in. She stood there, frozen to the spot, and then went to lie on his bed, and looked up at the ceiling, at the stars that she had glued onto it herself one year as a Christmas present. She could sense him lying next to her, his young slim body pressed against her, his hand holding hers, his face next to hers.

"Oh God, I miss you, Axie," she said out loud in the silent room. He had spoken English with her, and French with his father and everyone else. He had been perfectly bilingual. There were photographs of all his favorite soccer players on the walls, and a few Yankees stars. He loved baseball too. She had taken him to a Yankees game in New York and he loved it. They ate hot dogs and he jumped up and down and yelled every time they hit a home run.

She got up and walked over to his desk and saw a photograph of her and Matthieu there. He had been a good student, but most of all he had been a wonderful boy, the light of her life. She still couldn't believe that that light had gone out, and she would never see him again.

After looking at and touching everything, she called her bodyguard again, told him where she was, and asked him to bring her boxes. He appeared respectfully in the doorway, with the boxes, not wanting to intrude.

"Would you like me to pack up the room for you, ma'am?" he asked gently, and she shook her head.

"Just leave the boxes, thank you, Franck. I'll do it myself." He was German but spoke perfect English.

"Call if you need anything. I'll tape them up when you're finished," he said and went discreetly back down the stairs.

The movers had been instructed to take all the boxes to the apartment in the city. She was going to dispose of Matthieu's clothes, but she was planning to put all of Axel's things in his room in Paris. Even if she never unpacked them, at least she would know they were there.

It took her over an hour to pack up his room, all the mementos and silly things he loved, his old favorite teddy bear, which he still slept with at thirteen but pretended he didn't. He was just a boy, a little kid, and they had killed him. The police had said he hadn't suffered and she hoped it was true. He had been shot in his father's arms, with Matthieu trying to protect him, and then they had shot

Matthieu. The cruelty of it was beyond belief, and being in Axel's room now brought every moment of it back to her again. It was why she never could have kept the château, not with memories like this like a stake in her heart.

The room looked barren and empty when she had packed everything. She stood glancing around for a last time, wanting to be sure she hadn't missed anything. She had even packed his toothbrush and toothpaste. The bed had been stripped a year before, or she would have taken the sheets too, hoping to get some lingering scent of him on the pillow, but it was gone by then.

She walked slowly down the stairs with a heavy heart, her memories trailing along behind her, and she went back to her own room, feeling exhausted, as she had last time, but this time she wasn't confused. Every memory was etched in exquisite agony: Axel's voice, his smile, his laughter when they played together. She had taught him how to ride a bike, how to throw a baseball and a football, and Matthieu had taught him how to swim. A whole little life ready to launch into the world one day, and now he was a bright, shining star up in Heaven somewhere. She liked to believe that he was watching her and always near, since he had been only a child when he died. She hoped that there was a special place in Heaven for him.

She saw that her own dressing room was empty, as well

as Matthieu's, the boxes waiting to be taken downstairs and loaded onto the truck. And then she went down to the main floor to see how the movers were doing with the art. They were handling the paintings less gently than she would have liked. They had forgotten their gloves again, and the shoe coverings they were supposed to wear to protect the antique rugs from their rough, muddy boots. There were six of them, moving slowly, and not speaking to each other. She could see that there were five paintings already in wooden crates, and fourteen left to pack, some of them already off the walls and propped up around the living room.

She could hear her bodyguard and driver in the kitchen, talking while they replaced old kitchen items with the new things she had bought. They were speaking in low voices, they were trying to give her space so as not to intrude on her, although normally they would have been at her side to help, but they knew that it was an emotional day for her and wanted to respect it, so they let her move around the house alone and waited until she asked for their help. She approached the foreman of the movers to remind him about their wearing gloves and shoe covers again. As she walked toward him, she saw him look at one of the others and nod, and suddenly powerful arms grabbed her from behind and lifted her off her feet. Someone slapped a wide piece of strong tape over her mouth before she could scream, and she tried to struggle against them. All six closed around her, and the two who held her rushed her toward one of the long windows. She knew at that moment that this was exactly what had happened to Matthieu and Axel. She tried to kick them behind her, but nothing she did slowed them down. They carried her like a doll toward the windows, ready to run to the moving truck with her. She wondered if they were going to kill her, and for an instant she didn't care. With Axel gone forever, it didn't matter.

They tied her hands behind her, and she was making muffled sounds, which weren't loud enough for Franck and her driver to hear her in the kitchen. Just as they reached the windows, there was an explosion of sound near her ear, and she saw the leader standing only inches from her, with his brain exploding from his skull. He'd been shot in the head, and pitched forward, his brain splattering all over her face and chest, his blood splashing everywhere as he collapsed. There was a second explosion immediately, then two more, and the two men who had been carrying her collapsed behind her—one dead, and the other shot in the shoulder and the back of his leg. Both were lying on the floor in a pool of blood. She stood there trying to scream, with the tape over her mouth, and her hands behind her back, shaking violently. Franck and Christophe, her driver, came running into the room, while the three remaining movers fled through the long French windows they were intending to use as an exit to carry her to the truck.

Her two employees looked wild-eyed, there was blood everywhere and through the window they could see the French DGSE agent in hot pursuit of the three men, shooting at them as they leapt into the moving truck and took off at full speed. He was certain he had wounded one of them, and the one he had injured in the living room was too badly hurt to move. The other two were dead.

As soon as the truck sped off, he called in the description and license plate to his superiors, reported what had happened, and rushed back into the house to make sure that Theo wasn't hurt. She was badly shaken and sitting on the floor, the tape and rope binding her hands removed. She sat between the two dead men, and the DGSE man put handcuffs on the injured man who'd been shot in the shoulder and leg. The agent had saved Theo's life, and had been chosen for the detail for his expert marksman skills. He was well aware of the risk he had taken, shooting so close to her, but he was certain that if they took her, they would kill her sooner or later, probably after they got the ransom again. His shooting the foreman in the head had been an act of desperation, which had saved her.

She had bits of the dead man's brain all over her, and

Danielle Steel

blood smeared everywhere. The agent knelt beside her to make sure she wasn't hurt, and he asked her questions while carefully examining her. She was untouched. The bullet had gone right past her into its intended target.

"I'm sorry," the agent said kindly. "I had no choice, before they took you."

"Thank you," she said in a shaking voice. "I'm okay." She looked like she was about to faint. There was a pool of blood soaking into the Persian carpet, and more splashed on the upholstery. The agent helped her to her feet to lead her away from the bodies and the injured kidnapper, then asked Franck to take her to the kitchen and sit her in a chair. Her legs could hardly hold her as he walked her to the kitchen with an arm around her waist. The agent remained with his gun pointed at the injured kidnapper.

They could hear sirens in the distance by then. A moment later, the driveway was filled with police cars and an ambulance. And moments after that, an unmarked DGSE car arrived with two senior agents. The injured kidnapper was bleeding profusely but not at risk of dying, and a police paramedic tended to him. They wanted a statement from him before they took him away. They put him on a gurney where the DGSE sergeant gave him the opportunity to confess and inform on his co-conspirators, only to discover that he spoke no French and only Russian.

"Get us a translator," the agent in charge said harshly. "I want to know where the others are going." They hadn't loaded anything on the truck yet, so nothing had been stolen. Theo realized then that she had heard the foreman's accent but hadn't made the connection that these men were the same nationality as the original kidnappers, and possibly the same ones. She had been too overwhelmed by memories of Axel and Matthieu to pay close attention to them.

It was all a blur of activity after that. A forensics team arrived to collect fingerprints and samples of DNA to see if there was a match with Matthieu and Axel's kidnappers. Theo remained in the kitchen, and various people came to talk to her, including a female police sergeant and the senior DGSE agent. Franck helped her clean off some of the blood. Her sweater and jeans were soaked through with blood and her shoes were covered with it, but all of her clothes were packed.

Somewhere in the melee, Guy Thomas appeared and was very kind to her. She told him everything she had observed. She said that they hadn't worn gloves while handling the art, and he assured her they would get fingerprints from the frames, and the police uncrated everything they'd packed while the forensics team went to work.

The DGSE marksman assigned to her had saved her life.

But there were still three of the kidnappers at large, one of them possibly badly injured.

"We'll find them. We want to know if they're the same men who kidnapped your husband and son," he said, and she nodded. Guy had already advised Robert Richmond about what had happened. The British police and MI6 would be looking for them and for any information they could get from their informants all the way to Moscow.

Guy told her she could go home, and they would be in touch with her. He was going to provide four agents to protect her, until the remaining three kidnappers were caught, however long that took. As her own men drove her away, Guy called Mike Andrews in New York. It was three o'clock in Paris by then, nine A.M. in New York, and Mike had just gotten to his office and had his hands full with his own serious cases at the moment. The locals were restless these days, particularly in the drug world. They were waiting for a shipment to hit New York, via Bolivia, and Mike was determined to stop the activities of a particularly bad gang of Colombians he'd been trying to catch for two years.

Guy told him what had happened and Mike was worried sick as he listened, but grateful too. "Thank God for your guy at the scene. Do you think it's the same group?"

"I'm almost sure of it. I'd stake my life on it. They knew

the house, the whole style was very similar. We've got prints and DNA all over the place. We should have them all ID'd very quickly. Three of them got away, but this time we won't lose them, and one of them is badly injured. My agent is a great shot. He took a hell of a chance shooting the foreman, but Ms. Morgan is unhurt. They'd probably have killed her if they took her, just as they did last time with her husband and son. They're not the smoothest group." Even not speaking the same language, one could tell that they were rough and uneducated.

"Thank you for letting me know. Is the one you've got in custody liable to talk?" Mike asked Guy.

"I think that's a certainty," Guy said with a small smile at his end of the conversation. "We have a translator with him now. I hate to do it, but we'll offer him a lighter sentence if he talks."

Mike's hand was shaking when he hung up the phone. If they had killed Theo, or taken her, he would have been devastated, and he was still worried about her, with three of the kidnappers on the loose. He called Robert Richmond next. He had already been filled in by Guy Thomas. Mike wanted to call Theo, but Guy said she was on her way home and somewhat in shock.

"I don't know if they'll show up here, but I've reached out to all our informants," Robert said. "They may be a little sloppier now with their leader gone and one of them injured. I'll let you know if I hear anything. And the DGSE has her well protected. She needs to lie low for a while till we see what they do next. It must have been a hell of a scare for her."

"I'm sure it was," Mike said. "Guy said she was covered in their blood and brain matter when he got to her. The DGSE had one of their best marksmen with her. They don't want a replay of last time." Neither did Mike. "I'm going over in about a week, but I've got my hands full here right now, waiting for a big deal to play out. I can't leave at the moment."

"Good luck with that. I'll keep you posted," Robert said succinctly.

"Thanks, Robert," Mike said and hung up.

Mike decided to try calling Theo. She had just gotten home and was about to take a bath. She sounded stilted and strange and still in shock. It had been a hard morning for her, even before that, going through Axel's things and overwhelmed with memories. And now she had fully understood the danger she was in as long as the kidnappers were out there, even three of them. They were on a mission, with their own lives probably at stake if they didn't complete it successfully. Men who were after a fifty-million-euro ransom didn't take it lightly.

"Are you okay?" He knew she wasn't, but as much as she

could be in the circumstances. The terror she must have experienced when they grabbed her must have been even worse than being poisoned.

"Yes, I am," she said in a small voice. "I thought they were going to kill me."

"They probably would have," he said, and thought they still might. He just prayed that the DGSE agents were equal to the task this time, and able to protect her if the kidnappers tried again.

"Do you think they'll come back?" she asked softly.

"There's a chance they will. You have to be very careful. Stay below the radar right now, don't go out more than you have to, and I'll be back in a week."

She sounded very meek when they hung up.

Afterwards, she peeled off her blood-soaked clothes and slipped into the tub. Their blood was still on her skin and in her hair, under her nails, and on her eyelashes. She felt as though she would never be able to scrub it off her adequately. All she'd wanted to do afterwards was come home.

After the crime detail and forensics experts had gotten all the evidence they needed, the police had promised to bring her crates from the château to her apartment. She didn't want Axel's things to get lost in the shuffle.

She lay in the tub with her eyes closed, playing over in

her mind everything that had happened that morning. Her ears were still ringing from the shots that had been fired, and she could still see the foreman's head as it exploded inches from her. It could all have turned out so differently. She could have been tied up in the back of the moving truck by then, her fate sealed, in exchange for the rest of the ransom they hadn't gotten before.

Agent Guy Thomas called her at five o'clock. The fingerprints and the DNA were a match for all six of them. It was the same crew as before, but at least two of them were dead, and two were injured, one of them in custody. They didn't have the team they needed to pull it off smoothly now, which might mean they'd use greater force and more violence if they tried.

"We'll have your property delivered to you tomorrow," he promised her. "I'm sorry today was so traumatic."

"It's all right, if it leads to your catching them and putting an end to this," she said in a tired voice. She was exhausted. Guy Thomas knew that even if they did catch them, one day there would be others. She would have to be carefully protected forever. It was the legacy her husband had left her, along with his business and his fortune.

As promised, her crates and boxes arrived the next day in good order. She put all the wooden crates with the art in one of the guest rooms to deal with after the holidays.

She carried most of Axel's boxes up to his room herself, and supervised the others that were too heavy for her. It felt like her final act of motherhood for him, like his funeral with the small pine casket sixteen months before. They were acts she had never wanted to have to do for him. She wondered what the new owners of the château would do with the stars on his ceiling that she had put up with so much love and care, according to the real constellations. He had loved it. She hoped they'd leave them there, just as a tiny souvenir of him, the little boy who had lived there, the last of the Pasquiers. The family name had died with him.

Chapter 13

The search for the three remaining kidnappers was intense. One of them, the injured one, was picked up three days after the incident, on the Belgian border. He said he was going to visit a friend, and had been injured in a hunting accident. His fingerprints were a match and the DGSE brought him back to Paris for interrogation, which was carried on day and night until he broke down out of sheer exhaustion and confessed. As the murderer of two victims a year before, they had no inclination to go easy on him, especially since one of the victims had been a child. All he was willing to divulge was that they had been hired by a businessman in Moscow who had a score to settle. He didn't know what it was or the man's name. They were hired through an intermediary whose identity he claimed not to know either. They had been promised ten thousand dollars each to do the job, only received five thousand of it last time and were being paid another five thousand now to finish it. The ransom for Theo was going to be fifty million. It all matched up to the facts the DGSE had from their informants. Guy Thomas knew that the French government would never be able to touch the angry billionaire who had hired them. He was safely in Moscow, and too well connected with crooked friends in government who were protecting him, and who were probably getting a cut of the ransom too, if there had been one.

They didn't allow the two men in custody to speak to each other and the search for the two other men continued. They contacted every source they had who might know something about the plan, and their whereabouts now. The trail went cold for two days and then Robert Richmond heard a whisper of information in London. It wasn't much but led them to believe that the trail wasn't entirely cold. There was a rumor that one of the kidnappers was at a safehouse just outside London. Agents from MI6 raided it within hours of the tip, and there was evidence that someone had been there, but he was gone when they arrived. But now that they knew one of them was in England, Robert continued to shake the trees as hard as he could, and hoped something would fall out.

Mike hadn't been in contact with him since the day of the attempted kidnapping. He had his own problems to deal with, although he called Theo whenever he could to see how she was.

She was trying to repair the damage that had been done at the château when they tried to kidnap her. The Persian carpet in the living room was damaged beyond repair, drenched with blood, and she replaced it with one of her own. She found the fabric to re-cover the blood-spattered upholstery, so it wouldn't look like a butcher shop when the new owners arrived. She told the realtor there had been a security problem there with some damage that was being repaired, and all would be in good order shortly.

The new owner did not ask for further details, nor did Theo offer them. He knew about the abduction of Axel and Matthieu and it hadn't stopped him. And he was bringing a security team of his own. His realtor had already urged him to have maximum security on the grounds, and the new owner was confident that his own people would do a better job than Theo's.

She got her upholsterer to agree to re-cover the damaged chairs over the weekend before Christmas, for double the price. Daniel delivered them to the château as soon as they were done, and said everything looked fine.

She wasn't going out more than she had to, and had gone to her office with four armed guards.

The pop-up store on the Avenue Montaigne was doing an amazing business, as was the one in London in the rented townhouse. Business was excellent, for Matthieu's brands too. But the tension of waiting for them to find the kidnappers was extreme, and there was no further news of the remaining two.

The Christmas decorations were up all over Paris, and the city was in a festive mood. Most of the damage from the recent riots had been repaired and ordinary business was picking up again, although not quite as briskly as the year before. But luxury brands like Theo's, particularly with her online business, were extraordinary.

Mike hadn't been able to call her as often as he would have liked. She could tell that he must have been working on something big, and he sounded distracted when they talked.

When he arrived from New York to spend the holiday with her, she could see the strain in his eyes. He had been worried about her, and there had been a delay in the Colombian drug shipment coming from Bolivia, so they didn't know when it would arrive now, but they were trying to keep all the bases covered while they waited. They were no longer sure if it was still coming by ship, or being flown in. He was worried it would all happen while he was in Paris. His men were prepared, but he liked to be there for an operation as large as this one.

He and Theo had both been through the wars since they'd last seen each other, and it took him a few hours to calm down. But the warmth and pleasure of being with her eventually relaxed him and allowed him to put distance between himself and the complex operations he was responsible for. On her side, there had been no news of the kidnappers for several days.

They went to church together on Christmas Eve, and had dinner at the Ritz before that. Her four plainclothes DGSE agents were at a nearby table. Knowing the possibilities and risks for her in Paris, Mike had made arrangements and filled out the appropriate paperwork to travel with his own guns this time. He wanted to be prepared if anything happened like at the château. She was surprised when she hugged him when he arrived and discovered that he was wearing two guns, one at his waist and the other in a holster under his arm. He wore them every day in New York.

"Is that for me?" she asked him with a look of surprise, and he nodded.

"I promise not to sleep with them." He smiled.

"You'd better not." She was dreading another encounter with the kidnappers and hoped it never happened. The memory of the brains flying out of the kidnapper's head when the bullet hit him was still a vivid one.

Their lovemaking was especially tender this time and just as intense. He was so grateful she was alive and that the attempt to kidnap her had been foiled.

He had checked in with Robert Richmond when he got to Paris, but Robert had no news for them either. They were still on the lookout for the kidnapper who had fled to England. And both the DGSE and the DGSI were searching for the one in France. They weren't sure if he had successfully fled the country, or if he was concealed somewhere in France. No one had provided any further information, yet. Mike and Theo did their best not to think about it, and to enjoy the time they had, but it was ever present on their minds.

They spent Christmas Day quietly at home, and the city looked magical when it started to snow. It reminded her of how much she and Axel had loved it at the château when it was snowing and they had snowball fights in the orchards and on the front lawn. It made her wonder too if the new owner's wife would love it when she saw it. It was the perfect way to see the château for the first time, under a blanket of snow. She remembered how romantic it had been when Matthieu took her there for the first time. The new owners were arriving the next day and everything was pristine after the kidnapping attempt. Everything had been cleaned, repaired, or replaced. There was no sign of the carnage that had happened there.

Mike had been watching Theo as she sat lost in thought. He had made a fire in the fireplace in her study.

"What were you thinking about just then?" he asked her gently. Her face looked so innocent and faraway.

"I was thinking about the château and wondered if the woman will love it when she sees it. It looks so pretty in the snow."

"It's quite a Christmas gift," he said, thinking how far he had come from his own origins to his life with her. Her need for protection made him feel at home with her, and as though he could provide something useful in her life. "I'm sure she'll love it."

"She wouldn't have if she could have seen the mess it was a week ago. It looked like a horror movie." She smiled in spite of the impact of the memory. "I've never seen anyone get shot before," she said matter-of-factly.

"It's not a pretty sight. I'm sorry you had to see that, Theo."

"Thank God he shot him, or I'd be history by now."

"I won't ever let that happen," he said calmly, and she believed him.

They sat in front of the fire for a long time, talking about their Christmases when they were children. Hers had been everything traditional, with unexciting but rock-solid, loving parents, who had always given her their full support. They had been bothered about Matthieu because he was so much older, but they had eventually come around when they saw that it worked well and he was kind to her. And now all of her family was gone, her parents, her husband, and her son.

Mike's memories of his childhood holidays were less idyllic. His mother had managed as best she could, but they were always struggling and lacking something, and they'd all had small jobs, even as kids, to try to help her. He talked about the two brothers he had lost, and how great they were. They'd died at eighteen and twenty in the Persian Gulf. "War is always so senseless," he said, looking pensive as he stared into the fire. "I thought that when I was in Iraq, and in the military. It seems like I've always had a job where someone might be shooting at me." He smiled at her. "I'm getting a little old for that. I'll be fifty this year, and I've been lucky so far."

"Do you worry about getting hurt with the work you do?" she asked him, and he shook his head without hesitating.

"No, it goes with the territory. I'm not crazy. I wear a bulletproof vest most of the time, if I think I'll be in danger." He had never told her that before, and she looked surprised.

It was a reminder that the job he did was dangerous, even at his level. She understood that better now after the damage she'd seen so recently. But there had to be people like him, to protect people like her. Like the marksman who had shot the kidnappers. She knew Mike would do the same for her. He had been wearing his guns since he arrived.

"Shouldn't you always wear it?" she asked, worried.

"I'm not on the front lines often anymore, and they're hot and uncomfortable. I know when I need it and when I don't," he said confidently. And she hoped he was right.

The embers were dying in the fireplace when they went to bed. The snow was falling outside, and looked like lace on the streetlamps, and a white velvet carpet on the streets. There were no footprints in it yet. There were no cars moving outside. The city looked peaceful blanketed in white and sound asleep.

They were both tired and relaxed, but couldn't resist making love again. She felt so small and safe in his arms and he looked down at her for a moment with love in his eyes.

"I'll never let anything happen to you, Theo," he whispered, and she knew he wouldn't, as she gave herself up to him completely and felt like the luckiest woman in the world. And she firmly believed that no harm could come to her with Mike at her side.

Chapter 14

Guy Thomas called Mike the day after Christmas to tell him that they had found the fifth kidnapper hiding in the barn of a farm a few miles from the château. They had discovered the abandoned moving truck hidden in a clump of trees and made an intense search of the area, until they located him cold and hungry in the barn, with a horse blanket to keep him warm. The farmer and his wife were away for the holidays and their son was caring for their livestock, but he hadn't discovered the intruder in the barn. Two local policemen had found him. He had fired a round of shots at them and missed, and no one had been injured. They had overpowered him, and he was in custody now with a DGSE agent and an interpreter interrogating him.

So far, he said that he didn't know who the employer

was, but he admitted to kidnapping Matthieu and her son. It made Theo realize that this investigation wasn't just about protecting her, it was about finding Matthieu and Axel's killers and putting them in prison for what they'd done. He confessed to both crimes, and to attempting to kidnap Theo. He admitted that they were going to take her and demand a ransom of fifty million for her since they had gotten shortchanged last time, and the man who had hired them had been very angry about it. He had said that Matthieu owed him the money and refused to pay him, and this was the only way he could get it, by kidnapping him and his son. It seemed to make sense to them in a convoluted, twisted way.

The kidnapper in custody told the Russian translator that the man who had hired them had said the widow would pay, and if they weren't paid in full this time, they should kill her too. It was her last chance to pay her husband's debt. It was a sick way of thinking, but it explained the motivation and how the kidnappers expected to resolve it. He didn't seem too sorry to be in custody, he said that their boss would be very angry at them if they failed again in their mission to recoup his money, and he would kill them. And since it hadn't gone as planned, he felt safer in jail than at the mercy of the man who had paid them for a job they hadn't done.

He said he didn't know where the other kidnapper had gone. He knew he had a friend in England, and was going to try and go there, but this man hadn't heard from him, and he didn't know what part of England the friend was in.

"It's almost over," Guy told Mike. "We only have one more man on the loose." Mike had been right. The hundred-million-euro investor in Matthieu's two stores in Russia had decided to collect it or kill him, and he wanted the rest of the money from Theo after killing her husband and son. "It's very complicated and Russian. I don't think he'll come after her again if they don't succeed this time. It's too much trouble—he's lost too many men, and paid them for nothing. I want to put the last one away. We can't get to the man who hired them, but four people have died, and he got half his money back with the first ransom. That should be enough, even for a Russian," Guy Thomas said. It had taken an enormous amount of money and manpower just to get this far, and two people had been poisoned, which could have meant two more victims.

"Do you think he killed Matthieu's young actress too?" Mike asked, fascinated by how sick and how wrong the whole thing was.

"He might have, as a warning to him. Or she was killed by the FSB or SVR. She was double-crossing everyone, so it could have been them or Matthieu Pasquier's disgruntled investor. She was dispensable for them, a meaningless pawn in the game who probably betrayed too many people too many times. She was young and foolish and no match for the people she was cheating. Pasquier lost twice as much money as his investor on that deal, but he had a more pragmatic attitude about it, and he could afford it. So could his Russian associate, but he's known to be a hothead, according to one informant. Hopefully he'll let it go now. We've put the word out that we know who he is, and we'll make trouble for him with the SVR if he doesn't stop. I'm not sure they'd care, but it's one thing killing their own, and another coming here and killing respectable people and a child. We can make a request for extradition, but they'll never give him to us. They protect their own, no matter how bad they are."

"Robert says that too. They don't seem to hesitate to poison the people they're unhappy with. Theo is damn lucky they didn't use a more powerful nerve agent on her. Maybe de Vaumont is a casualty in this too. He took a lot of risks with the people he's been working for recently. Any news of him, by the way?"

"Nothing. He'll turn up one of these days, maybe he's on to some big deal. Or he's dead. He was playing with fire with the people he was dealing with. Very few people get away with that for long. Tell Mrs. Pasquier she has one less

Russian criminal to worry about. We're going to prosecute the guys we have in custody, and not send them back to Russia. It sends the right message. We're going to charge all three of the men we have with kidnap and murder. They'll be in prison here for a very long time. And hopefully, we'll find the last man soon. When we do, it will be over this time, and justice will have been served. It won't bring her husband and boy back, or keep her out of danger in future. But for now, and for a while, she'll be safe—as much as she can be."

"Thanks, Guy. And her DGSE detail?"

"Will stay in place until it's over, and maybe a while after that to make sure that it's really finished, and Dmitri Aleksandr will leave her alone. If he hires a new team, we'll do everything we can to stop him from here. This isn't the dark ages where you can go around killing anyone you want to. Even the Russian authorities won't approve."

"Thank you. She'll be relieved to have your men for a while, and I certainly am, for her."

"I knew months ago that you had a personal interest in the case, it wasn't even your case. And I was right." Guy laughed knowingly, and Mike smiled.

"I didn't even know I had a personal interest in it then. But I do now. She doesn't deserve any of what's happened to her, especially the boy."

Guy's face grew serious at that. "No, she doesn't. I hope she can find her peace about it someday. And she has you to protect her now."

"Your man did a fine job of it at the château. I'm not sure I'm as good a shot as he is," Mike said seriously. "I'd have been afraid to risk it with the kidnapper standing right next to her."

"He's a good shot and a good agent. Enjoy your holiday in France. I'll let you know when we find our man. Don't worry, we will. And Richmond is turning England upside down to find him. So are we here, in case he's back in France."

Mike thanked him and they hung up, then he reported the conversation to Theo, who looked somewhat relieved. There was only one kidnapper left to find, and it sounded like he was in England, not nearby. She was still trying to adjust to the idea that someone might try to kill her. It made Matthieu's fortune and her success more of a curse than a blessing. She had no one to leave it to now anyway. If something happened to her, she had designated half a dozen charities for children to be the beneficiaries. She had no one else, with Axel gone. And at least the money would do someone some good when she was gone.

For Mike, it got harder and harder to leave her every time. Mike spent New Year's Eve with her, and they had a lavish meal at Alain Ducasse. Mike liked treating her to special evenings, there was so little else he could do for her. He couldn't even buy clothes for her, since she sold them on her website and had whatever she wanted. He had bought her a gold bracelet with a large gold heart on it and had had their initials and the date engraved on the back, to commemorate their first Christmas. She had bought him a warm, fur-lined black leather jacket, which fit him perfectly, and he could wear in New York too.

On New Year's Day, he flew home to New York. He hated to leave her, but it was the life they led, with their respective jobs in different cities. It made their meetings more exciting, and the sex seemed new every time, but they were both lonely in between, no matter how busy they were in their work lives. He had hinted to her that he was going to have a lot to do when he got back. They had finally been alerted that the drug shipment they'd been waiting for, due in from Bolivia, had been moved and was coming from Ecuador now, in a week. Theo knew nothing about it.

The week after New Year's Day was busy for Theo. She was already working on their buy for the following fall and she had meetings in each of Matthieu's companies. She was essentially the fashion director of each of his brands, checking the orders for each product and each season. It was a huge job, and his brands were different from hers. His were more established with a design history and a look that had to be respected when they brought a new designer in, which she had just done in three of them, and the new designers had to be carefully supervised until they hit their stride.

Her own company kept her busy, making sure that the combination of the brands they offered were different enough but still worked well together to tell a unique fashion story that made women feel they had to have what she was selling. It was a constant marketing challenge, something that she was good at. She had a sixth sense for what look would be next in fashion and what styles and colors her customers would want to wear. That sixth sense and her flawless sense of style were what had made her business successful and had helped Matthieu with his too. When she was definite about something, he never questioned it. He followed what she said. He had enormous respect for her talent.

She was so busy the week Mike left that she never had time to call him at the right time, with the time difference between Paris and New York. Some days it was just always wrong. People came back with renewed energy after the holidays, and she had dozens of meetings to take advantage of that. She knew he was busy too—he had warned her he would be. On Friday, she realized she hadn't talked to him in three days, since Tuesday, which was unusual for them. They always spoke at least once or twice a day.

She waited to hear from him that night, and when he didn't call, she tried him on his cell and it went straight to voicemail. It seemed odd to her for a minute, and then she told herself that he must have been on some secret operation. She never questioned him about his work now since she knew he couldn't tell her anyway. She sent him a text to tell him she loved him, and went to bed, sure that she'd hear from him in the morning.

On Saturday, when she woke up, there was no return text, and for an instant she was annoyed, and thought how long could it take to write a quick text. By the end of another day of silence, she had a gnawing feeling in her gut that something might be wrong, and told herself she was being neurotic. She wasn't sure whether to be angry at him or scared, or if he was just being thoughtless or had the flu. She was sure it was something as simple as that. And maybe it was just some male side of him she hadn't seen yet, and he was starting to take her for granted or was tired of a long-distance relationship where they only saw each other every three or four weeks. She thought of a million reasons why he hadn't called, ranging from the banal and selfish, maybe he was out getting drunk with friends, to the truly terrifying, he'd been run over by a bus and killed, which seemed the least likely. She knew he was in a potentially dangerous line of work, but he played it down so she wouldn't worry. She was more inclined to be angry at him by Sunday, when she still hadn't heard from him in five days.

She lay in her bed on Sunday night, beginning to panic, and decided to call his main office line the next day. But with the time difference, she had to wait until three P.M. her time before there would be someone at his office to answer. She wondered at least once if he had decided to end the affair with her and didn't have the guts to tell her, but that was so unlike him, and nothing had gone wrong during his recent visit to Paris.

She hardly slept that night and had sent him half a dozen anxious texts by then, and left at least ten voicemails and an email. She wondered if he had lost his phone, which was the simplest explanation for his silence, and she hadn't even thought of that before. It had happened to her once and she was out of communication for a week until she got a new one. Matthieu had been very annoyed with her, but she hadn't had time to stop and pick up a new phone.

She got to her office promptly, her DGSE agents with her. They had a comfortable spot to sit outside her office where they could see her through a glass wall, without disturbing her. She checked her watch constantly for the next six hours, trying to get some work done in between, not too successfully. Her assistant Martine asked if anything was wrong, and she said there wasn't, but Martine could tell Theo was lying and hoped it wasn't something to do with the kidnappers again.

At five after three precisely, she took out the business card Mike had given her when they met, with his main office line on it, and she put the number into her phone and waited.

A serious male voice answered and gave the fictional name of the law firm he allegedly worked for. She asked for Michael Andrews in what she hoped sounded like a normal tone and not as hysterical as she felt by then, after six days of silence.

The male voice said simply, "Just a moment. Please hold the line." She had never spoken to any of them, since she always called him on his personal cellphone, not the office number. The wait seemed interminable and she assumed they were asking Mike if he would talk to her. She hadn't even had time to give her name before she was put on hold, and she wanted to scream while she waited. After five minutes, a female voice came on the line. She sounded serious and older, and not young and sexy, which reassured Theo since she had no idea why Mike was no longer speaking to her. Maybe he had fallen in love with his secretary.

"May I help you?" the voice said. "Mr. Andrews isn't available at the moment. He's out of the office." The only thing that reassured Theo was that since she hadn't given her name to the first voice, the refusal wasn't personal.

"I'm afraid that the call is important," Theo said politely, but with determination. "Will he be in shortly?"

There was the slightest pause, and then, "I'm sorry. He's working out of the office with a client today. May I help you with something?" Theo was at a loss for an instant. She knew his assistant's name but had never spoken to her.

"Could I speak to Jocelyn, his assistant?" Theo said. "I'm Theo Morgan." She hoped that Jocelyn knew about her, but she wasn't sure since Mike was so secretive about everything.

"One moment please, I'll transfer the call," the woman said, and Theo had another five-minute wait. She had never realized how complicated it was to reach him, since he called her most of the time. A younger woman's voice came on the line then, also sounding serious, and Theo identified herself again. And then in desperation, she added, "I'm the person he visits in Paris," hoping that Jocelyn knew about her.

"I know who you are," the girl said quietly, and there

was a tremor in her voice that Theo didn't like. "Mike isn't coming in today," she said in the same tone.

"Is he working out of the office?" Theo felt as though she had hit a stone wall and was looking for a door but couldn't find it. There was a long silence after her question.

"I'm so sorry," Jocelyn said, and Theo almost thought she was crying. "I'm not supposed to give out information. He had an accident last Tuesday night."

"What kind of accident?" Theo could feel her blood run cold, and she had a terrifying déjà vu of when she was told that Matthieu and Axel had been kidnapped, after she arrived and found Axel's running shoe on the front step and then found the château empty. "Is he all right?"

"No, he isn't," Jocelyn answered. "He's in critical condition, in the ICU. He was shot during a big field operation."

"Oh my God. Where?" She meant geography, not that it mattered.

"In the chest. They're keeping him in a coma, he's on a respirator. He joined the operation in the field at the last minute," she said. The floodgates had opened and she was crying, and so was Theo. She wasn't listed as an emergency contact for him, so no one had known to reach out to her, or that she even existed, if he couldn't tell them himself.

"What hospital is he in?"

"New York Presbyterian. He can't have visitors, just

257

family. He only has the office listed as his next of kin, so I don't think anyone is with him. He has a sister but he didn't want to worry her if he ever got injured." It was more information than he had ever given her. He was very close-mouthed about things like that.

"Is he going to be all right?" She held her breath after she asked.

"The bullet grazed his heart, but it didn't enter it. He was in surgery for twelve hours. I don't know more than that."

"Thank you," Theo said, feeling dazed. "Can I give you my number so you can call me if anything happens?" Jocelyn took down her numbers in Paris, office, home and cell, and her email address, and Theo thanked her for telling her the truth. She sat without moving in her chair when she hung up, and Martine walked in and stared at her.

"You're looking very pale. Do you feel okay?" She hadn't looked that bad when she was poisoned.

Theo glanced up at her with huge eyes in a snow-white face. "Mike had an accident. I need a ticket to New York, right away. I want to leave as soon as I can. I'll go home and pack. Call me there."

"God, Theo, I'm so sorry. A car accident? Will he be okay?"

"I don't know." She couldn't give Martine the details

because she couldn't explain why he'd been shot, and didn't know anyway, but it was in the line of duty, and no one except Theo knew that he was CIA. She got up quickly then, grabbed her purse, and headed out the door, signaling to her bodyguards to follow rapidly.

"I'm going to New York for an emergency. A friend of mine is very ill," she explained to them. They wondered if it was Mike, but didn't ask her. They just hurried after her, down the stairs and out the door to her car. Two of them got in with her, and the other two got in their chase car on the street. She went straight home and started packing as soon as she walked in, speeding around her dressing room, throwing black jeans, some sweaters, shoes, and underwear into a small valise. When she had almost everything she needed, she went to call the hospital, and asked to be connected to the ICU. She got the nurses' station and inquired about his condition, and the nurse asked immediately if she was related to him.

"Yes, I'm his sister," she lied to them.

"He's still in critical condition, there's been no change and he's still intubated."

"Is he still in a coma?" she asked in a choked voice.

"He's medicated," the nurse said more precisely, in a gentle but serious voice.

"I'm in Paris, I'm flying in to see him. I just heard about

it." She gave the nurse her name and cellphone number, and asked to be added to his contacts, and the nurse said she would. Theo didn't know if she was breaking any CIA rules, but she didn't care, she wanted to know what was happening to him.

Martine called as soon as she hung up. "You're on a seven forty-five flight to Kennedy tonight," she told her. "You have to be there at five forty-five to check in. You should leave in the next fifteen minutes. You're in business class, first was full, and I got a seat for Patrick to fly with you in business too. He was the only one who could do it on such short notice. He has clothes at the apartment. And you're staying at the Four Seasons. The Carlyle was fully booked. I got you a suite." It was everything Theo needed to know.

"Thank you. You're an angel." She went to get her passport out of her desk, checked that she had everything she needed, and closed her valise, just as Patrick came down the stairs carrying his suitcase. She had never traveled with him before, and she explained to the head DGSE agent that she was flying to New York to see a sick friend. They said they would advise Agent Thomas, and wait for further orders from him. He called her in the car on the way to the airport. She was staring out the window, feeling dazed. She couldn't believe that fate could be this cruel to her again. She had lost Matthieu and Axel, and Mike had fallen into her life like an angel from the sky. She couldn't lose him too. And regardless of her, he didn't deserve that. He was such a good person and kind man, who had spent a lifetime protecting others. He couldn't die at forty-nine. But another voice in her head said he could. If Axel could die, an innocent child, so could Mike.

She answered the phone when Guy Thomas called her.

"I understand you're leaving for New York to see a sick friend?" He sounded puzzled and surprised. "I hope it's not serious." But he knew it must be if she was leaving so hastily.

"It's Mike. He was shot during an operation last Tuesday. I just found out. He's in critical condition, in a coma, in the ICU in a hospital in New York."

"Oh, I am sorry. He's a good man, and a strong one. He'll pull through it," he said with a conviction he didn't feel but thought he should show to her. The poor woman had been through enough. "Give him my best. We'll handle everything here. And hopefully we'll have your other problem taken care of by the time you get back. I'm in close communication with MI6. They're combing England for our man. My men will be waiting to take care of you when you get home. I hope everything turns out well in New York." He hoped that fervently for her. If anyone ever deserved not to lose another person close to her, it was Theo. She had been unspeakably brave through some of the worst that life had to give. Then he added, "I'll say a prayer for him." It wasn't something he offered to do often, but he thought it was warranted in this case, for both of them.

Her eyes filled with tears and she could hardly speak when she answered.

"Thank you. I will too," was all she could say for a minute. "I'll be at the Four Seasons Hotel in New York, if you need to reach me."

"I'm sure I won't," he assured her. "Take care of yourself," he said kindly, and they hung up. She sat staring out the window after that, thinking of Mike, with tears running down her cheeks.

Chapter 15

The DGSE agents got her past the security lines and onto the plane before anyone boarded. She and Patrick settled into their seats. First class had been fully booked, and she didn't care how they got there. She would have flown coach if she had to. She texted Martine once she was on the plane, and thanked the DGSE agents before they left. They waited just outside the plane to observe the other passengers boarding, and would stay there until the doors to the plane were closed and the flight took off. They had already shown their badges and credentials to the cabin crew, who had been notified that they had a VIP on board, with special government protection. They texted ahead to New York to be sure she got VIP service when she disembarked. The captain had been advised too. He recognized the name and knew who she was.

She reclined her seat immediately after takeoff, and lay wide-awake, thinking about Mike, willing him to live. This couldn't happen to him, and to her again. They had only been together for four months, but he had become an integral part of her life in a surprisingly short time and had turned a tragic time into something she could live with. He made her happy. She would have sacrificed anything if she could make a deal for his life now, even give her own.

She couldn't sleep and didn't watch a movie, and she declined the meal when they offered it to her. The flight would take eight hours and arrive at ten P.M. New York time. She knew it would be too late to see Mike at the hospital. The other patients would be settled in for the night, although the ICU never slept and tended to their critically ill patients round the clock. They had told her she could come to see him at nine A.M., so it would be a long night once she got to the hotel around eleven-thirty. She knew Martine would have arranged a car and driver for her and advised Patrick. All Theo had to do was get to the hotel and to the hospital the next day. She had read somewhere that people in comas could hear you speak to them, and all she wanted to do now was sit next to him and hold his hand and tell him how much she loved him.

She finally dozed off halfway through the flight. Patrick covered her with a blanket and turned off the overhead light. Most of the passengers slept after the meal, and a few watched movies. He watched one, sitting next to her, and checked on her from time to time. Her eyes were closed and she was sleeping peacefully, but once in a while he saw a tear on her cheek. He had been told the reason for their trip to New York and felt sorry for her. She had been through so much, and the American who had been visiting her periodically seemed like a good man. He appeared to have a close connection with the DGSE detail, and Patrick wondered if he did police work of some kind, but didn't want to ask. He seemed to be fully trained in security operations and Patrick had noticed that he was armed, which meant he was probably a federal agent of some kind.

Theo woke up on her own half an hour before they landed. She hadn't eaten during the flight. She went to wash her face and brush her hair, and she looked serious and worried when she got back to her seat. She didn't like being out of touch for so long. If anything had happened while she was on the flight, she had no way of knowing. The thought of it panicked her. What if he had died while she was on the plane? She tried to force the thought from her mind.

When they landed at Kennedy and the plane stopped at the gate, two Homeland Security officers came on board to escort her and Patrick off, as the other passengers watched and wondered who she was. A movie star maybe, or someone important. She followed them with a serious expression, and Patrick walked close to her. They were escorted rapidly through immigration and customs, and their bags were among the first ones off, with the first-class baggage. They had given her every privilege possible, even though she wasn't flying first class. The Homeland Security officers and the airline's VIP agent walked her to the SUV waiting for her at the curb. They couldn't have done it faster if they'd flown, and she thanked them before they drove away. Patrick was sitting in the front seat with the driver of the SUV. She called the hospital as soon as they left the curb, and spoke to the nurses' station again, and got the same report she had before. There had been no change, but at least he was still alive.

It took them an hour to get to the hotel, and she was escorted to her suite, with an adjoining room for Patrick, for security reasons. The last thing they wanted was for her to get kidnapped in New York, but she knew that wouldn't happen. The men who were after her were far away now.

The view from the living room of her suite on the forty-eighth floor was amazing. Room service had left wine and pastry, chocolates, fruit, and champagne for her, but she paid no attention to it. Mike was all she could think about.

She was only sorry she hadn't called his office sooner,

but she kept thinking he would call and was just busy or sick or thoughtless. It never dawned on her that he might have been shot. It occurred to her that they led strange lives, the two of them, he in law enforcement, and she as a target for people who poisoned her and wanted to kill her and hurt the people she loved. They were two sides of the same coin, facing the same evil forces every day, she as a target and potential victim, and he as the hero who protected and saved people like her. In an odd way, they complemented each other, and completed each other.

She slowly undressed and took a shower, then realized she had forgotten to bring a nightgown with her. She was going to sleep in one of the hotel's terrycloth robes that came with the suite. It was one in the morning by then, and she had another eight hours to get through before she could see him. It was already seven in the morning in Paris by then, and she was wide-awake. She lay on the bed and turned on the TV. She paid no attention to what was on the screen, but it was comforting to hear voices in the room.

She finally closed her eyes at three in the morning, and woke up at six. She called the nurses' station again then, and there was still no change. She wondered how long it could go on that way and what it meant.

Finally it was eight-thirty and, wearing black jeans and a black sweater under a black coat, she went downstairs with

Patrick to find her car and driver and go to the hospital. She had forced herself to drink a cup of coffee and eat a piece of toast before she left the suite. She had no idea how Mike would look when she saw him, and she was bracing herself for whatever she found in the ICU. She had never been through anything like this with Axel and Matthieu. They were taken from the château, and when they were found they were already dead. There had been no bedside vigil, no wait at the hospital, praying that they'd live. She had never seen or spoken to them again after they'd been taken. She'd never had a chance to touch them or kiss them goodbye.

She didn't speak to Patrick on the drive uptown and he could see how tense she was, so he made no attempt at conversation. He hoped things hadn't gotten worse.

When she got to the hospital, she made her way to the information desk after going through a metal detector, with Patrick following her discreetly. He had to show his French government badge to pass the metal detector while armed, and they let him through. It was a confusing maze of hallways and elevators, and the man at the desk told her how to get to the ICU. She went up what she hoped was the right elevator, followed his directions, and found herself outside locked doors, where she pressed a buzzer to be admitted. They let her in immediately. Patrick waited at the doors, and she went to the nurses' station, asked to see

Michael Andrews, and told them she was his sister, as she had on the phone.

"Of course," a nurse said to her, then came around the desk and led the way to his cubicle. There were no rooms in the ICU. All the patients had to be instantly accessible, with monitors to read and nurses and attending physicians observing them at all times. A curtain could be drawn for privacy if a family member was visiting, but the rest of the time, each patient's bed was positioned in such a way that the nurses could see them.

The nurse passed a line of beds, as Theo tried to look away discreetly, so she didn't intrude on the other patients in their misery. The nurse stopped at the third cubicle and walked in quietly with Theo right behind her. There was another nurse standing at the head of the bed, watching the monitors and his vital signs. It shocked Theo when she saw him. He was stretched out to his full height, deathly pale and unconscious, with a breathing tube in his mouth, and a machine breathing for him. There were IVs in both arms, and heavy bandaging on his chest. Theo gently touched his hand and his cheek, and then stroked his shoulder. She stood next to him and wasn't sure she would have recognized him. He looked so severely ill and badly damaged that it shocked her. The nurses retreated to the foot of the bed to leave them alone, and conferred quietly, then added the latest data to a computer on a stand.

"Hi, Mike," she whispered softly to him. "It's Theo, I came to make sure you get better. I'm here with you, and I love you." Tears filled her eyes and spilled down her cheeks as she said it. There was no reaction, and she hadn't expected there to be one. He was in a deep coma. She couldn't imagine that he could hear her, but on the slight chance that he could, she wanted him to know that she loved him. "I'm sorry you got hurt, but you're going to be okay now. You're going to be better soon, and your heart will be fine . . . I love you, Mike."

She kept talking to him, and the nurse who had brought her to him reminded her gently that visits were for ten minutes, so she could come back again an hour later. They kept visits short so the most severely ill patients could rest. In most cases, ten minutes were all they could handle. Theo gently stroked his forehead with light fingers and smoothed his hair down. He hadn't shaved in a week, which added to his ravaged look. Another nurse came in to replace a bag of fluids for one of his IVs and checked the oxygen clip on his finger. There were wires and tubes and monitors attached to every part of him. At the end of ten minutes, the nurse standing next to his bed signaled to Theo to leave.

Theo bent low near his ear then. "I'll be back in a little

while. I love you, Mike. I'm right here." She left him then and went back to the nurses' station and thanked them.

"There's a waiting room around the corner, or you might want to get something to eat downstairs." As she said it, a man in a gray suit approached the desk.

"Michael Andrews?" he inquired, then glanced at Theo. She looked somber and upset.

"He's just had a visit with his sister," the nurse explained. "You can see him in a few minutes."

"You're his sister?" the man in the suit asked Theo, and she hesitated.

"Yes. I just flew in from Paris."

"Why don't we go and chat for a few minutes," he suggested, and Theo wondered if he was going to expose her as an imposter, and then they wouldn't let her see him again. She was going to ask him not to, if he told her he knew she was lying. Luckily, there was no one else in the waiting room when they got there and both sat down.

He looked at her seriously and explained who he was. "I'm Mike's senior supervisor. I came up from Washington to see how he's doing. Paul Blakely."

"I'm Theo Morgan," she admitted to him. "I'm a friend of Mike's from Paris. I flew in last night as soon as I heard."

"I know who you are," he said quietly. "Mike has told me about you." He knew the rest of her story too, Mike's interest in her case and his concern about kidnappers taking her too. "Mike and I were in the military together, that's where I met him. I was the one who talked him into leaving the navy and signing up with us. He's had a bad break here. You can't keep a good agent away from fieldwork. We had a big operation going last week, and he showed up as it was going down. He was supposed to supervise from the base. Things started to go wrong, and he flew out of his office to help. He got there in time to save the operation and the lives of three of our agents. He got shot in the process. He must have left his office so fast he forgot his vest. He probably didn't even think about it. All hell was breaking loose when he got there. He wouldn't even have had time to put a vest on then. He was lucky. The bullet grazed his heart but it didn't kill him. They're keeping him in a medicated coma to give his body a chance to heal after the surgery. They may keep him like this for a couple of weeks," he explained, "but the doctors think he'll pull out of it. We just have to wait and see how he does. He's made it for six days, which is a good sign." He tried to reassure her, she looked so devastated. He looked about five years older than Mike. He was well dressed and had gray hair, and she assumed that he must be high up in the CIA if he was Mike's superior.

"I told them I'm his sister," she confessed, "but they wouldn't have let me in otherwise."

"I'll put your name on the list. I'm glad to meet you, Ms. Morgan. You mean a great deal to our boy here. He's been very worried about you in Paris." Theo was touched that Mike had told his friend about her. "Mike actually has a sister, but she's not on his list of next of kin, and I haven't called her, if that's not what he would have wanted." Theo knew she wasn't on the list either, but she had come anyway.

"I don't know how close they are," Theo said. "I don't think they're very close, but she's the only relative he has."

"He's not one to make a big fuss. He was injured in Iraq, when a bomb went off in a restaurant, and he got through it on his own, and didn't want anyone around. He's a strong guy and he's got nine lives. He'll come through this," Paul Blakely said firmly, wanting it to be true. He was worried too but didn't want to scare her.

"Well, I'm staying till he's better," Theo said with a stubborn look in her eyes, and he smiled.

"I think he'd be glad you're here," he reassured her. "Give me your contact numbers, and I'll let you know if there's any change, if you're not here." He stood up to go and see Mike then, and she jotted down her hotel and her cell number on a piece of paper, and he slipped it in his pocket. She walked out of the waiting room with him, and she saw him show his badge and ID card at the desk. The nurse nodded and stood up immediately. They knew that Mike was CIA, several of the senior agents had been in to see him, and there was a special code for no information on his chart. They didn't want anyone to come in and finish the job, which was a risk with law enforcement officers, especially those of Mike's high rank. Killing a senior CIA agent would have been a feather in the cartel's cap.

Paul Blakely nodded at Theo and walked into Mike's cubicle. She turned to walk down the long hall to help pass the time. Paul only stayed for a few minutes, and then asked the nurse some questions before writing Theo's name down on a list of approved visitors. There were only a few names on it, and then he left and took the elevator back downstairs.

Theo was back an hour later, and the nurse nodded and pointed at Mike's bed. Theo was approved now. "You can go and see him." Theo took her place near his head again and spoke to him in gentle, soothing tones, telling him again how much she loved him. They let her stay fifteen minutes that time. She went outside to get some air after that, and Patrick followed. She walked around the block, and he kept a discreet distance from her. She continued coming back on the hour to visit him all day. Patrick tried to get her to eat between visits, but she wouldn't.

"There won't be much change in his condition, as long as he's this heavily medicated," the nurse told her. "They want to keep him this way so he doesn't do any damage to his heart moving around so soon after the surgery. He might be this way for another week," she told Theo, and she nodded.

"I understand. I just want him to know I'm here, on the chance that he hears me."

The nurse smiled in response. "A lot of patients tell us that they did hear their loved ones when they were comatose. There's a lot we don't know about the human mind. Just keep talking to him, it will be good for both of you," she said kindly.

Theo stayed until eight o'clock that night. She had been there for eleven hours when she left, and had seen him eleven times.

"See you tomorrow," she said to the nurses as she left.

"Do you know who she is?" one of the nurses said after the doors closed behind her. Theo had a look about her even in black jeans and a black sweater. "I think she owns that online shopping site that I spend my whole damn paycheck on every time I check it out. Theo.com." The others smiled when she said it. They knew the site.

"She said she was his sister," one of them said.

"I don't think so, if you listen to her talk to him. Girlfriend more like," one of the other nurses said.

Another nurse lowered her voice conspiratorially. "He's some big-deal CIA guy. Half the CIA was in here when it happened last week. It didn't look like he would make it at first, but these guys are tough. He's hanging in. All the big-gun surgeons were called in for the surgery when they brought him in. Two flew up from Washington." They all went back to work then.

Patrick was still waiting for her when Theo left the hospital and got back in the car to go to the hotel.

"I'm sorry it was such a long day," she said to Patrick and the driver.

"How's Mr. Andrews?" Patrick asked her.

"He's in a medically induced coma, so it's hard to tell right now. He's on a respirator," she said, and melted into the seat. She was exhausted. The emotional strain of seeing him so sick and watching the machine breathe for him left her so drained that she could hardly get out of the car when they got back to the hotel. Patrick gave her a hand, which she accepted gratefully, and she asked the driver to be back again at eight forty-five the next morning, then she and Patrick rode up in the elevator. He was looking forward to a good meal from room service. Theo had had two bites of a sandwich Patrick bought from one of the shops in the lobby and she ate in the ICU waiting room. She wasn't hungry now but knew she had to eat.

She ordered a cheeseburger from room service, and it reminded her of their first date at the diner. She was going to remind him of it the next day when she saw him. She had talked to him about inane things all day, about what they were going to do when he was better, the places they wanted to go. She reminded him that he had promised to take her to Venice, and they wanted to go to Rome too. She wondered if they ever would. He seemed so close to death that it was hard to imagine him surviving, but she wanted to believe he would. She had to, she couldn't bear the thought of losing him. She refused to believe that would happen, but she was scared for him every time she looked at him.

She managed to eat half the burger and a few French fries, took a shower and put the cozy robe on again, and lay on her bed. She fell asleep and the next thing she knew it was seven in the morning. She ordered oatmeal for breakfast and turned on the news, where she saw a big story about a major drug bust the week before. Literally tons of heroin and cocaine had come in by plane from Ecuador, and one of the biggest Colombian drug lords had been captured in a gunfight with federal agents at the airport. She knew as she listened that that was when Mike had gotten shot. It said that three of the drug runners had been killed in the process, and two federal agents had been killed, and three others had been saved by a heroic senior agent who had been shot in the process and was in critical condition. She understood what he did better now. And all she hoped was that he'd survive. She hoped that Paul Blakely was right and Mike had nine lives.

Theo was back at Mike's bedside at nine-thirty. The nurses smiled when she arrived, and she took up her gentle patter of one-sided conversation with Mike. She reminded him of their first date at the diner, and told him she wanted to go back there with him again. And she reminded him about Venice and Rome. She talked about anything she could think of, and told him again and again how much she loved him.

The days ran into each other as she arrived in the ICU every morning. She brought a big box of chocolates for the nurses, which pleased them. And on her third day there, she saw the doctors examine him. They pulled the curtain around his cubicle and looked satisfied when they emerged. She asked one of them how they thought he was doing.

"We're pleased with his progress," he said conservatively, once she introduced herself and he saw her name on the approved visitors list. "He's been stable for ten days, we may wake him up a little and take him off the respirator next week." It sounded like good news to her, and later when she asked, one of the nurses told her it was.

"He's getting stronger," she said. "It's hard to see progress while he's on the respirator. When they lighten the sedation, you'll start to see some improvement," she encouraged her. They had all been impressed by how faithful Theo had been. She was there every day for ten or twelve hours, and there were dark circles under her eyes. She was obviously very concerned about him.

Theo had gotten texts from both Guy Thomas and Robert Richmond. The last kidnapper was still at large somewhere, but both men were concerned about Mike's condition, and they told Theo to wish him well and a speedy recovery. She told him about it during one of her fifteen-minute visits with him. She told him everything she could think of to encourage him.

She called her office occasionally, but everything was running smoothly there and they didn't want to burden her.

She maintained her hourly visits with Mike for an entire week, and on Monday, almost two weeks after his long heart surgery, they let him out of the medical coma, and he opened his eyes for the first time. He looked surprised to see Theo. He couldn't speak while he was still on the respirator, but she thought his eyes were smiling and he squeezed her hand. He was still very weak, but his color was better.

They took him off the respirator that night. He ran a fever, which panicked Theo, but the nurses said that happened sometimes, and the doctors weren't concerned. His temperature was normal by morning.

She was gently stroking his hair and speaking softly to him when he said his first words to her.

"Love you, Theo . . ." he said in a hoarse whisper. His throat was irritated from the respirator, and she kissed him gently on the cheek.

"I love you too. How do you feel?"

"Better than when I went to sleep." He smiled at her. "I owe you a burger and a trip to Venice," he said in a raspy voice, and she looked surprised.

"Did you hear me when I talked to you?"

"I don't know . . . I don't know if I dreamed it, but I thought I heard you."

"I've been talking to you for a week."

"How long have you been here?" he whispered.

"A week today."

"You're an amazing woman." He dozed off then, and slept a lot for the next few days, still lightly sedated so he didn't have pain. At the end of the week, they moved him out of the ICU to a private room, with a federal agent standing guard at the door. He could sit up by then, and the next day, he took a short walk down the hall with Theo next to him, pushing a wheelchair in case he needed to sit down. By the end of the following week, they said he could go home. He had been in the hospital for four weeks, and was eager to leave. He looked at Theo seriously then.

"My apartment is a mess, you can't stay there with me. It's more like an office with a bed in it."

"Then we'll go to my hotel. You can have room service, and whatever you want."

He had to admit he liked the idea, but he didn't want to take advantage of her. "If I stay with you, then I'm paying for the hotel."

"Don't be ridiculous. I've been there for three weeks, another week or two won't matter. And if they let you, you can come back to Paris with me. How much sick leave do you have?"

"Another month or two, whatever I need."

When they asked, the doctors weren't keen on his traveling too soon. They wanted him around for the next month, in case he had any problems. But he agreed to go to the hotel with Theo, and when she left, he'd go back to his apartment.

He was thrilled to leave the hospital two days later, and they moved into her suite at the Four Seasons. He laughed when he saw it.

"I should have just stayed here for four weeks," he said, and Theo grinned at him. She was so relieved to see him up and around again. He looked normal, but he wasn't supposed to exert himself or overtax the surgical site. The bullet had done a fair amount of damage, even though the repair work had been skillful and the doctors said he'd be as good as new in a month or two. The doctor was amused at his last question before they discharged him.

"Give it two more weeks, and don't go too crazy at first." His actual heart hadn't been damaged, but the structure and muscles supporting it had been, and he had had an enormous amount of internal stitches. But his heart was sound.

"The doctor said we can have sex whenever we want," he said to Theo, as he lay on the bed in her suite and was smiling broadly.

"No, he didn't. You're a liar, and a sex fiend, Mike Andrews. I asked him, and he said not for two more weeks."

"Shit, why did you ask him?" He looked disappointed and she laughed at him.

"Because I don't trust you, and you just lied about it, which proves I'm right. Do you want to rip all your stitches open?"

"Hell, I was shot. I deserve some TLC and cheering up."

"You can have all the TLC you want, but no wild, crazy sex for two weeks."

"I'm having withdrawals," he complained.

"We can play cards and watch TV, and go for walks," she said, handing him the room service menu.

"And take cold showers."

The doctor had said that he could go out, as long as he

didn't do anything strenuous or exercise, so the first time they went out, they went back to the diner and had a good time. Patrick went with them and sat in a separate booth.

Mike took her to his apartment just to see it, and it looked even worse to him than he remembered.

"It looks like a computer lab," she said, frowning. "I'm not even sure decorating would help. All you have is office furniture."

"Courtesy of Goodwill and the Central Intelligence Agency."

"You get an F in decorating."

"I was afraid you'd say that."

When they got back to the hotel, she told him she wanted to meet his sister, if he was willing. He looked sheepish when she said it.

"I never told her I'd been shot. She worries about me, that's why I don't have her on my emergency list. She thinks I'm invincible."

"So do I, but shit happens," Theo said calmly, grateful beyond words that he'd survived. She had been terrified he wouldn't.

"She's going to be shocked to see me at this hotel. That might shock her more than my getting shot. She's kind of an oddball, but I love her."

"We can meet her at a restaurant if you want."

"No, let's do it here. She thinks being poor is admirable. She's suspicious of rich people." But he called her anyway, he wanted to see her too. When he called, he told her he'd been injured but he was fine now, and he was staying with a friend at a hotel uptown. She was visiting from Paris, and he wanted them to meet.

"Is she French?" she asked suspiciously.

"No, she's American, but she lives in Paris."

"Are you getting married?" Fiona asked him, while Theo was at her desk in the living room of the suite. Her office had been sending her work by email every day, ever since Mike was better. She was struggling to keep up with it, after being away for three weeks.

"No, I'm not getting married, but she's important to me. And so are you, and she wants to meet you."

"Can I come to the hotel the way I am, or do I have to get all dressed up to get through the door?"

"You can come however you want. She's a good person, Fi, you'll like her."

"The last girl you said that about was in college, and she hated me, and I hated her more."

"You won't hate this one, and I happen to love her."

"Oh God, that's bad. You've never said that about any woman. Now I'll have to be nice to her."

"Be yourself. Do you want to come to dinner tonight?"

"No, but I will, because I love you, you jerk. And why didn't you tell me you got hurt?"

"I didn't want to make you nervous."

"What happened?"

"I got shot. But I'm fine now."

"Okay, I'll come. What time and where?"

"How about seven? Do you want to bring Ian?"

"No, he's teaching an art class tonight." She'd had the same boyfriend for fifteen years but they didn't live together and didn't want to get married, and she was happy that way.

He gave her the address of the hotel and their room number, and she said she'd be there. He walked into the living room to tell Theo. She looked up from the computer and smiled. She was so happy to see him up and around and looking like himself again.

"She's coming, at seven. I told her I got shot. She took it well. I didn't give her the details." Theo could sense it was going to be an interesting evening.

Mike opened the door when his sister rang the bell promptly at seven, but he had forgotten to tell Theo that Fiona had pink hair. She had had it for as long as he could remember, and the bright pink pixie cut looked good on her. She was wearing paint-splattered sneakers and a matching shirt, torn blue jeans, and a synthetic leopard coat. She looked about twenty years old, not forty-two.

Theo crossed the room to meet her and was glad she'd worn jeans too. Fiona had a wild teenage style to her, but the whole look worked on her, and she had brightly colored flowers tattooed on the insides of both arms, that actually were cute on her. Theo was wearing a pink Chanel sweater and black and pink Chanel ballerinas with her jeans. They were both good-looking women but in entirely different ways. Fiona was hesitant as she greeted Theo, but Theo was warm and welcoming, and Mike looked like a proud papa bear with two cubs.

He offered his sister a drink and she asked for white wine.

"What kind of art do you do?" Theo asked her as they sat down.

"Street art, like graffiti," she said, and Theo smiled.

"I love street art," she confirmed.

"I've been doing it for about twenty-five years, before everyone knew about it and people started paying a fortune for it. My gallery says I should raise my prices, but then no one will be able to afford it except rich people, and it should be for everyone. What do you do?" She looked like a model to Fiona.

"I sell clothes online. Do you sell your work online?" Theo asked her.

"I have a website. I do pretty well with it," Fiona said as she sipped her wine and relaxed a little. She didn't want to like Theo and she thought the hotel was ridiculous, but she had to admit, her brother was right. Theo was nice, and although she was wearing expensive clothes, she wasn't pretentious or a phony or a snob. She was a normal person, in fancy clothes and rich surroundings, and she could see why Mike liked her. Fiona did too. They talked about art, and life, and work, and Fiona told funny stories about Mike as a kid.

"He used to lie all the time. Biggest liar I ever knew. He probably still does. But he got all holier-than-thou and honorable when he joined the CIA. He was kind of a pain in the ass for a while, playing Mister Secret Agent, but he's almost normal these days." Theo laughed at her irreverent description of him.

"He lied to me too. He told me he was a lawyer when I met him."

"He does that. I think they tell them to," Fiona said in his defense, "but if you're going to go around getting shot, you might as well tell people the truth, otherwise they'll either think you're a cop or a drug dealer."

They ordered dinner then. Theo said the burgers were pretty decent, and the roast chicken was good, but the pasta wasn't so great. In the end, Mike had a steak and Fiona, who was a vegetarian, had a veggie plate she liked. They had ice cream sundaes for dessert, and Theo told her about their banana split on their first date.

Fiona stayed until ten o'clock, and Theo noticed that Mike looked tired by then. The two women hugged before Fiona left, and Mike hugged Theo after Fiona was gone.

"You were fantastic. She loved you, and you were so nice to her. I never know what she's going to do or say."

"She's terrific." Theo smiled at him. "The only thing I want to know is how you could let me sell you that red purse for her. She'll never wear that in a thousand years. I would wear it, she wouldn't, not in a million years. Did you give it to her?" Theo asked him, and he looked sheepish.

"No, I didn't. I was so excited to meet you, I'd have bought anything."

"It's a good thing you didn't buy the red mink jacket, she would have hated that more."

"It was too expensive."

"Yes, it was," Theo agreed. "It's overpriced."

"I still have the purse if you want it."

"Never mind. I know exactly the right one for her. What did you give her instead?"

"Nothing. It wasn't her birthday."

"You lied to me about your sister's birthday? Oh my God, you are a liar. She's right!" Theo was laughing and he grinned.

"Maybe introducing the two of you was a mistake. I'm starting to think so, if you're going to gang up on me." He kissed her then, and was dying to get her into bed in a serious way.

"Remember what the doctor said," she warned him. "Two more weeks!"

"I hate you," but the way he kissed her said otherwise. It had been a fun evening for all three of them. Fiona texted him as she rode back to the Village on the subway.

"She's terrific. Marry her," was all it said.

Theo sent a quick email to her office before they went to bed. Two days later the package arrived of what she ordered that night after meeting Fiona. It was the Balenciaga City bag with multicolored graffiti all over it, and it was perfect for her. She showed it to Mike and he grinned when he saw it. It looked like it had been made for her or that she'd made it herself. Theo sent it to her address by messenger, with a note hoping to see her soon, and Fiona was bowled over. She sent Mike another text after that. "If you don't marry her, I will. Best purse I ever had."

"It's complicated," he responded to his sister.

"She's already married?"

"Widowed. A year ago. Bad story."

"I'm sorry. I love her," Fiona wrote back.

"Me too," Mike wrote to his sister.

The meeting between the woman he loved and his sister had been a resounding success.

Chapter 16

Theo spent another week with Mike at the hotel in New York, and then she had to get back to work. She had been gone for four weeks to see him through his recovery, and he was going to take another month off, but couldn't travel. She had to catch up on all the things she hadn't done while she was in New York, but they were closer than ever when she left. Her standing by him while he hovered between life and death had created a bond between them that deepened their relationship immeasurably, the way nothing else could have. They had been through the worst together.

He had been in touch with both Guy Thomas and Robert Richmond, and the remaining kidnapper was still floating around somewhere just out of reach. Robert's sources told him that he was still in England, but no one seemed to know where. He had gone underground and was staying out of sight.

Both men were immensely relieved that Mike had survived his ordeal.

Daniel had changed places with Patrick halfway through the New York trip.

Theo was sad to leave Mike, but he knew she had to get back to work, and he was grateful she had stayed for so long.

"I'll come over as soon as they let me travel," he promised her before she left. And they had decided to take the trip to Venice and Rome when he felt up to it, maybe in the summer.

She was swamped when she got back, but they spoke several times a day. The four agents from the DGSE were assigned to her again, and they were in evidence. She couldn't enjoy the same freedom she'd had in New York, and she missed it.

She'd been back for a week when Robert got word of a sighting of the Russian they'd been looking for since December. They followed the leads he had to the Cotswolds, where they saw the kidnapper coming out of a supermarket and closed in on him before he could flee. He tried to run and fired a shot at one of the MI6 agents pursuing him, missed, and the agents caught him and pinned him to the ground, and delivered him personally three days later to Guy Thomas, who arrested him and added him to the others to stand trial for the kidnap and murder of Matthieu and Axel Pasquier, and the attempted kidnapping of Theodora Morgan Pasquier. Guy went to Theo's office to tell her in person. Mike already knew, but Guy wanted the pleasure of telling her himself. It had taken more than a year to find them, but justice would be done in the end.

Theo looked incredulous when he told her. "Does that mean I'm a free woman?" she asked him.

"Not totally, I'm afraid. You will need to be careful in the future. You will always be a target. Your success and your fortune are both a blessing and a curse. I'd like to keep our detail with you for another month, just to be comfortable, and after that your own private security should accompany you publicly. There will always be someone envious and ill-intentioned. There are unseen evils in this world, and you need to protect yourself against them."

"I have ever since my husband's death," she said sadly. "I suppose I'll never have the freedom I had before." Her life had changed radically. But the daily tension and terror would no longer be there, knowing that they were after her to settle an old score that should never have been held against her, or her husband, and surely not their son. She had paid a terrible price for what had happened, a price that could never be reversed.

"I hope you can live in peace now," Guy said sincerely. She wasn't too old to marry again and have other children, but he didn't know if she would. Theo had already decided that having another child would have been a betrayal of Axel, and she would live in constant terror that another child could be taken from her, or killed simply because of what she had. She couldn't imagine living with that kind of fear as a constant presence in her life, and she didn't want to try. She knew she couldn't endure it again. Axel had been her bright shining star, and the only one she wanted now, in her heart forever. But at least her life would be relatively normal again, with the four surviving kidnappers in custody. Until the next time, or the next threat, if it ever happened. It would always be a possibility. She had to learn to live with that now. She was almost used to it, but not quite. And maybe she never would be, having bodyguards around her for the rest of her life.

And the DGSE and MI6 had passed a serious message, both through underground channels and with an official warning to his government connections, warning Dmitri Aleksandr that if he pursued the Pasquier matter again, he would be prevented from entering England and France in the future, which he did not want. So it was over.

A week later, Guy contacted her again, by phone this time.

"I thought you'd be interested in knowing that Pierre de Vaumont has turned up." She wasn't surprised and was sure he was off taking advantage of someone, making a deal and a commission at someone's expense. He was a lowlife and would always find a way to make use of someone.

"Where was he?" She was sure he would say Dubai, or Morocco, or someplace where deals were made and rich people congregated.

"He turned up in the Seine, early this morning. His body was dumped there sometime in the last day or two. He didn't drown, he was strangled." He had been found with a thin wire around his neck. "He made a few too many deals for his own good. I don't know where he's been since he disappeared—Russia probably, or maybe he's been in hiding somewhere. I think he made promises he couldn't deliver on. I'm not sure who his client was for your château, but he may have already taken an advance on a commission and couldn't return it, or perhaps he promised your husband's angry investor that he could deliver you this time for the balance and it all went awry. The kind of people he dealt with don't take kindly to not getting their way, and there's a price to be paid for that. His matchmaking was bound to catch up with him one day. It did. He poisoned you, and God knows what else he would do for money. Money is a god to some people, and it's a dangerous one to have."

There was a final sense of closure with Pierre de Vaumont's death. He had led an empty life. His victories were hollow, and none of the people who had known him and profited from the connections he made seemed to miss him. Many didn't even remember him. Men like Pierre de Vaumont were soon forgotten.

Mike was relieved to hear the news of the final kidnapper being arrested and Pierre de Vaumont's ignominious end. He was satisfied with the stern warning to Dmitri Aleksandr from the British and the French. And he was relieved for Theo, as much as he could be. None of it would bring back the people she loved. But at least the criminals would be punished for the crimes they had committed. Two of the kidnappers had died, the first ransom had never turned up, and had been laundered somehow, somewhere, and whatever part Pierre de Vaumont had played in it had cost him his life. Theo's life had been altered forever, in ways that could never be repaired or replaced. The life of a thirteen-year-old boy had been snuffed out like a brightly burning candle, which was the cruelest of all.

* * *

Theo took a long drive to Deauville with one of her body-guards after she heard all the news from Guy Thomas. She needed time to absorb it and think about what the future would look like without the people she'd lost. She was still working it out in her own mind.

They stopped for lunch at a little café, and she looked at the ocean and the beach. She thought of when she had gone there with Mike. He was recovering in New York, missing Theo and chafing to get to work. He was almost back to full strength, but not fully there yet. His doctors were pleased and told him every time they saw him how lucky he had been. He knew it in many ways, and a woman like Theo crossed your path once in a lifetime.

She and the bodyguard drove past Deauville after lunch, and she noticed a large Norman farm on the other side of the road, with tall old trees around it. There was a small sign that said it was for sale. She asked the bodyguard to drive up the long driveway. There was a high wall surrounding the property and an iron gate standing open. There was a beautiful old farmhouse inside the walls, and a stone cottage near the gate. She looked around, and an old caretaker came out to ask what they wanted. Theo asked him about it, and he said that the property was for sale. The elderly couple who had lived there had died, and their children didn't want it. They all had left France and lived abroad now and weren't planning to return to France, so they were selling it.

"May I look around?" Theo asked. She had a strange feeling being there, as though she had been led there by some inexplicable force. He asked if she wanted to look inside the house, and she said yes.

It was beautiful and charming with heavy wood beams and a wood-paneled dining room. There were fireplaces everywhere and an old-fashioned kitchen. It needed to be modernized, but it was big and rambling and comfortable, the kind of place you'd want to come to on a weekend. Theo could see the ocean from the master bedroom.

She thanked the caretaker and wrote down the number of the realtor, to call him on Monday. She thought about the house all the way back to Paris. The rooms had been sunny and just needed a fresh coat of paint in light colors. It was a house to fill with friends or children or to spend time in alone. It was the perfect counterpoint to a city existence, where you could get away from all the pressures of a fast-moving urban life. The house she had seen was a place to slow down, look at the ocean, and smell the sea air.

She was still thinking about it on Monday when she got to her office, and called the realtor. The price was absurdly low, given the area and how popular Normandy was. It needed work but she had the feeling it could be turned into a magical place, and the stone cottage at the gate could house all the bodyguards she needed.

Mike called her that night. He had just seen the doctor and he was cleared to travel in two weeks. He couldn't wait to see her, and he had another month off from work to recuperate if he needed it, which he said he didn't. He felt fine.

"You sound dangerous," she said and laughed. She knew what he had in mind the minute he got there. They hadn't made love in almost two months, since his last trip to Paris. Spring was in the air, and she couldn't wait to see him.

Chapter 17

Theo tried to catch up on all her work before Mike arrived. She was buying for fall and winter for Theo.com, and trying to solve a problem with one of Matthieu's brands. It was what she always did, and had done for a long time, but she was feeling excited about it these days, and wanted to put new life into their companies.

She finished the last of her big projects the night before he arrived. She felt liberated, and he had told her he wanted to go back to Deauville and walk along the ocean with her. He was feeling a rebirth too. After almost dying from his gunshot wound, every day seemed more precious, everything looked beautiful and vibrant to him, and he couldn't wait to do things with Theo that he had put off for too long. Venice, Rome, or wherever she wanted to go.

There was so much they could do together, and she said she wanted to too.

He had lunch with Fiona before he left, and she was carrying the purse Theo had given her. She loved it, and told him what a fantastic person Theo was. He told her the story of how she had lost Matthieu and Axel. Fiona was sobered by it and felt deep compassion for her.

"How do you live past something like that? How do you wake up every day and keep going, and find meaning in life?"

"I don't know," he said, "but somehow she does. She's a powerhouse, always full of new ideas and things she wants to create. She has an amazing head for business, and a vision of things. She can make something out of nothing. I've seen her take empty spaces and turn them into magic with a roll of fabric and a staple gun. She's an inspiration."

Fiona talked about her own relationship with Ian. "I don't even know why it works. He drives me nuts some of the time, but the rest of the time I think he's fantastic. He's a terrific artist, and he thinks I am too. We've been thinking about going to city hall one of these days and getting married, but I'm afraid it'll ruin everything."

"Why? Because Mom and Dad were such a mess? That was them. This is you. Don't let that stop you from leading a life, Fi. Marry him if you want to. You've been together for fifteen years."

"I know. Isn't that ridiculous?" she laughed. "It shows an epic lack of imagination on both our parts. We've never even cheated on each other. That's pathetic."

He laughed at his sister's view of things, but he loved her, as funny and odd as she was.

"Don't get married until I can give you away," he called down the subway steps after her and she turned back and laughed.

"Yeah, count on it. I wouldn't do it without you." But she would do, one day on the spur of the moment, and they both knew it. Their mutual acceptance of each other's foibles had always made the relationship work, and he loved that she and Theo got along. It was important, and one more point in Theo's favor, because she accepted her too, and even enjoyed her, and saw the beauty and talent in her, pink hair, paint-splattered clothes and all.

It reminded him of the red purse he wanted to give back to Theo so she could use it, and he put it in his suitcase to take with him.

Theo was waiting for him at the airport when he arrived. She was standing with Daniel when Mike came out of baggage claim, and Daniel took the suitcase from him and walked away as Mike pulled Theo into his arms and kissed her.

"I thought I'd never get back here. All I could think of was coming home to you." She loved that he felt that way about her and coming to Paris. He appreciated the beauty of it and the home she had there.

They talked nonstop all the way into the city, laughing together, with his arm around her in the back seat, holding her close to him. The driver and bodyguard talked to each other in low voices in the front seat, kept their eyes forward, and paid no attention to them.

Mike walked straight into her office when they got home, and from there straight into her bedroom. He closed the door behind her and didn't wait another minute to start peeling her clothes off. She saw the scars from his surgery when he took off his shirt. They looked angry and raw, and she touched them gently.

"It's a miracle that you're here," she said and looked up at him. He kissed her and a moment later they were in her bed, thirsting for each other, and everything they brought with them. They were so much more together than apart, and their lovemaking drove them both into a frenzy of ecstasy. It had been so long this time because of his surgery. They couldn't get enough of each other. It was hours before they emerged, and it was dark outside by then. They put on robes and walked into the kitchen. No one was around. She had bought the robe for him for his homecoming, for him to keep in Paris.

They sat at the kitchen table and shared what they found in the fridge that appealed to him. She had bought foie gras and some cheese and there was a roast chicken. It seemed like a feast to them both. The simple pleasures were so much sweeter together.

"I have a proposition to make to you," he said when they finished eating. "I was going to wait till tomorrow, but I'm too excited about it to wait to tell you."

"What kind of proposition?" She looked nervous when he said it. Everything was so perfect between them, she didn't want to spoil it.

"I'll have twenty years with the CIA in June. I want to retire. I know that sounds crazy at my age, but I'm ready and I know it's the right thing for me. It's not that I don't enjoy getting shot in the chest every now and then. I love it. But I have a better idea for the next twenty years, or thirty or forty." He smiled at her.

"But then what are you going to do, if you retire? You're too young to retire, you'll be bored stiff." It didn't sound like a good idea to her, even though she didn't like the dangers he dealt with every day. He had been lucky this time, but he might not be the next time.

"I want to run your security, all of it: the people, the technology, your alarm systems, who you hire, how you train them. It's a full-time job for someone and I want to do it. You could have the most state-of-the-art security setup, your very own little CIA." He was beaming as he said it.

"You want to be my employee?" She looked shocked. "And give up a prestigious high-security-level government job? You're crazy."

"I've done that, for twenty years. That's enough. I want to reinvent myself, and I can't think of anyone I'd rather do it with, and do it for. Theo, I want to be with you, but I don't want to be deadweight around here. I'm not a gigolo. I need to work, and I could give you something you really need, and I can do well. I've had twenty years of training for it. And you're going to need bodyguards and a sophisticated security system forever. That's real job security," he said, and leaned across the kitchen table and kissed her. "What do you think?"

"I think you kiss better than any man I've ever met, *and* you make love better."

"That's separate from the security job." He grinned at her.

"Oh, I thought it was included."

"It's a perk, for me," he added, and she laughed.

"For me too. For a minute I thought you were going to propose to me." She grinned at him.

"That can happen too, when you're ready for it," but he knew she wasn't yet. The look of panic in her eyes a moment earlier had confirmed it. All the bad things that had happened were still too fresh.

"Speaking seriously for a minute, I want you here with me, but do you really want to give up the CIA for that?"

"Yes, I do." He was sure of it, and had been working it out in his head all month. His pension after twenty years would be a good one. A lot of CIA agents retired at fifty and started new ventures.

"You wouldn't miss New York?"

"Maybe, but Paris is pretty damn great too. And you're here. I don't want to be in New York without you."

"What about your sister?"

"She can come visit. I can put her up in a hotel if she drives you crazy."

"She won't. I love her. She'd be fun to have for a visit."

"I'm ready for a change. Getting shot in the chest told me that. I don't want to do the same thing for the rest of my life. Setting things up right for you would be a challenge. Everything you have in place right now was done in a crisis. You needed to make choices and decisions and set things up fast. Now you can set things up in a way that really works for you. You know more about it yourself now. I can design it just the way you want it. I have to wait till June to leave the job, but I can be working on it before I start. You don't even have to pay me, my pension is great."

"If you're going to perform a major function like that, you should be paid for it and have a title."

"However you want me to do it."

She liked the idea. He had given her advice before, but this would be different. It would be entirely his bailiwick, and given his training, it would be perfect.

"Let's sleep on it, and decide before you go back, so you can get the ball rolling in New York."

"That sounds perfect." He looked pleased.

They went back to her bedroom then and made love again. She loved the idea of his moving to Paris and living with her. It was just right for right now, and it could grow into more later. He had touched on it, and she hadn't responded. But he was letting her set the pace, which was what she needed.

They fell asleep with his arms around her, and she hadn't slept as well since he left Paris the last time.

When they woke up in the morning, the sun was shining and it was a beautiful day.

"What are we doing today?" he asked her as they got dressed after breakfast.

"You said you wanted to go to Deauville again, and it's the perfect day for it." They both dressed accordingly in comfortable warm clothes and boots with rubber soles. "Do we need a bodyguard?" she asked him.

"I can drive us," he said easily. And twenty minutes later they were in her car with down jackets and warm scarves. The air was still chilly.

They drove to Deauville and had lunch in the same restaurant they had loved before. She had a delicate sole, and he had lobster. He looked up at her for a minute.

"I thought I'd never get to do this again. There was a moment after I was shot when I was sure I was going to die. I'm still stunned that I didn't."

"You scared the hell out of me," she said. "I'm glad you're retiring." She didn't want to lose him.

After lunch, they walked on the beach, and when they got back to the car, she asked him if she could drive. She hadn't been allowed to drive herself since the first kidnapping. He hesitated and then nodded, handed her the keys, and got into the passenger seat next to her.

She started the car and headed out of Deauville, and a few minutes later, he pointed to the signs on the road.

"I hate to be a backseat driver, but you're going the wrong way. Paris is behind us."

"I know. There's something I want to show you before we

go back." He enjoyed the scenery then, and a little way up the road, she turned into a long driveway, and rode up a hill to the old farm she had seen when she'd gone there alone.

"Do you know the people who live here?" he asked her, and she nodded. "It's a beautiful old place."

"I think so too. Let's get out and look around," she suggested, and they both got out. The old caretaker came, recognized her and greeted her, and they had a brief conversation in French. "He told us to go wherever we want. Come on, I want to show you the house." The door was unlocked as it had been before. Mike followed her in, hesitantly, but was immediately taken with the warmth and charm of the room.

"I love this place. Why is it empty? Who lives here?" He looked puzzled and she put her arms around him when she answered.

"We do," she said, smiling at him. "I just bought it. And there's a cottage for the bodyguards right near the house. It's an old farm. The people who owned it died, and their children have all moved away. And now it's ours to do whatever we want with it. And you can have a ball with the security. Nothing has been touched here since 1950. It all needs to be redone, however we want to do it."

He looked shocked at first and then grinned. "You're a little monster, up to mischief the minute I turn my back.

I get shot in the chest and what do you do? You buy a house."

"Well, we don't have the château anymore, and it's nice to have someplace to go on weekends. And we like it here. Do you like it?"

"I love it. And more than that, I love you."

"You have a new job and a title, we should have a house to go with it."

He glanced around the house again with pleasure, and then down at her. "It really was destiny, wasn't it? Destiny brought us together—and Pierre de Vaumont."

"What does he have to do with it?" Theo looked puzzled.

"I was following him, or having him followed, and I fell over you. You were on the same plane he was, which started everything. Now here we are, five months later."

"You work fast," she said, smiling at him.

"No, we do. Because it was so right, right from the beginning. I felt like I was being pulled by a giant magnet the moment I laid eyes on you."

"Then you lied to me," she said, grinning.

"I did not. What did I lie to you about?"

"The red purse. It wasn't your sister's birthday, she wasn't turning forty, and she would have hated it."

"I would have bought the chandelier if I had to. By the way, I brought you back the red purse, it's for you."

"Thank you," she said and kissed him, and he kissed her back. They had come a long way to find each other, through some terrible times, and now the good times were rolling out like a red carpet ahead of them.

"I love you," he said, pressing her close against him as he held her.

"Don't ever lie to me again. I love you too," she said in a whisper of desire, and he laughed.

Danielle Steel

Have you liked Danielle Steel on Facebook?

Be the first to know about Danielle's latest books,
access exclusive competitions and stay in touch
with news about Danielle.

www.facebook.com/DanielleSteelOfficial